A TOOTH FOR A TOOTH

A ROY BALLARD MYSTERY

This one is for Martha Lind,
a sweet friend and avid reader who will be missed.

ACKNOWLEDGMENTS

I'm lucky to have the best editing and proofreading team in the business, along with friends and family members who provide expert-level input on a variety of topics. Much appreciation to Tommy Blackwell, Becky Rehder, Helen Haught Fanick, Mary Summerall, Marsha Moyer, Stacia Miller, Linda Biel, Leo Bricker, Kathy Carrasco, Naomi West, Martin Grantham, John Strauss, Betty Blackwell, and Tony Turpin. All errors are my own.

1

People were stupid. No question about that. What kind of idiot leaves his car door unlocked all night in his driveway? A frigging retard, that's who.

Lennox had no qualms about stealing all their shit. They deserved it, basically. It would teach them a lesson, if they had any brains at all. Lock your damn doors. That was the lesson. Don't be a retard.

He was using the same method tonight that he always used. Drive out to one of the decent neighborhoods west of Austin—out near Driftwood or Dripping Springs or Spicewood—where each home sat on a couple acres of land. Because the houses were spread out, the neighbors couldn't really see what was going on next door. Especially when it was two in the morning, when all the idiots and retards were sleeping.

This particular neighborhood was called Sunrise Vista Estates. How stupid. Marketing bullshit. Lennox had driven around the neighborhood a few days earlier and scoped it out. His ancient Honda Prelude didn't fit in too well with the newer cars parked in front of the homes, but that was fine. Anyone seeing him drive around at the time probably thought he was there to fix a sink or deliver a pizza. Morons.

Now, in the darkness, he killed the headlights and continued slowly down a long, straight road, using only the moonlight to guide him. He coasted to a stop on the shoulder beside a vacant lot, tapping the brakes for only a few seconds.

Then he sat in the Prelude quietly and waited. It was harder than hell, sitting there all fidgety and jittery, but he had to do it. If anyone had seen him pulling over and wondered what the hell he was doing— and then decided they'd come out and investigate, like some kind of neighborhood badass enforcer—they would likely do it pretty quickly.

Ten minutes passed. The street remained dark.

Twenty minutes. He wasn't concerned about the cops. If someone called the sheriff's office about a strange car in the neighborhood, it wasn't like a deputy would rush over to check it out. That kind of call was low-priority bullshit. A deputy might not show until morning, or maybe not at all. The sheriff would simply log the call and forget about it unless there was a repeat call about the same car.

At the thirty-minute mark, Lennox was satisfied that everything was cool.

He opened his door—still in darkness, because he'd disabled the interior dome light—and stepped out. Closed the door quietly with a gentle push.

Then he set out on foot, taking quick but light steps on the asphalt. He was wearing dark clothes. Not using a flashlight.

Most of the homes were cloaked in near-total darkness. No porch lights burning. No lights illuminating the vehicles in the driveways. Perfect, but Jesus, how stupid could you be? Lennox knew for a fact that lights kept people like him away, but some of the retards out here in the boonies were too concerned about "light pollution," or a high energy bill, or annoying the neighbors, or whatever.

Lennox had two ground rules. First, he didn't break into vehicles. The door had to be unlocked. And second, he didn't mess around with any vehicle that was parked more than forty or fifty feet from the street. That way he could check the doors and get back on the street real quick. Less risk. Easier to haul ass if he had to. Lennox figured some angry homeowner would be less likely to shoot him once he'd reached the street. That was his theory, anyway. Nobody wanted to shoot a prowler and have him die on the street, because you could supposedly get in trouble for that shit.

Lennox stopped for a moment near a circular driveway in front of a large home built of sandstone. Parked right out front was a white Land Rover SUV. He didn't know what model it was. He didn't care. Why the hell would he care? What difference did it make?

He waited again. Just listening for any noise that might indicate someone was awake inside the home, or in any of the nearby homes.

But there was nothing. Just the sound of crickets or frogs or whatever that noise was.

Without wasting any more time, he followed the driveway around to the SUV and went to the driver's-side door—the side closest to the street—and tried the handle. The door was unlocked. Frigging owner was a retard. Lennox quickly climbed into the SUV and closed the door behind him, to kill the interior lights.

Now he used the muted light from the screen of his phone to take a closer look around inside the SUV—and he immediately saw some high-dollar equipment. Like a GPS navigation unit mounted on the left side of the dash. He pulled it loose and stuck it inside a plastic grocery sack. Then he grabbed a nice dash cam that was suction-cupped to the inside of the windshield.

He looked inside the center console and found a wallet. What an enormous idiot. Lennox took a quick glance inside and saw several hundred dollars in tens and twenties. He stuffed the cash into the sack. Left the rest.

In the passenger seat, underneath a gym bag, was an iPad. Now it was his. He made sure it was powered off and stuffed it into the sack.

He popped the glove compartment and saw a small silver handgun inside a holster. Lennox paused for a moment. He wasn't into guns, and in fact he was a little bit scared of them. He'd stolen a couple, but he'd never fired one. This one was probably worth several hundred dollars.

Just as he reached for it, the porch light of the house popped on.

Lennox laid his phone flat against his thigh, killing the light, and froze.

Nothing happened for a full minute. Maybe the person inside was looking out the window, too scared to come outside.

Then the front door of the house slowly swung open.

Jesus frigging Christ. Lennox had never been caught before. Not for burglary. Should he jump from the SUV and try to run? If the owner of the SUV had a gun in his car, he probably had several more inside the house, right?

After what seemed a very long time, a man appeared in the doorway. Middle-aged dude. Thin brown hair and a paunch. Wearing a blue T-shirt and sweatpants.

And holding a shotgun loosely in his left hand.

Lennox didn't dare move. Despite the porch light, the interior of the SUV remained bathed in shadows. The man with the shotgun probably couldn't see Lennox. He stood in the doorway for thirty seconds, then raised his right hand and pointed it at the SUV.

Lennox jumped ever so slightly when the doors locked and the hazard lights flashed once.

Now his heart was galloping and his palms were beginning to sweat. The gun was right there in the glove compartment if he needed it. Could he do it? Could he shoot someone? He had no idea.

The man in the sweatpants turned and went back inside.

The porch light went out.

Lennox exhaled.

The hazard lights had flashed just once. He was pretty sure that meant he could unlock the doors from the inside without triggering the alarm.

He let some time pass. He wasn't sure how much—at least fifteen or twenty minutes. It was surprising how difficult it was to remain still that long.

Time to bail. He grabbed the gun from the glove compartment and stuffed it into the sack.

Took one more deep breath, then unlocked the doors. No alarm— thank God.

He opened the driver's door, hopped out, and hit the ground running.

NINE WEEKS LATER

2

I was seated in the waiting room at my doctor's office—listening to one elderly woman tell another elderly woman in graphic detail about the constipation she'd been experiencing recently—when I received a text from Jonathan, one of my biggest clients. Also one of my favorites. Young guy, but thoroughly competent and detail-oriented. Had a sense of humor, which was a bonus.

Got time for a case? he asked. He worked in the fraud unit inside one of the largest insurance companies in the world. His job, unlike mine, primarily took place behind a desk. Poor guy.

You bet, I replied.

Talk now? he asked.

I went to the reception desk and let the harried young woman behind the counter know I would be just outside the front door. Could she wave at me if my name was called? The waiting room was nearly full and she didn't appear too happy to accommodate this special request, but my charm won her over.

I stepped outside to a gorgeous November day and Jonathan answered on the first ring.

"If it isn't the groom-to-be," he said. "Getting the jitters yet?"

"My only jitter is that she might come to her senses before then."

"Yeah, I wouldn't rule that out," he said.

"I appreciate the support."

"Happy to help. Let me tell you about this case."

"Please do."

"Okay, back in September, one of our customers hit a pedestrian with his car, and at first it looked pretty cut and dried, but not when I dug deeper. Right now, we have no plans to pay any of the medical bills."

"What's the story?"

"Something isn't quite right. The claimant has a colorful history—couple of drug charges, passed some bad checks, had one count of credit card fraud, and—wait for it—he tried to pull a slip-and-fall routine in a grocery store about six years ago. Took several hours to find that one, but, fortunately, I'm damn good at my job."

"Despite what everyone says."

"That sparkling wit. No wonder Mia loves you."

"Indeed. But don't let me sidetrack you."

"Okay, what we're thinking is that this guy was trying to get hit, and he's either faking his injuries or he got hit harder than he intended and really did get hurt."

"Either way, it's on him," I said.

"Exactly," Jonathan said.

"What injuries is he claiming?"

"It's almost all soft tissue stuff—ligament and cartilage damage in his back and hips. Stuff that's hard to disprove. He did break his right arm, and I would guess that was unintentional, but that's already healed."

"I worked a case where a guy fractured his arm falling off a ladder at home, and he didn't have insurance, so he went into a Blockbuster and pretended to trip over a loose video on the floor that his wife put there five minutes earlier. Trying to get them to cover his bills. Might've worked if the store hadn't had a good camera system."

"What kind of store?"

"A Blockbuster." There was a brief silence. "Good God, do you really not know what a Blockbuster was? How young are you exactly?"

"I think I sort of remember them," he said.

A man who appeared to be in his fifties walked past me, coughing from deep in his chest, and entered the doctor's office. I could smell cigarette smoke trailing behind him.

"Any chance it happened just like he said?" I said. "Dude was walking down the street, minding his own business, and your guy creamed him?"

"If that's the conclusion you reach, then we'll reconsider."

"No pressure, though," I said. "How's your guy's driving record?"

"Average."

"What time of day was it?"

"Around nine in the evening. The claimant was jaywalking across

Exposition Boulevard."

Which was a fairly busy street that ran north-south for about a mile through west Austin.

"Any witnesses?" I asked.

I was looking through a window into the waiting room. I couldn't see the door the nurses opened to call the next patient's name, but I was keeping my eye on the young woman behind the reception desk and she hadn't even glanced this way. As far as I could tell, all of the same patients were still waiting. Good thing I'd blocked out the morning. I'd told Mia, who was out of town, that I was getting the tires on my van aligned.

"One, but she didn't see much," Jonathan said. "She looked up right after it happened. Wanna hear something ironic?"

"It's what I live for."

"This particular customer used to have a dash cam in his SUV, except his vehicle was burglarized about a week before the incident and the camera was stolen. He hadn't bought a new one yet."

"Sucky timing," I said.

"Indeed. Would've been nice to have video. Anyway, I'll send you the file, and just let me know if you have any questions. It's pretty detailed, and if anything important is missing, I know you'll find it online somewhere in about five minutes."

"That's flattering, but sometimes it takes six."

"Anything else you need from me right now?"

"What's your customer's name?"

"Joseph Jankowski."

That name sounded familiar, but I couldn't place it. Maybe I was mistaken. "Okay if I contact him?"

"Yep. I already told him you might, but be warned that he isn't the friendliest guy you'll ever meet."

"Yeah?"

Jonathan lowered his voice. "Dude has a stick up his butt, big time."

"That's unfortunate," I said. "He should have that removed."

"I think it's permanent," Jonathan said. "Anyway, his contact information is in the file."

"What's the alleged victim's name?" I said.

"Armbruster," Jonathan said. "Lennox Armbruster."

I went back inside and sat down. Ten seconds later a text arrived from Mia. A photograph. She and three of her friends were standing on the beach in bikinis, skin golden, facing the camera, the Atlantic Ocean behind them, shimmering in the sunlight. They were all laughing, and one of the women, Karen, was covering her mouth, as if somebody had just said something entirely inappropriate. Or maybe I was projecting.

I see three nines and a ten, I replied. Then I added, *If I were the type to objectify women in that fashion, which I'm not.*

She didn't reply right away. Had probably already put her phone away and gone back to her fun—a girls' getaway to Miami Beach for a week. She'd only been gone for two days, but I missed her so much that I literally felt an ache in my chest.

How had I gotten so lucky?

It wasn't a simple story, but it wasn't that complicated, either. See, once upon a time, there was this gorgeous woman named Mia Madison who worked as a bartender at a tavern I frequented on North Lamar Boulevard. I suspect some customers stopped in solely because they were smitten with her. Couldn't really blame them. Mia stood five foot ten in flats. She had lustrous red hair that cascaded to her shoulders and dimples that could make your knees buckle. And to top it off, she was intelligent and witty. Quite a combination.

Occasionally I would pay Mia a reasonable amount to encourage men—and some women—to lift items they shouldn't be able to lift, because they were claiming to be injured. Like, say, she might follow a subject to a home improvement store and ask him to lift a bag of concrete. Or wait outside his apartment and ask him to load a bookcase into the back of my van. Worked like a charm ninety-nine percent of the time, and I would surreptitiously record the action on camera, which was usually enough for that person to drop the insurance claim in an effort to avoid criminal charges.

Of course, all along I knew that Mia was more than a head-turning fraud-buster. She also had the brains and the savvy and the creativity to make a great business partner. So I mulled that over for a while—did I really want a partner?—and when I decided the answer was yes, I ran the idea past her. Despite some initial trepidation, she eventually went for it.

Did I mention that, by that point, I knew I was in love with her? Head over heels. Lock, stock, and barrel. Plus other clichés. Not just a crush, either. Hopelessly in love. The kind where you don't realize a traffic light has turned green because you're lost in thought. Took me a long time to admit it to myself, and just as long to tell her.

Problem was, at the time, she was seeing someone—an idiot and abuser named Garlen Gieger. She didn't see it at first. Didn't realize the kind of man he was. Or maybe she just didn't want to admit it to herself. I don't mean that to sound patronizing, and I freely acknowledge that Mia has better sense and judgment than I do in almost every possible way. Garlen was the rare exception.

But as you would expect from that type of person, Garlen eventually sabotaged the relationship himself—a couple of times—and then he decided it was all my fault, and that he should confront me, and a car chase ensued. Didn't go well for him. Or his BMW.

Once Garlen was in the rearview mirror, so to speak, I finally realized I would regret it forever if I didn't tell Mia how I felt. So I did, knowing it might change things forever—for the worse. But my wildest dreams came true. Not only did we start seeing each other, it wasn't long thereafter that Mia caught me by complete surprise and proposed to me. I said yes, of course. In a heartbeat. With no reservations whatsoever. Now two months had passed and our plans were beginning to take shape. We'd chosen a date in November of next year. One year from now.

But there was a problem. A rather large one.

There was an important piece of information I'd failed to share with her as our relationship progressed, and now it had reached the point that I needed to tell her as soon as possible. Right now, in fact. Before the planning went any further, because it was the kind of thing that might cause her to call it off. Seriously. It might not, but it very well might. And it had to do with my reason for visiting the doctor today. And there would likely be another visit after this one, with a different doctor, because this condition would require a specialist.

3

The following morning, I was waiting again, this time in the lobby of JMJ Construction. It was 9:38 and Joe Jankowski had agreed to meet with me at nine o'clock.

The receptionist—a tall, pretty brunette who appeared to be in her late twenties—hadn't said anything about the delay or given any indication as to whether Jankowski was even in the office. A nameplate on her desk told me her name was Brandi Sloan. Brandi had pointed out the coffee maker when I'd first arrived and hadn't paid me much attention since.

That was fine. I could use the time productively to do more background research.

Not long after my doctor's appointment yesterday, I'd read the file Jonathan sent and remembered why Jankowski's name was familiar. He was the forty-two-year-old CEO of JMJ Construction, which specialized in mid-sized commercial and retail projects—chiefly strip centers, if I were to guess based on the projects they featured on their website.

I'd also done some googling and learned that some time back—maybe a year or so—JMJ had experienced a case of fraud involving one of his construction workers. The employee—I'll call him Brent Donovan, because that was his name—sustained some injuries when he was pinned between a brick wall and the dumping chute of a concrete truck, but it was later learned that he was thoroughly intoxicated at the time. Then another member of the work crew revealed that Brent had been planning this little scheme for some time, and he'd needed to get drunk to have the guts to follow through. He intentionally placed himself in harm's way and things didn't work out as he had planned. He spent a week in the hospital recovering from broken ribs and a lacerated liver.

He'd picked the wrong company to rip off. He was fired immediately, of course, and JMJ refused to pay any of the medical bills. They also pursued criminal charges. "This punk needs to pay for what he done," Jankowski said in an interview. "Fraud like this cripples companies like mine and harms all of our honest, hardworking people. I want this loser to serve some serious time."

That kind of talk was typical Joe Jankowski, from what I'd learned. The articles I'd read about him in the business section of the newspaper described him as "brusque" or "no-nonsense" or "straight to the point." I figured all of those descriptors were subtle ways of saying he was an asshole.

The criminal case had been working its way through the legal system when Brent Donovan disappeared, apparently deciding to run for the hills.

"Good riddance to that coward," Jankowski said at the time. "You ask me, that's as good as a confession. He ran so he wouldn't become someone's girlfriend in prison."

Jankowski's bio on the JMJ website was a little more diplomatic. Apparently Joe had pulled himself up by his bootstraps, starting as a general unskilled laborer fresh out of high school, learning at the elbows of plumbers, electricians, and heavy equipment operators, as well as designers, architects, and project managers. Being a fellow with lots of pluck and initiative, he opened his first business at the age of 23 and it had become an immediate success. But he'd never forgotten his blue-collar roots, and that point was made over and over on the website. Most of the photos of Joe showed him in work clothes, wearing a hardhat. He got the job done. Didn't put up with any slackers. Real he-man stuff.

"This is a nice space," I said to Brandi, the receptionist. "Did y'all build it?"

The place was modern. Sleek. Lots of sharp angles, high ceilings, and recessed lighting. Brandi stopped what she was doing on her computer and said, "Honestly, I don't know. Nobody has ever asked that. I assume so."

"How long have you worked here?"

"Almost a year."

"You like it?"

"I guess so, yeah."

"A ringing endorsement if I've ever heard one."

"No, I do. It's fun. Everybody here is fun."

I had seen several people coming and going through the lobby, disappearing down various hallways. None of them had appeared to be fun. Rushed and focused, maybe. Not fun.

"How about Mr. Jankowski?" I asked. "Is he fun?"

"He's nice," Brandi said, nodding. "I like him."

I couldn't tell if she was sincere.

"You know what else he builds very well? Suspense." She looked puzzled, so I smiled and said, "Any idea when he might be able to meet with me?"

"Oh!" she said, and laughed. She looked down at a piece of equipment on her desk. "He's still on the phone right now, but as soon as he's done, I'll take you back. I'm so sorry for the wait. That was funny, though. Very clever."

I started to point out that I'd had forty minutes to come up with that line, but referring to the long wait a second time would've made me sound like a real jerk, and I am just an artificial jerk, and only on select occasions. Instead, I said, "Thanks. Hey, this is great coffee. Is it Norwegian?"

"I'm not sure, but I'm glad you like it."

"Those Norwegians have a way with coffee," I said.

"You're being silly," she said. "Norway doesn't have the right climate for coffee."

"That's true. In my defense, I get Norway and Colombia mixed up."

"Uh-huh. Oh, good. He just got off the phone."

"I'm really not sure how I can help, and I'm afraid I don't have a lot of time," Jankowski said, and he waved half-heartedly toward the two chairs in front of his desk. I sat in the one on the right. He was wearing black slacks, loafers, and an expensive golf shirt. No hardhat anywhere. No dirt under his nails. Just a wedding band on his left hand.

"I'll try to keep it short," I said. "I guess Jonathan mentioned that I'm looking into the situation with Lennox Armbruster."

"I thought you were trying to keep it short," Jankowski said, and he wasn't kidding. "Yes, he mentioned that. Let's try not to cover old ground."

"Okay, then please tell me about the night you struck Armbruster."

"Didn't you read the police reports?"

"I did, but it might be helpful if you would share your account with me."

"How would it be helpful?"

"I said it *might* be helpful. Or it might not. But I think you are misunderstanding the situation here. My job is to find out whether Armbruster is committing fraud—if he jumped in front of your car on purpose."

"Yeah, I get that. So what?"

"You're a fun guy," I said.

"Pardon?"

"I heard rumors that you're a fun guy. I'm glad to see they're true."

He frowned, as if I'd just passed gas. "What are you talking about?"

"The fact that I'm trying to *help* you, which means I'm hoping we can work together."

"We are working together," he said. "That's why we're sitting in the same room, talking. But I'm starting to wonder if it's worth the time. If you got some questions, ask. Otherwise—"

"Did you know Lennox Armbruster before the night of the accident?"

"No. How would I?"

"No chance you might've run across him somewhere and he might've held a grudge?"

"About what?"

"I have no idea. That's why I'm asking. I'm just trying to weigh the possibility that he picked you specifically."

"The cops are doing that."

Was this guy just genuinely stubborn and argumentative, or was there something else at play?

"I understand, but there's no reason I can't look into it, too," I said.

"I thought you were, like, a video cameraman. That sort of thing."

"I'm a legal videographer."

"You follow people around with a camera, right?" Jankowski said.

"That's part of what I do," I said.

Legal videographers record all sorts of things on video—depositions, wills, scenes of accidents. But Mia and I specialize in insurance fraud. It's all we do. It's our specialty—what we're known for. Basically, we spend a lot of time doing exactly what Jankowski suggested—following a subject around and hoping to gather evidence proving he or she is faking an injury.

Other times, our activities veer into territory that requires a private investigator's license, but my criminal record prevents me from being licensed, just as it prevents me from obtaining a concealed-carry permit. Mia, on the other hand, already has a carry permit, and we've considered the possibility of getting her a PI license. For now, sometimes we operate in a gray area. Nobody has taken issue with that yet, or questioned our tactics.

"So why are you acting like a cop?" Jankowski asked.

I paused for a moment in an effort to keep my cool, running the risk that he might call an end to the meeting just because I wasn't using every second wisely.

Then I said, "I'm trying to help my client—your insurance company—keep you from being screwed sideways by this guy, Lennox Armbruster. I'd love it if you'd help me, but if you don't want to, I'll still do my best. Only problem is, I'll be operating at a disadvantage—kind of like a backhoe operator who doesn't know where all the underground pipes are buried. I need all the information I can get."

It was a clumsy analogy, but it seemed to have gotten through, or to at least make Jankowski understand he'd be better off cooperating, instead of fighting with me.

He sighed deeply because I was putting him out so much, then said, "There's not a lot to it. Driving down Exposition and suddenly the guy was right in front of me. I hit him and he sort of bounced back off the front of the car and landed near the curb. If it had knocked him straight ahead, I probably would've run right over him. He'd be dead now."

"How fast were you going?"

"About thirty-five, forty. No more than that."

"The police report said you stopped about seventy yards down the road."

"Yeah."

"Why did it take so long?"

"Ever hit anybody with your car? It freaks you out and you're thinking about all these other things—like calling 911 and getting him to the hospital—instead of hitting the brakes. And wanting to make sure the witness hung around. There was a woman that saw some of it. I just barely remember passing her right after I hit the guy. It was dark out there, but I saw her standing in the parking lot next to that grocery store."

"Randall's."

"Yeah."

"So it looked natural to you—the way he appeared in front of your car? It wasn't like he was trying to get hit?"

"I got no idea about that," Jankowski said. "How could I tell? My understanding is most of those cheating scumbags are pretty smooth. They make it look like an accident. We had an incident on a job site where a guy got pinned by the chute of a concrete truck. Luckily he'd blabbed his big mouth about what he was gonna do."

He was referring to Brent Donovan.

"The report says you tried to comfort Armbruster as EMS loaded him into the ambulance. Did he say anything relevant?"

"I don't know about comforting, but yeah, I felt bad for the guy, and I wanted to see how bad he was hurt, even though it was entirely his fault. I get over there and he's screaming and moaning, and then he asks how fast I was going—like trying to accuse me, like I was going too fast, instead of him stepping right in front of my car like a jerkoff."

I asked questions for ten more minutes, and Jankowski's antagonistic demeanor settled down somewhat, but nothing he told me was particularly helpful, nor could I see any inconsistencies with the account he'd given in the police report. I thanked him for his time and he grudgingly agreed that I could call him if I had more questions later.

On the way out, I nodded to the receptionist and said, "That's the most fun I've ever had."

Her reluctant smile told me she wasn't convinced.

4

Now the grunt work began.

Time to locate Lennox Armbruster and put him under surveillance. According to Jonathan's report, Armbruster's hip and back injuries resulted in a limp and some immobility that should be obvious to the eye.

I had Armbruster's address, so I headed that way in my beige Dodge Caravan. If there was a vehicle more suited to my line of work, I hadn't found it. Nobody noticed a nondescript vehicle like mine, in traffic or parked. The windows were tinted good and dark, so I could hang out in the van for hours at a time, cameras ready to record.

The interior had plenty of storage, including a secret compartment under the rear bench where I stashed various valuable equipment, including a nine-millimeter Glock. I'd dealt with enough criminals and scumbags to know it made sense to have protection close at hand, in a place where they wouldn't find it and use it against me.

I went south on MoPac, east on William Cannon Drive, then a short distance on Brodie Lane to an apartment complex. I love apartment complexes. Compared to a residential neighborhood, it's much easier to park and hang around an apartment complex as long as necessary, without anyone getting suspicious or curious.

The complex consisted of at least a dozen rectangular three-story buildings, but I knew Armbruster's building number and I found the unit easily enough. Got lucky and immediately spotted his faded Honda Prelude. Maroon, with one rear window replaced by cardboard and duct tape. I could tell from the tape that it had been in place for a good while. Keep it classy, Lennox.

I drove past his vehicle and found a spot about eighty feet away, but as I began to pull in, I realized that it was an assigned space. Curses. So I backed out and continued around the lot, until I saw a short row of spots marked as visitor parking. One space was available, so I grabbed it. It wasn't in an ideal location for watching the Honda Prelude, but it would have to do. I also noticed there was a surveillance camera mounted on a nearby pole, aimed directly at the visitor spots. Smart. Get a video record of any non-residents coming and going. Didn't bother me that I was on camera. I wasn't doing anything illegal.

It was a reasonably balmy day for November, so I lowered the windows a few inches and got myself situated for a long wait. I started by moving to the bench seat directly behind the front seats. I could get comfortable here. Stretch out. Have some snacks if I got hungry. Soft drinks in a cooler. Even a plastic milk jug if I needed to take a leak. Hey, it ain't pretty, but it works.

See, this is often how a case starts. Lots of enthusiasm. Plenty of patience. I could listen to some tunes, while keeping my eyes peeled for Armbruster, while also reviewing the file a second time on my laptop. Which is what I did.

According to Armbruster's statement to the police, he was attempting to cross Exposition at about nine in the evening when he heard a car accelerating rapidly and realized he was about to get creamed. He tried to jump out of the way, and he almost succeeded, but not quite. He took the hit in the pelvis and legs and was thrown toward the curb on the east side of the road. He said the driver must not have seen him, because it almost seemed as if the person was *trying* to hit him.

The police report confirmed that Jankowski had never hit the brakes. He said headlights from oncoming traffic got in his eyes and he didn't see Armbruster until it was too late. And, yes, he had probably accelerated, because he had just turned the corner at Lake Austin Boulevard, heading north on Exposition, so it was only natural to hit the gas and get up to speed.

It all made sense, except something was missing. Armbruster's destination.

I scanned the report again and still didn't find it. Where was Armbruster going when he was trying to cross the road? On the east side of Exposition was a Randall's supermarket, and then a Maudie's Tex-Mex restaurant and a liquor store and a Goodwill store.

But Armbruster had been trying to cross to the west side of Exposition, and the only thing over there was Lions Municipal Golf

Course. Why would he have been going to the golf course well after sundown? His car had been parked at the Randall's.

If he hadn't been going to the golf course, then where? The golf course occupied the northwest corner of the intersection, and there was literally nothing to the south of the T intersection that looked like a likely destination. Just a handful of offices, and not even the type of offices a person might routinely visit. For instance, the closest building south of the intersection housed the Brackenridge Field Laboratory, which was part of the University of Texas's Biodiversity Center. I had no idea what they did there, and I doubted Lennox Armbruster did, either. Besides, the place had parking. Why would he park at Randall's? I could understand why the police might not ask him where he had been headed, but I was damn sure curious.

I froze for a moment as a young guy with longish hair got into the car next to my van. Ten seconds later, he pulled away without having noticed me inside the van.

I went back to the file.

Was Armbruster a golfer? Did he have friends who golfed? Was he joining some friends for a beer at the clubhouse that long after dark? I jumped online and saw that the snack bar served burgers and sandwiches, but it didn't mention beer, and it didn't give the hours.

Why was I bothering with this? The perimeter of the golf course was fenced, and even if Armbruster hopped over a low point, it was still a good half-mile walk or further to the clubhouse, following a straight line across greens and fairways. It made no sense that he had been going there.

But there was one answer that made sense—or at least it made sense to me.

I texted Jonathan. *Any idea where Armbruster was going that night?*

What with Jonathan being a millennial, he almost always had his phone on him. He texted back in less than fifteen seconds: *hang on, i'll check.*

I had now been staked out in the van for more than two hours and there had been no sign of Armbruster. Not surprising. He might not leave today. Or tomorrow. Or in the next week. That's when the gung-ho attitude created by a new case starts to fade a bit.

Jonathan sent another text: *thats weird. i see what you mean. it doesnt say.*

Millennials and their indifference to proper punctuation. Nutty kids.

Then he said: *looking at a map now and all i see is the golf course. thats probably your point huh?*

I said: *Yep.*

He said: *on the other hand, if his intent was simply to step in front of a car and he wasn't really crossing the street to go anywhere...*

That's the answer that made sense. I said: *You have a mind like a well-oiled sundial.*

He sent back one of those smiley faces.

I added: *If he did step in front of the car on purpose, the question is, was it random or did he pick Jankowski?*

A minute passed.

Then he said: *i have full confidence in your ability to answer that question.*

I set the phone aside and waited for another two hours. I was tempted to call Mia and tell her about the case, but she was on vacation. I should let her have some peace and quiet, without having to think about work.

My next step would be a tactic Mia and I used regularly, even though it wasn't, strictly speaking, legal. I would attach a GPS tracking unit to Armbruster's car. That way, I wouldn't have to sit here—perhaps for days or weeks—and wait for him to go somewhere. I could go about other business and wait for an alert telling me that his Honda Prelude was on the move. In the hour or so it would take me to catch up to him, there was a chance I might miss an opportunity to record him moving or lifting something, but it sure beat the tedium of waiting.

But I waited some more, for now, and the most interesting part of my day came when a young man and woman—college-aged kids— stopped near the van while having an argument.

Him: "...don't even know her that well, but you think I'm sleeping with her? Why would I do that?"

Her: "Why *wouldn't* you do that?"

Him: "I've only met her one time and we talked for like five minutes!"

Her: "Then why is she sending you pics with her tits hanging halfway out?"

Him: "I'm just lucky, I guess. Hey, that was a joke!"

Her: "Not funny, Michael."

Him: "I'm sorry. Here, look, I'll talk to her about it." He raised his phone and began to recite what he was typing. "Britney, please stop sending me photos. I told you before that I have a girlfriend and she is getting pissed off."

Her: "Wait. You said you talked to her for five minutes, but she knows you have a girlfriend?"

Him: "What?"

Her: "She seriously asked you about your dating status in like five minutes?"

Him: "Well, it was maybe fifteen minutes and I'll admit she was hitting on me, but is that *my* fault? I didn't *do* anything."

Her: "Tell her I said she's a bitch."

Him: "Come on, we don't need to say that."

They began to wander away from the van.

Her: "She's trash and I want her to…"

That was the last remark I could make out. I bet that couple was fun at parties.

I was still grinning about it when Lennox Armbruster made an appearance. I wasn't really expecting him at this point, but there he was, emerging from a breezeway that cut through the center of his building.

Over the years, I'd watched dozens of hours of footage of genuine accident victims to study the way they moved, and Armbruster would've fit right in. He carried himself like a man in pain. Like a man with physical limitations. The intuition I'd developed was telling me he wasn't faking it. People committing fraud simply didn't know *how* to move the way Armbruster was moving. They tended to overact—to grimace and make exaggerated expressions of discomfort.

I had a super-zoom camera mounted on a tripod, just waiting for some action, and now I started recording as Armbruster stepped down from the sidewalk and began walking across the parking lot, toward his car.

He showed a mild limp, but not as much as I was expecting. His posture was slightly hunched. He seemed to have a bit of trouble walking a straight line. Perhaps it was the pain meds, or the effects of the accident.

He cut through one row of cars and headed for his Honda Prelude in the next row.

Imagine my surprise when he passed the Prelude and approached an Alfa Romeo Stelvio instead. Nice car. *Expensive* car. A recently purchased car, based on the temporary dealer plate on the back. I don't mean to sound like a snob, but it wasn't the kind of car you normally saw parked in a mid-level apartment complex.

Armbruster raised the key fob and unlocked the doors. Climbed inside slowly—and a little unsteadily, I might add—then backed up and drove away.

It doesn't take a brilliant investigative mind to conclude that something was peculiar about this scenario. I could picture a guy like Lennox Armbruster driving an Alfa—*after* he'd received a big settlement for being struck by a car. But before?

I followed him, of course, but he simply went to the grocery store and then returned to the complex. By then it was nearly nine in the evening.

I did some more waiting, but it appeared he was in for the night.

So I went ahead and stealthily placed a GPS tracker on the underside of the Alfa Romeo, plus one on the Honda Prelude, too, just in case.

I thought I would head home and get a full night of sleep. I was wrong.

5

Tarrytown is a quaint, historic neighborhood in west Austin—a highly sought-after area—but it is not immune to crime.

I arrived back at Mia's house—now my house—at five minutes before ten o'clock. I pulled into the driveway and killed the engine. Everything appeared to be fine. The porch light was on, because I'd turned it on when I'd left, knowing it would likely be a late night.

I stepped out of the van, locked it up, and began the thirty-foot walk to the front door. I was vaguely aware of headlights splashing through the trees and shrubs from down the street somewhere. Someone parking along the curb a few houses down?

Here's a cruel fact of life: Criminals often have the upper hand. Even if you go to great lengths to make yourself less of a target, they can prey on you during an unsuspecting moment, when you are vulnerable, because you can't keep your guard up all the time. It's simply not realistic. You can be alert, sure, but you can't be prepared to fend off an attack every minute of every day, especially when you have no reason to think you are in immediate danger.

Like now.

What was I supposed to do? Walk to the door with a gun in my hand? Truth is, even that wouldn't have worked.

I had the key in the front door when I heard someone behind me—a slight scrape of a shoe on the concrete—and then something cold pressed hard against my neck, behind my right ear.

"Don't turn around," a rough voice said. Sounded like he'd been swabbing his throat with a toilet brush. Gritty. That was the best way to describe it.

"Wasn't planning on it," I said. "You after my wallet?"

"Shut up."

"I can do that."

"I said shut up."

"Shutting up."

"You wanna get shot, just say something else."

We were standing in the glow of the porch light, but the porch wasn't visible to our neighbors on either side, and the neighbors across the street probably wouldn't be able to tell what was going on, even if they happened to be looking at us right now, which was doubtful.

The man had his left hand pressed against the small of my back, and he quickly felt around my waistband and under my armpits for a gun. I wasn't carrying one.

"What's your name?"

What? That wasn't a question I wanted to hear in this situation, because it indicated that this wasn't a random robbery or a carjacking. This man was looking for someone in particular, and that person was almost certainly me.

"Ernie," I said.

"Ernie what?"

I could smell cigarette smoke and a day's worth of sweat clinging to him. Pretty gross.

"Hungwell. Ernie Hungwell."

"Bullshit. You're Roy Ballard."

"Then why'd you ask?"

"Hands behind your back."

I did not comply. I simply remained silent. Never let an armed man—or even an unarmed man—restrain you if you can help it, because then he will take you somewhere, and wherever that destination happens to be, it's a given that nothing good will happen there. It's better to resist.

He pushed the barrel of the gun harder into the spot behind my ear.

"Put your fucking hands behind your back, smart guy."

"Not gonna happen," I said.

He shoved me roughly against the front door.

"Then I'll just kill you here instead," he said.

"See, that means you're planning to kill me somewhere else, so why would I go along willingly? You need to think these things through before you speak. There are three cameras aimed at you right now. Are you wearing a mask?"

"Liar."

I was running out of time. And options. I doubted he would actually shoot me here on my porch, with neighbors nearby, but I could be wrong.

"You're right," I said. "There are only two cameras. Ever heard of Krav Maga? My partner practices it."

"Just put your damn hands behind—"

I spun quickly, bringing my right elbow around with as much force as possible, and I caught him squarely in the jaw. In fact, the impact was greater than I could have hoped, and his knees buckled—but he didn't go down. However, he did drop the gun. I didn't see it, but I heard it clattering off the porch.

The man was smart enough to abandon his plan and run, and I could see that he was unsteady on his feet as he reached the street and lurched in the direction of the earlier headlights. An accomplice waiting for him? I considered chasing him, but that didn't seem to be a risk worth taking. I stood behind a brick pillar for safety.

Sure enough, a minute later, I heard a vehicle door slam, then an engine revving, and then tires squealing as reverse lights came on. The driver attempted to back into a nearby driveway but missed, and I could hear his tires hopping the curb and his bumper crashing into the mailbox. Then more squealing as he gunned the engine again and raced into the darkness.

I took a moment to catch my breath. Then I called it in.

"Know anyone who might want to harm you? Let me rephrase that. Have you pissed anyone off more than normal lately?"

The question came from an Austin Police Department patrol cop named Ursula Broward who was currently standing on Mia's porch. My porch. I had to stop forgetting that. It was my porch, too.

Broward knew me from previous interactions, and whereas some cops didn't have much patience with me—because my investigations sometimes interfered with theirs—Broward usually seemed more amused than annoyed.

Her question made me think about Lennox Armbruster. Had he

spotted me tailing him? He was physically impaired, but had he recruited a friend to try to scare me away? I figured that was a long shot.

So I said, "Well, I did find a horse's head in my bed last week, but other than that, I've been my typical charming self."

"Meaning you've probably created half a dozen enemies just this month."

Broward was maybe five foot four and one hundred and twenty pounds, but she exuded the kind of confidence necessary to take command of any situation she might encounter. I liked her.

"My charms are sometimes misunderstood," I said.

She shook her head as she took notes. She was an efficient and detail-oriented officer. She'd arrived in less than five minutes after my call, and right now several other units were patrolling the area, looking for anything unusual. The problem was, I could only give a limited description of the suspect, and as for the vehicle, I said it might have damage to the rear bumper.

"What about the cameras?" Broward said. She'd noticed my security cameras hanging under the eaves at each corner of the house. "Tell me they aren't dummies."

"They're as real as your stunning green eyes," I said.

"Knock it off."

"They're real."

I hadn't checked the video footage yet, because I'd been babysitting the forty-caliber semi-automatic Ruger I'd spotted in the grass to the left side of the porch. Hadn't touched it, of course.

Broward took some photos of the Ruger where it lay, then snapped on a pair of powder-free nitrile gloves and gently picked it up. She ejected the magazine into her free hand, then opened the slide to check the chamber, which contained a live round.

"He wasn't fooling around," she said. "You got lucky he didn't accidentally jerk the trigger when you pulled your Kung Fu move."

"Krav Maga," I said. "And I was kind of running out of choices. I have a disarming personality, but it didn't work on this guy."

"Been saving that line for the right moment, huh?" she said.

"Maybe. It's still good, though."

She studied the Ruger closely, then wrote in her tablet again.

"Got a serial number?" I asked.

"Yep."

"Think it's stolen?"

"Good bet."

She slipped the empty gun, with the slide locked open, in one evidence bag and the magazine and the loose round in another.

"Think we'll get any prints?" I asked.

"We?" she said.

"We, meaning all of us who side against evil and corruption in the world."

"Maybe," she said, "if he wasn't wearing gloves."

She looked at me now, an eyebrow raised quizzically, basically saying, *You didn't even have the guts to take a quick peek at him?*

Totally teasing me, though. I think. I shrugged.

She jotted some notes on the outside of the evidence bags. If there were prints on the Ruger or the ammo, then I'd have to hope there would be a match in AFIS to identify the guy.

She stepped down from the porch and shined her flashlight around in the nearby grass. I waited patiently.

"Which way did he run?" she asked.

"Right in that direction," I said, pointing at an angle toward the street.

She walked slowly, sweeping the flashlight along the ground. Then she stopped. Bent over and studied something closely.

"Dude, you must have hit him hard. You knocked one of his teeth out. A premolar, I think."

"Is it wrong for me to take pleasure in that?" I asked.

She took some photos of the tooth on the ground, then collected it in an evidence bag.

"DNA," I said.

"Yeah, if you don't mind waiting a couple of months," she said. She looked at me again. "You can't think of anyone who might've done this?"

"Nobody I pissed off recently," I said.

The problem was, Mia and I exposed people who were committing fraud—that was what we did for a living—and some of those people held grudges, especially if they served time on account of us. So, yeah, there was a long list of people who might've wanted to put a gun to my head and take me to an undisclosed location for undisclosed purposes.

It's a risk of the job, and there are times it keeps me awake at night—mostly worrying about Mia.

"How about we go inside and check your cameras?" Broward said.

"We?" I said.

6

Both cameras caught the entire incident, but the footage wasn't very useful. We could tell that the man in question was rather large, and he was probably white or Hispanic. He hadn't shaved in several days. But the light was too low and there were too many shadows across his face to make out more than that. He could grab a shave and walk right past me on the street and I wouldn't be able to positively match him to the video.

So, the next morning, I made a note to mount a camera directly over the front door, and to install additional lights, motion activated, around the exterior of the house, including the back.

Then I sat down and made a call I couldn't put off any longer.

Mia answered on the second ring. "Hey there."

"Am I calling too early?"

"No, we're all up."

"How's it going down there?"

"Good. I've been eating and drinking way too much. We went to a place called Pao last night and it was amazing. The pork belly was incredible. They even flash grill the salad."

"I'm not sure what that means, but it sounds all fancy-schmancy."

"It is. Then we had dessert, of course, and I was so stuffed."

"Are you still nubile?"

"At the moment, I don't feel nubile," she said.

"I'll feel you when you get home and let you know," I said.

"I'm ready to be home, to be honest," she said. "This has been fun, but I'm worn out. And I need to start planning a certain event."

"My bris?"

"I know firsthand that has already been taken care of."

"I miss you," I said. "A lot."

"Ah, I miss you, too."

"And I need to tell you something."

"What?"

"You got ten minutes?"

"Uh-oh. What's going on?"

I told her what had happened in the past twenty-four hours, starting with the new case and ending with the incident on the porch last night. I didn't leave anything out.

First thing she said was, "I'm glad you're okay."

"Me, too."

"I should come home right now."

"You'll be home in three days," I said. "I'll be fine until then."

"How do you know for sure?" she said.

"The guy is going to lay low for a while to see if the cops ID him," I said. "And his buddy driving the car, too. They lost the element of surprise and now they can't afford to make another move without knowing if they blew their cover or not."

Mia remained silent for a moment, then said. "I should be there to help."

"I appreciate that, and I'd feel the same way if the situation was reversed, but I'll feel awful if you cut your vacation short. Please stay in Miami Beach. Hey, it just occurred to me that 'Miami' has your name right in the front of it."

"You are getting weird."

"Maybe."

I walked over to a window and looked outside. It was dreary, with a low-hanging carpet of gray clouds.

"Any guesses on who it was, or why?" Mia asked.

"None," I said. "I'm lovable. Forthright. An all-around good citizen. Who would want to do such a thing?"

She didn't laugh and I didn't blame her.

I added, "Of course, we know that anyone we've ever busted could be looking for some payback."

I could hear other voices in the background—Mia's friends moving around the condo they'd rented for the week. Oh, to be a fly on the wall there. South Beach would never be the same. I could only imagine how many oiled-up bros and dudes had hit on them—and been rejected. I was afraid to ask.

"Payback would be a busted windshield or, worst case, maybe a black eye," Mia said. "This guy wanted to take you somewhere else. We both know that wasn't going to end well."

There was no use in arguing, because she was right.

"If it's any consolation," I said, "there's a very good chance I broke his jaw. Minimum, he won't be eating with much enthusiasm for a week or two. I have you to thank for that."

She'd taught me some basic self-defense moves.

The line was silent for a moment.

"I'm guessing you were tempted to keep quiet about all this until I got home, but I'm glad you told me now," she said.

"I also forgot to take the garbage cart out to the street this morning. Do I get a pass on that?"

"It's like I go away for a few days and everything goes to hell," she said.

"I'll be fine," I said. "Promise. Just have fun, and maybe send me an occasional intriguing photo, if you know what I mean."

"Perv."

"This is news?"

"If anything else happens, call me," she said.

"I will."

"Or if you learn who the jerk was."

"I will."

"I don't care what time it is."

"Okay."

We were both quiet for a moment. I didn't want to hang up. This was the first time we'd been apart for an extended time since we'd been a couple.

"I miss you," I said.

"You already said that," she said. "Now you're just getting repetitive."

By ten o'clock that morning, neither of Lennox Armbruster's cars had moved, according to the GPS app on my phone, so I placed a call to Sarah Gerstenberger, the witness who'd been nearby when

Armbruster got hit by Joe Jankowski's car. She worked at the library at the intersection of Bee Caves Road and Cuernavaca and said I could swing by anytime before five o'clock for a chat. I agreed that I would be there in the early afternoon.

I stepped onto my front porch and looked around, checking for any small piece of evidence that might remain. Ursula Broward and I had missed nothing the night before. Or if we had, I was still overlooking it.

The neighborhood was quiet—a mid-morning lull. No traffic. No walkers or joggers. The air felt damp.

I walked down the street and stopped in front of the home that had had its mailbox run over. Nothing much to see here, either. Just a dented black mailbox mounted on a black metal pole that was now bent parallel to the ground. I managed to bend it straight again—good enough for mail delivery—and then I went to the front door and knocked. Nobody answered. I'd exchanged waves from a distance with the young couple living here, but they hadn't been here long and we'd never met. I left a note. *I'm going to replace your mailbox and post. Sorry for any hassles. Please call me if you have any questions.* I jotted my phone number underneath. I snapped a photo of the mailbox and the post.

Last night, Broward had searched for pieces of broken taillight lens and come up empty. Likewise, she'd found no automotive paint on the mailbox, indicating that an unpainted steel bumper had likely done the damage. Not much chance of identifying the type of vehicle without any evidence.

I studied the house itself for surveillance cameras. None that I could see. Same with the houses on either side, and the ones across the street. Didn't these people realize that security cameras were cheap and easy to install nowadays? Then again, mine hadn't done much good, had they?

Broward had knocked on some doors last night, but nobody had seen anything. Here at the house with the damaged mailbox, the young couple had heard the squealing tires but didn't know where the noise had come from and didn't go outside to investigate.

Unless Broward got a hit on AFIS, it appeared my assailant was going to get away clean, for now.

"Thanks for taking the time to talk," I said to Sarah Gerstenberger three hours later.

"Oh, no problem," Gerstenberger said. "I'm happy to help however I can. I feel bad for that poor guy. I could tell that he was in a lot of pain. But I'll admit I'm a little unclear as to your role in the investigation. You said you were with the insurance company?"

She'd sounded about thirty years old on the phone, but in person, she appeared to be in her mid-forties. She had a wide, friendly smile, medium-length sandy hair, freckles, green eyes, and deep dimples. She was dressed in a white sleeveless blouse and a denim skirt that hit mid-thigh.

I said, "That's right, and we just want to make sure we understand how everything happened. It's pretty basic."

We'd found a table near the back of the library. So far, I'd seen only six or seven people browsing the stacks or using the computer.

"Okay," she said. "But do you mean you're with the insurance company for the man in the SUV or the man who was hit?"

Smart. The majority of people wouldn't even think to clarify the distinction. It might also present a roadblock.

"I'm a freelancer hired by Joseph Jankowski's insurance company," I said.

"He was the driver, right?"

"Right."

She was shaking her head, confused. "I'm afraid I'm a little slow today. I still don't understand what's going on. You're a videographer?"

"That's right, yes."

"Hmm," she said.

"I can see that you're hesitant to talk, and that's completely understandable. I'd be hesitant to talk to me, too. I mean, come on, just look at me. I have 'disreputable' written all over my face."

The levity didn't work. She smiled, but she said, "Is the insurance company trying to avoid paying the claim? Is that's what's happening?"

"I wouldn't categorize it that way," I said.

"Okay, humor me. How would you categorize it? What exactly did the insurance company hire you to do?"

"Sure," I said, all breezy-like. "Have you ever seen clips of people committing insurance fraud? They're usually all grainy, because they are shot from a distance and—"

"Because somebody follows them around with a camera," she said.

"Right. Well, that's part of what I do. I try to catch people who are committing insurance fraud. But sometimes the opposite is true—sometimes I report back to my client that the person in question appears to have a legitimate injury."

"Your client is under the impression that this man, Lennox…"

"Armbruster."

"They think he's committing fraud?"

"Not at all. They just want to rule that possibility out."

"But how is it even a possibility? The man got hit by a car."

Now I realized I was dealing with someone who was naïve about the lengths to which criminals will go to earn a dollar.

"You'd be surprised what some folks will do," I said. Then I added, "But that doesn't mean that's what's happening here. In fact, it makes my job easier if everything happened exactly the way it seems. Then I can move on."

She was looking at me, wondering if I was simply telling her what she wanted to hear. Finally, she decided to talk.

"Okay, well, I'll tell you the same thing I told the police. I was leaving the Randall's, walking out to my car, which was in the row nearest Exposition, when I heard someone scream. So I looked up, and by then I'd already heard a big thump, and I see a body flying through the air. It was kind of dark over there, but I could still see it clearly, and it was pretty gruesome. You don't expect something like that to happen, and I was just frozen for a moment. You never really know how you'll react in a situation like that, and I was basically sort of hypnotized, like…Did that really just happen?"

"So you didn't see the actual moment of impact?"

"I did not."

"Did you see or hear the SUV—Jankowski's vehicle—before you heard the scream and the thump?"

"No."

"Did you notice Lennox Armbruster before then?"

"No, I had no reason to look in that direction. I was walking to my car, answering a text at the time."

"And how did you react when it happened?"

"As I said, I froze for just a moment, and then I ran over there to see if the guy was okay. He was still on the street, right near the curb, sort of just piled there. I could hear him moaning, so I knew he was alive. I knelt beside him, checking for bleeding, in case I needed to apply pressure to a wound, but all he had was one small cut to his forehead. His arm, on the other hand—I could tell right off it was broken. So I figured the first thing I should do is call 911, which I did."

"And where was Jankowski's SUV during all this?"

"Right when I reached Lennox, the SUV was still moving down the street, slowly, and then he eventually pulled over."

"Were you close enough to the street to get a good look at him right after the accident?"

"At Jankowski?"

"Right."

"Not really, no. The inside of his vehicle was too dark, and by then he was already down the street."

"Could you ID the make and model?"

"You mean if he hadn't stopped?"

"Yes."

"Maybe if I had photos to compare it to."

I knew that it was a Land Rover Discovery.

"Would you have been able to get the license plate?" I asked.

"If I'd thought about that, yeah, I probably could have."

"Do you think he saw you?"

"Probably, yeah. The parking lot at Randall's has some lights." She looked at me more closely. "Wait a second. Are you thinking he stopped only because I was there?"

Sharp lady.

"I try not to think too much," I said. "It makes me dizzy."

"Cute, but you're dodging my question," she said.

"Fair enough," I said. "The truth is, I'm just asking questions right now, and then I'll see where it leads. I do know that some people zone out after a wreck, almost like they're in shock, and they just keep driving until it sinks in what happened. Then they stop or turn around and drive back to the scene. That might be what happened with Joe Jankowski."

7

She told me more, but nothing that wasn't already in the file.

Joe Jankowski pulled over, but he didn't get out of his vehicle to see if Armbruster was okay until three or four minutes later. By then, a patrol cop had already arrived, responding to Gerstenberger's 911 call.

When Jankowski walked back to the scene from his car, he didn't appear particularly distressed or traumatized from having hit a fellow human being with his car. Truth is, some people react that way in stressful situations. They zone out.

Jankowksi freely gave a statement and checked on Armbruster as he was loaded into the ambulance. Armbruster responded with agitation and asked Jankowski how fast he'd been going, which matched what Jankowski had told me when I'd interviewed him the day before.

It was entirely possible Jankowski had been tempted to keep driving, even if he had zero culpability in the accident. It's a natural instinct to flee from trouble.

According to the officer, Jankowski showed no signs of impairment from alcohol or other drugs—but what if he'd had just a drink or two a few hours earlier? Wouldn't that have made him panic, even if the accident would have happened anyway?

Why was I letting myself get sidetracked with this? If Jankowski had been on the verge of hauling butt, what did it matter? It had no bearing on whether or not Armbruster had intentionally stepped in front of the car. My objective remained the same: determine if Armbruster was committing fraud.

Oh, and catch the bastard who'd held a gun to my neck.

I called Ursula Broward, got voicemail, and left a message.

"Good afternoon, Officer Broward. This is Roy Ballard calling to light up your day. Assuming you haven't already captured the notorious scalawag who accosted me last night, I'm wondering if a detective has been assigned to that case. I know I might seem pushy, but I prefer to think of it as proactive. Sure would like to know if you get a hit on the serial number from that Ruger, or if you can pull any prints. Thanks for your time and for being a valuable asset to our community."

What to do next?

I was still wondering where Lennox Armbruster had been going on the night of the accident. I was also curious about his new Alfa Romeo. Where had he gotten the money for that?

I checked the GPS app on my phone just to make sure it wasn't malfunctioning. Nope. Working fine, and Armbruster still hadn't gone anywhere in either vehicle. Not surprising. There was a slim chance he might be doing things around his apartment complex that would prove useful to me—carrying a loaded basket of clothes to the laundry hut, for instance—so I returned to his apartment complex and parked in the same spot I'd occupied yesterday.

And I waited. One hour. Then two.

The gray clouds had grown thicker, and then a light drizzle began to fall on the van's windshield. No arguing couples wandered past to keep me amused.

I was dozing off—sure, I'll admit it—when Broward called me back and informed me that a detective named Billy Chang was now assigned to my assault case. Not great news. Chang was a good detective, but he was tight-lipped and was unlikely to share any information with me. Still, I called his number and left a message, indicating that I'd love to talk when he had a moment. I knew he wasn't going to call me back, but I'm an optimist. What can I say?

Now it was raining so hard I wouldn't be able to identify Armbruster even if he walked right past the van, so I returned yet again to the case file on my laptop. Went through the reports and notes, line by line. Nothing new.

Studied the photos from the accident scene snapped by the responding officer. It wasn't necessarily standard operating procedure for a cop to take photos at a scene like this one, but in this case, I think he was wanting to document the distance Jankowski had driven after impact. Just in case.

The officer had taken several photos while standing in front of Jankowski's Land Rover, aiming back toward the spot where his marked police unit was parked. Obviously, it was nighttime, so it was difficult to gauge the distance perfectly, but however you looked at it, it was a good long way.

The front end of Jankowski's SUV was dented, but not as badly as one would expect.

The heavy rain lightened up a little. Another hour passed.

My phone chimed with an incoming text from Mia. A selfie of her standing in front of a bathroom mirror, wearing a green bikini, but cropped to show just her torso, from her collarbones to the middle of her thigh.

Like my new suit? she asked.

I studied it—and wow!—but hang on a second. I realized what she was doing, that little trickster. The woman in the photo wasn't Mia. It was Leann, one of her friends with a similar build.

That's one hot body, I said. *Almost as good as yours.* And, of course, I added an obligatory laughing-face emoji.

She sent back a kissy-face emoji and said, *Off to the beach.*

I replied: *Don't break too many hearts.*

Another hour passed and I was getting restless, so I opened my laptop again, and one of the photos of Jankowski's SUV was still on the screen.

This time, however, I noticed something immediately—something that should've been obvious from my first viewing. How had I missed it? How had the cops missed it?

Inside the SUV, suction-cupped to the windshield, was a dash cam. That meant Jankowski had likely captured the accident on video. Why wouldn't he mention that? It should exonerate him, if everything had happened as he'd said.

And now I remembered that Jonathan, my client, had mentioned that Jankowski had a dash cam stolen sometime before the accident, and that was ironic, because if that hadn't happened, there would've been a video record, and wasn't it a shame that Jankowski hadn't bought a new one yet.

But he had. And he'd apparently lied about it later.

Why?

At four o'clock, there was a break in the rain, so I decided to get a jump on rush hour traffic and head for home, stopping at a Home Depot along the way for a mailbox, mounting post, and bag of ready-mix concrete.

When I got home, the rain had started again, so I couldn't install my neighbor's mailbox right then. Instead, I worked under the cover of my front porch, mounting a security camera directly above the front door, aiming at the steps. This time I chose a battery-powered model, so I wouldn't have to run a power cord into the attic or through a wall. Connected it via Wi-Fi and all was good. Took about eight minutes total.

Then I went inside and sat quietly on the couch in the living room and tried to think.

Possibility: Jankowski's dash cam wasn't working when the accident happened. His failure to mention that he had a dash cam wasn't any kind of cover-up on his part. He simply left it out because there was nothing of value on it.

Another possibility: The accident happened exactly the way Jankowski described, but he was exceeding the speed limit, and he was afraid the video would act as evidence against him.

One thing was for certain: If the camera was working that night and caught something good, Jankowski had deleted it long ago—probably immediately afterward.

I took a break at seven and ate some leftover pizza.

Tuned ESPN to a game between the Dallas Cowboys and the Washington Redskins. The Cowboys were having another mediocre year. No surprise.

Billy Chang hadn't called me back. Also no surprise.

By eight o'clock, the rain had stopped again and the moon was rising in a clear sky.

I texted Mia. *Staying out of trouble?*

Thirty seconds later, she replied: *Riding the trolley to Mango's.*

The trolley? I said. *Like common people?*

I hadn't heard of Mango's, but their website told me you could have "an epic party in South Beach's most legendary nightclub" where you could "keep the excitement flowing all night." I'm guessing the scantily-clad showgirls and enormous frozen drinks helped the party along. A page about bachelorette parties featured video of muscular bare-chested male dancers pumping and grinding for gleeful young ladies who might have had a few drinks. "A night she will never forget!" Yeah, I'll bet.

I'd be lying if I said I wasn't concerned about the kind of people Mia and her group might encounter in such a hard-partying nightclub—but then she sent a photo from inside the place. It was dead. For the moment, anyway. Further reading told me it didn't get going until late in the evenings, and not so much on weeknights. Mia and her gang would be gone by then.

Let me know if you see Lola, I texted. Good Lord, a Barry Manilow reference. Grounds for her to call everything off.

I was waiting for a reply, phone in hand, when an alert popped up on my screen. It was a notification from the GPS tracking app. Ah, man. I wasn't in the mood for it, but Lennox Armbruster's Alfa Romeo was on the move. I didn't *have* to go. I could monitor him on the app and see where he stopped, and then decide if I wanted to follow. His destination might make all the difference.

If he went to a movie theater or a restaurant, for instance, it was unlikely I would document any strenuous physical activities on his part. But if he went to a gym, or a Home Depot, or a driving range, then he might do something worthy of capturing on video. Problem was, he might hit a bucket of balls and be gone before I could get there.

I reluctantly pulled my shoes on and went out to the van.

Ten minutes later, before I'd caught up with the Alfa Romeo, it was already parked in a residential area in east Austin, along a short street called E.M. Franklin Avenue, which ran north-south between East 12th Street and Manor Road.

Odd to be making a social call at 9:33 in the evening, but not everyone keeps regular hours. Some people work evenings or overnight shifts. It also meant this trip was probably going to be a waste of time. Armbruster would be inside someone's home at nighttime, meaning I probably wouldn't be able to see what he was doing. They could be swinging from the chandeliers in there and I wouldn't be able to see it or film it.

I drove a few blocks past E.M. Franklin and hit a red light at the intersection of Martin Luther King Jr. Boulevard and Springdale Road. When the light changed, I pulled into a Valero and tried to decide how to proceed.

The Alfa Romeo hadn't moved. I was reluctant to drive past the home where it was parked. I didn't want Armbruster to see the van, even as nondescript as it was. I was wishing I'd brought my Toyota Camry—my secondary surveillance vehicle—but the van had some of my best surveillance gear in it.

The tracker is accurate to within twenty or thirty feet, so, out of curiosity, I checked for an exact address. It appeared the Alfa was parked at the curb in front of a house on the west side of E.M. Franklin, just a few doors down and across from the Austin Moose Lodge.

So then I checked the tax rolls to see who owned that home—and I nearly choked on my Dr Pepper.

Holy hell.

It was Brandi Sloan.

Joe Jankowski's receptionist.

8

"There's no way it's a coincidence," I said to Mia on the phone the next morning. "Jankowski didn't just randomly run down some guy who happened to know his receptionist."

It was just past eight o'clock and I was drinking coffee on the back porch. The neighborhood was quiet, although I could hear traffic in the distance. Still hadn't heard back from my neighbors regarding the note I'd left about their mailbox.

"And if he did," Mia said, "that's something he would've mentioned to somebody by now. The receptionist—"

"Brandi," I said. "With an *i*."

"Really?" Mia said.

"Yep."

"Okay, well, Brandi with an *i* would've pointed out that she knows the guy."

"Absolutely."

"How long did Armbruster stay there?"

"About nine minutes. Then he went back to his apartment. Hasn't moved since."

Earlier, when Mia had woken up, she'd texted me a photo of herself in bed. I won't go into detail, but the photo managed to be exceedingly erotic without being lewd or obscene, and I would treasure it until the day I died.

"You sure it was Armbruster?" she asked.

"Yup. I got a good look when he walked from his car to his apartment."

We were both quiet for a moment.

"I bet you have some theories," she said.

"Yup."

"The most obvious one being that Brandi and Armbruster are

pulling a scam together. Ripping off Jankowski."

"That's in the lead right now," I said. "Mostly because it's the only one I have. You got some others?"

"Let me think," she said. Then, a moment later, she added, "Nope. That's it."

"You think Armbruster knew Brandi before she started working for Jankowski?"

"Hey, I'm on vacation," Mia said. "This is too much thinking right now."

"How does it benefit them that Brandi works for Jankowski?" I asked. "I mean, couldn't Armbruster just as easily have jumped in front of some other wealthy dude's car?"

"I hear some of the other girls getting up," Mia said.

"In fact, doesn't the fact that she works for him make the risk that much greater—because some genius like me will come along and figure out the connection?" I said. "Assuming Brandi and Armbruster really are working together. But I can't think of what else it might be. Why would he be going over there if they weren't working together?"

If Brandi Sloan and Lennox Armbruster had a relationship prior to the accident on Exposition Boulevard, I would need to find solid evidence confirming it.

"I smell coffee," Mia said.

I said, "Now I'm wondering if Brandi Sloan applied for a job at Jankowski's place specifically to rip him off. Now, granted, that would be some long-range planning, but I've seen more elaborate scams. Then the question is…why? Would she and Armbruster go to that much trouble just so he could jump in front of Jankowski's car?"

I was just brainstorming and throwing out possibilities, which was often very helpful. It opened your mind to all kinds of scenarios you might not otherwise envision.

"Hey, I have an idea," Mia said.

"Excellent. What is it?"

"Solve this whole business before I get home, and then we can spend my first day home in bed together."

"That's a fantastic idea," I said. "But can't we do that anyway?"

"We'll see," she said.

"Will you wear the same item you're wearing in this picture?" I asked.

"We'll see," she said. "And delete that, by the way."

"After I have a poster made," I said.

I drove the van—with the new mailbox, post, and bag of concrete still in the back—to my neighbors' house. No answer when I knocked. So I spent the next thirty minutes pulling the old mailbox out of the ground and installing the new one. Looked good as new by the time I was done. Left another note on the door asking them to call me if they were unhappy in any way.

I went back home, showered, then grabbed my laptop and returned to the back porch. Time for some research. I started with the basics—social media and readily available public records. I quickly discovered the following:

Brandi Sloan was 33, which was a few years older than she appeared. Good for her. Maybe she had an effective skin-care regimen.

She had been arrested once, nine years earlier, for writing a bad check under the amount of $500. Those charges had been dismissed, meaning she had probably reimbursed the person or business to whom the check was written. Otherwise, her record was clean.

She was not registered to vote, nor had she made any political donations, as far as I could tell.

Prior to working at JMJ Construction, she had worked at a real-estate brokerage as an administrative assistant for several years, and prior to that, she'd worked a variety of retail customer-service jobs.

She had gotten a bachelor's degree from Texas State University in San Marcos, about forty-five minutes south on Interstate 35.

None of this appeared particularly helpful.

She was on Instagram and Twitter, with both accounts set to private, but much of the content on her Facebook account was visible to a stranger like me. I saw that she had a brother in Georgetown, a sister in Ruidoso, New Mexico, and her parents lived in Spicewood, just west of town. I assumed she was from this area originally.

I scrolled through all of her photos—thousands of them—going back nine years. No sign of Lennox Armbruster. It was possible she had also gone through them and deleted a bunch, or set them to private, but most fraudsters weren't smart enough to stay on top of stuff like that.

She was a big fan of UT softball, and it appeared she ate barbecue several times a week. She regularly jogged on the hike-and-bike trail along the lake. I discovered that she'd bought the house on E.M. Franklin about four months earlier. If there was a spouse or significant other, I couldn't find him or her, or even an ex. In that case, I could believe that she had gone in and deleted some photos, which is what a lot of people do about their exes.

I googled "lennox armbruster" combined with "brandi sloan" and came up with nothing.

I spent some more time studying the photo Mia had sent me this morning, just in case it held a clue. It didn't.

Went back online and spent another solid hour trying to find any trace of a relationship between Brandi Sloan and Lennox Armbruster. Found nada. Nothing. Zilch.

I didn't have a lot of options at this point except to wait, because Armbruster still hadn't moved today.

Patience.

Okay, then what to do with my day? More research?

Or should I get out and shake things up? If so, how?

I was pondering this very matter when hell flew and pigs froze over. That's my clever way of saying I received a call from Detective Billy Chang. As I mentioned, this gentleman wasn't big on sharing information with anyone outside the police force.

"That Ruger comes back as stolen," he said. "Case was never solved, so that's a dead end."

"From where?" I asked.

"A duplex in south Austin."

For Chang, this was a veritable verbal avalanche, or some other more artful turn of phrase.

"Were you able to pull any prints?" I asked, figuring I might as well try to get everything I possibly could while Chang was talking.

"Nope. Not even a partial."

Okay, now I could understand the reason for the call.

"So..." I said.

"Yeah."

"I shouldn't expect the guy to be identified anytime soon."

"Not unless something changes," Chang said.

"That's disappointing," I said.

"Tell me about it."

Reading between the lines, Chang wasn't going to work the case anymore unless some new evidence or information fell into his lap. Guess I couldn't blame him. Like most police investigators, he had more cases than he could possibly handle. He had to prioritize.

"Mind telling me the person who owned the gun?" I asked.

"So you can call her and make a pest of yourself?" Chang said.

"No way. Of course not. I mean yes."

A fat squirrel jumped from a nearby oak tree and landed with a thump on the roof of the porch.

"You think you're gonna find something I missed?" Chang asked.

"I wouldn't put it that way," I said. "I just know that every detective up there is absolutely buried, and that means there isn't enough time in the day to mess around with the smaller cases, like this one. If I'd been shot, sure, it would be a priority, but getting a gun pulled on me? Happens every day, and you've got more important things to do."

"You're a pretty good bullshitter," he said.

"Maybe, but it's also the truth."

"Tell you what. I'll give her your number and if she wants to call, she can."

"Fair enough," I said. "I appreciate it."

As I was walking outside to the van, I spotted Regina, our next-door neighbor, rolling her garbage cart up her driveway from the street.

I walked over and said, "Manage to sleep through the fun the other night?"

"I was watching through the window," she said. "Halfway expected that cop to slap the cuffs on you and haul you away."

"But you would've bailed me out, right?"

"Uh, yeah, sure," she said. "You can always count on me."

I felt a special connection to Regina because there had been an incident a while back in which a suspect in one of our cases had set fire to Mia's house. Fortunately, Regina was home and spotted the flames in time to put them out before they got completely out of hand. For that, she would have my everlasting gratitude.

On top of that, she was just a warm, funny person in general—someone you couldn't help but like. Great neighbor to have, and, quite frankly, it bothered me that my line of work could bring trouble or violence into our neighborhood that might potentially impact people like Regina.

I quickly told her about the man who accosted me on my porch and the vehicle that picked him up, doing my best to neither overstate nor underplay any possible risk to anyone else living nearby.

"Dude," she said. "You need to be careful. I've grown rather fond of you, but don't tell anyone."

"Never."

"Think they'll come back?"

"I seriously doubt it," I said, "Not here at the house. But I can't guarantee it. I don't even know who it was or what they wanted."

"Could've been random?" she said.

"Could've, but I don't think it was."

She grinned and shook her head. "Living next to you and Mia is an adventure."

"I'm glad you feel that way. That's better than saying we bring turmoil and danger into your life."

"I've always been a diplomat," she said.

"And a first-class human being," I said.

"Thank you. I'll check my cameras," she said, looking proud of herself.

Cameras? I'd been after her for quite some time to install surveillance cameras at her place. These days, there's no reason not to, regardless of who lives next door. Cameras are relatively affordable and easy to set up. The peace of mind they can provide is invaluable.

"So," I said, "you got some?"

"Yep. Last week. Four in total. Meant to email you."

"Excellent," I said.

"I'm just leaving now for a meeting, but when I get back, I'll take a look."

"I appreciate that," I said. "And if you happen to see anyone hanging around who looks out of place…"

"Other than you?" she asked.

"Oh, man. That's just mean," I said.

She laughed. "I'll let you know, but I'm leaving town tomorrow for a week."

"Where you headed?"

"Big Bend. Just going to hike and bird watch and pretend the rest of the world doesn't exist."

"Sounds nice."

"In the meantime—and I realize I've said this before—try to stay out of trouble."

9

If Brandi Sloan was upset about anything, I couldn't see it. There she sat, smiling and upbeat, behind the reception desk at JMJ Construction. A real sweetheart. A doll.

Then again, when I worked as a camera operator for one of the local news stations some years back, we had a receptionist who could charm a client as he came in the door and cuss him like a sailor after he'd left. We're talking world-class two-faced potty mouth. Great actress, really.

"You're back," Brandi said, as I made my way toward her desk.

"And my front," I said. "All of me is here to see Mr. Jankowski again, if possible."

"Is he expecting you?"

"I'm afraid not," I said. "I was in the neighborhood—not just a figure of speech, but for real—and I realized I needed to talk to him again, if he can spare a few minutes."

"Oh," she said, "I'm afraid he's not here right now. He's at a meeting and I think he'll be gone all day."

I had to wonder why she would ask if he was expecting me, and then reveal that he wasn't even here. Maybe she was simply wondering if Jankowski had forgotten about an appointment he'd had today. With me. I had no problem with the situation. In fact, I preferred it. I'd made the trip for the sole purpose of interacting with Brandi.

"Bummer," I said. "Well, that's okay. It can wait. Maybe I'll call him tomorrow. Nothing urgent."

"I'm sure he'll be happy to hear from you. Should I let him know you stopped by?"

"That would be fine," I said. "Thank you."

I made a show of turning to leave, but then I pivoted back around.

"Hey, Brandi, can I ask you something?"

"Sure," she said, all smiles. Just as friendly as can be.

"Okay, it's kind of…forward," I said. "I don't want to make you uncomfortable."

She didn't appear uncomfortable in the least, but she also didn't appear to understand where I might be going with the conversation.

"That sounds mysterious," she said.

"Not really, and just let me know if I'm overstepping any boundaries. See, I have this good friend—he's going to be one of my groomsmen, actually—and he's single…"

She laughed, because she finally got where I was going.

I said, "He's a great guy. Smart, handsome, funny. He can juggle chainsaws."

"A blind date, huh?"

"That's what I'm thinking."

"Oh, God. That's so sweet! But I'm seeing someone."

"I kind of figured you might be," I said. "All the best ones are taken, you know? I mean that in the least creepy way possible."

"That is absolutely the way I took it," she said. "You are so nice."

"Is it serious?" I asked.

She nodded enthusiastically. "It's been a year now."

A middle-aged man in a necktie came through the door and hurried through the reception area and down a hallway without the faintest acknowledgment of the two human beings he was walking past.

"Who's the lucky guy?" I asked.

"Well," Brandi said slowly, and I could tell now that she was deciding how much of her personal life she wanted to share with a man she hardly knew. Or perhaps she was stalling to make something up. Finally, she said, "His name is Karsten, and he's from Denmark."

"That's cool," I said.

"He's a software engineer," she said.

"Interesting," I said. "How did you meet?"

"In a bar. Doesn't that sound awful? I don't *ever* talk to men in bars! But I'm glad I made an exception."

The incoming line began to ring.

"I bet he is, too," I said. "And with that, I'll stop prying and let you get back to work."

"Okay. Good to see you again," she whispered as she answered the phone.

I stepped through the office door into the central atrium for the office building, and then headed for the double doors leading outside.

Hadn't really learned all that much from Brandi, except that she and Lennox Armbruster were not an item. Didn't mean they weren't scamming Jankowski together, but they most likely hadn't hatched the scheme while lying in bed together. Or maybe they had. You never know.

I exited the building and moved toward the steps leading downward to the parking lot. A woman in a suit was walking toward me, hurrying inside for a meeting, and I could smell the cigarette smoke from a man to my right talking on the phone. He was roughly twenty or thirty feet from the doors, as was required per the Austin smoking laws enacted back in 2005. Who would've guessed those laws would've impacted one of my cases so many years later?

Because I recognized his voice. Gritty. That was the best way to describe it.

He hadn't said anything of importance—"I'll be back over there in another hour or two"—but that was enough.

It was him. The man who had accosted me on my front porch. I was sure of it. The voice was too distinctive to be anyone else. There was one small difference this time, though. He was speaking as if he wasn't opening his jaw all the way—as if it had been recently injured. Maybe even lost a tooth.

That cinched it.

How to react? I had to make up my mind in in instant. I could approach him and lose the element of surprise, but then I would get a good look at him and could probably snap a decent photo with my phone. Or I could try to ID him without being seen, which was preferable, so I simply veered to my left when I reached the bottom of the stairs and walked away from the main entrance to the office building.

I snuck a quick backward glance and could see him now, leaning against the side of the building, phone to his ear and a cigarette dangling from his left hand. He hadn't seen me or even noticed me. Too focused on his call. I quickly jogged around to the rear of the building and found another set of double doors into the atrium. Went inside and hurried to the front again. Found a bank of windows to the right of the doors, and from there, I could catch a glimpse of my assailant from the side.

Couldn't see much, though. And there was too much glare on the window to get a decent photo. He was still on the phone, and the way he had his head down made it even harder to get a good look at his face.

I waited.

I had the advantage at the moment. I could stay right here, hoping to get a good photo, and then possibly follow him discreetly to his car, or to one of the offices, if he entered the building.

If for some reason that didn't work, I would simply walk right up to him, phone in hand, shooting video. See how he reacted.

I waited some more. He dropped his cigarette butt and crushed it with his shoe. Still talking on the phone.

Then I saw Joe Jankowski walking toward the building from the parking lot. He was also talking on the phone. He disconnected. So did my assailant, who now stood waiting.

Waiting on Jankowski.

What in the actual hell was going on here?

Jankowski mounted the steps and the gritty-voiced dude walked over to join him.

I snapped out of my bewilderment long enough to realize they were going to enter the building, and unless I hid somewhere fast, one of them would probably spot me.

I literally ran for the men's room door, forty feet away, and made it inside just in time. I ducked into a stall and locked the door behind me.

Waited some more.

Nobody entered.

I waited another full minute.

Joe Jankowski had sent that man after me with a gun. The question was why?

Less than thirty minutes later, Mr. Gritty Voice exited the building, and I got my first good look at him. Big guy, but big in the way of a man who needed to lose twenty pounds. Unkempt dark hair. Broad, flat nose. Thick eyebrows. Couldn't tell if his jaw was bruised, because he needed a shave. Close to forty years old. I snapped several photos of him as he walked through the parking lot to a white Chevrolet truck. I got a clear photo of the license plate.

Then I followed him at a safe distance as he drove north, to a three-story building under construction on Burnet Road, a few blocks south of 45th Street, with a large sign out front proudly identifying it as a JMJ Construction project.

Who would've guessed?

He drove into a parking lot surrounded by chain link—for authorized personnel only—and I parked at the next lot over, with a clear view of the building site. I figured he was going back to work and wouldn't be coming out for a while, possibly the end of the day. I was too curious about him to wait until I got home to do research. I got out my laptop, logged on to one of my favorite sites, and ran his plate.

Registered owner of the Chevy was Damon Tate. Switched to a different site and saw that Tate's driver's license photo matched the man inside the building.

Next I checked Mr. Tate's criminal history.

Good Lord.

Tate had been arrested nearly twenty times since the age of eighteen, including a couple of felony charges for assault and armed robbery. He'd been incarcerated four times. This was the man with a gun to my head a few nights ago. He wasn't the type to play around.

He'd been turned loose on an innocent public yet again just sixteen months ago, after serving three years for beating up a guy at a high school football game. The man was interviewed after the arrest, right after the game, and he'd said that Tate "thought I was staring at his junk in the bathroom, so he punched me in the side of the head."

At nineteen, Tate had been dishonorably discharged from the U.S. Army, but available records didn't say why. My understanding is that you had to do something fairly flagrant or stupid to get booted from the military. They didn't ditch people for getting drunk or having shoes that weren't quite shiny enough.

I dug some more but didn't find anything else relevant. I concluded that Damon Tate was just an all-around bad dude. A social misfit who couldn't contain his violent urges. The perfect man for Jankowski to send after me. But why? What was Jankowski trying to hide?

Tate was still inside the building, but I waited some more, just in case he went anywhere else. It would be great if I could slap a tracker on his truck, but the parking lot was just too busy for that.

While I was in research mode, I decided to see if Brandi was telling me the truth about her dating life. I went to her Facebook page and checked her friends list, and sure enough, there was a friend named Karsten. Yep, he was from Denmark. And he was a software engineer. She'd told the truth about that.

But I noticed that there wasn't a single photo of Brandi and Karsten together. She never mentioned him in any of her posts. Not once. No date nights. No selfies of the two of them on vacation or out on the town.

Then I went to Karsten's page and noticed that he was married. Happily, from what I could tell. For several years. To a man named Clarence.

10

Two hours later, after no further sign of Damon Tate and no new discoveries online, I drove toward home, pondering everything I'd learned.

Frankly, I was baffled, but as long as I kept acquiring facts and information, eventually I would be able to piece it together. One thing was for sure: This was not a simple accident involving an automobile hitting a pedestrian. There was something else behind it. Had to be.

Joe Jankowski had recruited Damon Tate to either do me great harm or attempt to scare me. What possible explanation could there be for that, except that Jankowksi was guilty of something and didn't want it exposed? That also explained why he didn't mention the dash cam in his SUV. He'd forgotten about it, and it had recorded the incident. I could only assume Jankowski had intentionally run Lennox Armbruster down.

But why?

Then there was Brandi. What role did she play, if any? I could believe that an attractive, single woman like Brandi had a ready-made excuse to fend off any unwanted suitors or matchmakers, but that didn't explain Lennox Armbruster's visit to her house.

I stopped for a late lunch at a Chinese buffet, and as I walked back to the Toyota afterward, I got a text from Regina, our next-door neighbor. She'd attached a video clip from one of her new surveillance cameras—a car passing by on our street exactly one minute before I'd called the police about Damon Tate. The getaway car. This clip was dark. Not a lot of help. Not yet.

I couldn't make out much about the car. It had two doors. I think. It was a mid-sized car. It looked gray, of course, because most cars looked gray at night through a camera using infrared light. White was an exception. I knew the car wasn't white. Yippee. Big progress. I froze the video to get a still shot of the car, but that wasn't much better. Honestly, a lot of today's cars look the same to me. Even if I had a clear photo, it wasn't like I could immediately identify it.

Just as I was about to get back on the road, my phone pinged with another incoming text, this one from an unfamiliar number.

My name is Claudia Klein and Detective Chang gave me your number. I own the gun that was pulled on you. Sorry about that! Feel free to call or text anytime.

She even added a smiley face.

I replied immediately. *Could we meet somewhere? Coffee shop?*

She was tiny. No more than five feet and maybe ninety-five pounds. In her late twenties, I guessed. Medium-length blonde hair, with a small swatch dyed bright pink in the back. She carried herself with confidence. As we talked, she struck me as the type you could easily imagine smiling at the top of a cheerleader pyramid ten years ago, but also the type that would make light of the whole cheer experience later.

"I really appreciate your willingness to talk," I said after some introductory chitchat.

"No problem," she said. "I don't know if I can help, but I'll try. Detective Chang didn't tell me much about what happened to you, just that a gun was pulled on you and it was mine. The one that was stolen."

We were seated at a two-top table at a place called Blue Dahlia Bistro on Bee Caves Road, west of town. Busy. Lots of women in yoga pants. Claudia Klein was having a strawberry cream cheese croissant. I was sticking with coffee.

"Tell me about that, if you don't mind," I said. "Were you burglarized?"

"Exactly," Claudia said. "Came home and found the back door open. Someone had broken one of the little glass panes and unlocked it. They got some jewelry, my laptop, and the gun—a forty-caliber Ruger."

"Do you live alone?"

"My ex-boyfriend was living with me at the time, but we were both gone. I was at work and he was out of town. Cheating on me, as it turned out. The jerk."

"That's not cool," I said.

"No kidding. Tell me you don't cheat on your women."

"Well, I don't have *women*," I said. "But I'm lucky enough to have one woman. A fantastic woman."

"Well, cute guys can get away with all kinds of nonsense, so I'm impressed that you don't."

"That's nice of you to say. What time of day did it happen?"

"The cheating?" she asked. "Just kidding. You mean the burglary. Sometime between eleven in the morning and eight that evening. Probably before sundown, because the scumbag hadn't turned any lights on, or at least they didn't leave any of the switches in the on position. If it had happened after dark, he probably would've turned on some lights and left them on."

"That's what the cops said?"

"No," she replied, showing a little faux offense. "I figured that out all by myself. I'm clever that way."

"I'm sure you are," I said. "Most people don't think of things like that."

"I guess he could've used a flashlight, but from what I understand, most burglaries happen in the daytime. Or a lot of them, anyway."

"That's true," I said. "Was your routine fairly regular, or did you work different shifts at different times?"

She laughed. "You're asking more questions than they did, and you actually sound like you know what you're doing."

"The cops didn't?" I asked.

"No, it wasn't that. It was just obvious that there wasn't much they could do about it. They'd open the case and that's about it, unless somehow I got lucky. Which is what happened, huh? I never expected to get my gun back at this point. Anyway, yeah, my hours changed pretty regularly on that job. Some morning shifts, some afternoon, and some evening."

"Where did you work?"

"A bakery on Congress Avenue. It closed down last year. They had the best baklava, but that wasn't enough to keep them going."

"Hard to beat a good baklava," I said.

"Isn't it?" she said.

"If only I knew exactly what baklava was."

"Oh, come on. You've never had baklava?"

"Not intentionally," I said.

"It's a dessert," she said. "Did you know that?"

"I did not. You must have quite the metabolism."

"Fortunately, yeah, I do. Can't put weight on if I try. Anyway, baklava is basically a pastry filled with chopped nuts and then soaked in honey."

"Okay, I'll admit that does sound good."

"Everything is better soaked in honey," she said. "And I mean everything."

She raised an eyebrow at me.

"I'll have to remember that," I said.

"Tell your woman," she said. "She'll appreciate the suggestion."

What were we talking about? I wasn't sure at this point.

I said, "How much did Chang tell you about my case?"

"The cop? Almost nothing. Just that someone pulled a gun on you and it turned out to be mine. Did the guy drop the gun or what?"

"I managed to take it away from him."

"Jeez, really? How?"

"I got lucky with a roundhouse elbow," I said.

Her eyes widened. "Seriously? You clobbered the guy?"

"Well, I don't want to sound like some sort of bad-ass street-fighting machine, but that pretty much sums it up. Knocked one of his teeth out."

"That's pretty amazing," she said.

"I didn't have a lot of options."

"So, why was this guy holding a gun on you?"

I told her what I did for a living and how that occasionally irritated some people. I didn't mention anything I had learned about Damon Tate or his connection to Joe Jankowski. I was saving that.

"That sounds like a pretty exciting job," she said.

"It can be, at times," I said. "But mostly it's just following people around and waiting for them to do something stupid."

"Ever see anyone do anything really weird?" she asked.

I had learned by now that Claudia was great at taking conversations off on tangents. It was a price I was willing to pay to ask her questions.

"Oh, sure. One time I was following a guy and he stopped at a bank for a roll of dimes. Then he went into a Taco Bell and ordered four burritos, and as he ate them, he swallowed the dimes with his food, one by one. And I could tell that part of the thrill for him was doing it out in public, and trying to be secretive, so nobody would notice what was going on."

Claudia stared at me for a long moment, confusion on her face. Then she said, "I could see one or two dimes, uh, working their way through your system, but an entire roll? Wouldn't that kill you?"

"Apparently not, because he did the same thing two days later."

"Wow. Please tell me it wasn't the same dimes."

I laughed. "I hadn't thought of that. I hope not."

She tore off another small bite of her croissant and held my eyes for a long moment as she nibbled it. Then she smiled. A couple of years ago, when my social circumstances were different, I might've tried to decipher the meaning of that smile.

I said, "Hey, let me ask you something. Do you know a woman named Brandi Sloan?"

"I don't think so. Doesn't ring any bells."

"How about Joe Jankowski?"

"Nope."

Now the big one.

"Damon Tate?"

"Sorry, no," she said. "Who are these people?"

How much to tell her? How much could I trust her?

"I'm not positive about this—not yet—but I think Damon Tate was the man who threatened me the other night. The man with your gun. I was hoping his name would be familiar."

"Damon Tate," she repeated. "If I've ever met him, I don't remember that name at all. Who is he?"

"He works at Joe Jankowski's construction company," I said.

"In addition to being an asshole burglar who steals stuff that isn't his?" she said.

"Well, we don't know for sure that he burglarized your place," I said. "Maybe he bought the gun from whoever stole it. He might not have even known it was hot."

"What did he tell the cops?" she asked.

"About possessing your stolen gun?"

"Yeah, and coming after you with it. What was he trying to

accomplish?"

"Well, here's the deal," I said. "The cops don't know about Tate yet. This is stuff I've dug up myself."

"Ooh, so I'm privy to top-secret information. Are you going to tell the cops about him?"

"Maybe later. Right now, no."

"Why not?"

Partly because they would tell me to stay away from him. They'd warn that I was interfering with an investigation. She didn't need to know that.

"Still piecing things together," I said. "Besides, would you rather have me working on the case, or them?"

"Okay, that's a good point. But if this Damon Tate is the dude who ripped me off, I want him nailed for it. Can you promise me that?"

"I can promise to do my best," I said.

"I want my laptop back. And my jewelry."

"Understandable," I said. "But don't hold your breath."

"Yeah, I know."

I had one more long shot—one more name associated with this case. "Ever hear of anyone named Lennox Armbruster?"

Her expression changed quickly to surprise.

"Oh, that idiot," she said.

"You know him?"

"He was my next-door neighbor back then. Is he somehow involved in all this?"

11

That was one of the many questions I needed to answer.

How did Damon Tate end up with a forty-caliber Ruger stolen from one of Lennox Armbruster's former neighbors? Was there a connection between Armbruster and Jankowski that I was somehow missing? Or maybe a connection between Armbruster and Tate? Frankly, that made more sense, what with both of them having criminal backgrounds. Maybe they'd met in prison.

And, of course, the central question remained: What was Jankowski trying to hide? He'd sent Tate after me for a reason, but what was it? What was so serious that Jankowski would hire an armed man to attempt to abduct me?

I was home again, sitting quietly on the back porch. An ice-cold bottle of Lone Star was resting on the top of the handrail. It was 3:38 in the afternoon.

Lennox Armbruster's Alfa Romeo was currently on the move, heading north on MoPac, but I didn't see any value in keeping him under surveillance anymore. Not right now. This case had grown much larger than his alleged injuries, which seemed to be real. It appeared there was some sort of conspiracy going on involving Joe Jankowski, Damon Tate, and possibly Lennox Armbruster and Brandi Sloan, and I needed to focus on unraveling it.

Claudia Klein had told me she'd lived next door to Lennox in a duplex for roughly a year. Didn't know him well, and that was by choice, because he was a rough type of guy, and she quickly suspected he was dealing drugs. This was based on lots of people coming and going from his place, staying for just a few minutes, and from snippets of conversations overheard through walls and fences. He was a meth user, at a minimum, she thought. He and his friends were often awake at all hours of the night. Sometimes they partied. Sometimes they got into heated arguments.

One time he tried to sell her a high-end stereo system at a huge discount, and that's when she wondered if he was fencing stolen goods. She'd mentioned Lennox's name to the deputy who'd written the report about the burglary of her residence, but if Lennox was ever questioned, she was unaware of it.

She noticed that Lennox seemed to avoid her after the burglary. Maybe he wasn't good at keeping secrets. Or maybe it was one of his friends or customers who had ripped her off, and he was embarrassed about it. Honestly, she said, she didn't know if Lennox had anything to do with it, but it was difficult to dismiss the suspicions. Drug users usually resorted to burglary, right?

After I'd given her some additional details of the case, she'd said, "Does this guy Damon Tate know Lennox?"

I said, "So far, I haven't been able to make a connection."

"But it seems weird that my gun got stolen, and it was later used against you, and you've got Lennox under surveillance, and Lennox lived next door to me."

"That sums it up," I said.

"How did Damon Tate end up with the gun if he doesn't know Lennox?"

"I'm working on that."

"No way that's a coincidence," she said.

"Probably not," I said.

I could tell she was enjoying the process of playing detective and trying to figure out the details of the case—enough that she might want to tell her friends about the excitement she was having.

So I said, "I would also consider it a big favor if you wouldn't discuss this with anyone else."

"I won't."

"Are you good at keeping secrets?"

"Pretty good, yeah."

"I don't need word to get back to anyone—Lennox or Damon Tate, especially—about what we've discussed. I can't afford to let them know what I know."

"No problem," she assured me.

Before we left the bistro, I promised to keep her posted, mostly because she deserved to know what was happening.

As much as I'd learned today, I felt like I'd hit a roadblock at the moment, which always made me restless, so I texted Mia.

Having fun?

I took a long drink of the Lone Star and enjoyed the way it cooled my throat. It was a nice moment out here on the patio, with doves cooing in the trees—but my mood was dampened when I remembered the secret I still needed to share with Mia. Maybe I was blowing it out of proportion. Maybe it wouldn't matter at all.

Mia sent back a photo of a plate of Cuban-style shredded beef, with yellow rice and plantains on the side. Looked pretty damn tasty.

Early dinner? I asked.

Late lunch, she said. *How are you?*

Making headway, I said. *Will fill you in later. So to speak.*

She sent me the emoji of a face with shocked, wide-open eyes.

Right then I received an alert that the tracker on Lennox Armbruster's Alfa Romeo had stopped sending a signal. I waited a full minute—hoping the car was simply in a dead spot—but it didn't come back online.

Could the battery have died already? Seemed doubtful, but it was possible. I knew that at least half the charge remained yesterday. Could be defective. Batteries only lived through so many recharge cycles.

Another possibility was that Armbruster, or someone else, had discovered the tracker and disabled it. Crushed it with a hammer. Dropped it into a toilet. Whatever. But I'd hidden it well.

I opened the app and checked the recent activity. Armbruster had still been on MoPac, up north near Parmer Lane, moving along at 77 miles per hour, when the tracker had stopped working. That ruled out anyone finding it.

Had to be the battery or some type of electronic malfunction.

I went inside and grabbed another Lone Star out of the refrigerator. I'd decided I was done for the day.

But I stood in the kitchen with the capped bottle dangling from my hand, unsure of what I wanted to do next. Still restless. I could see out the window above the sink to the street in front of the house. Craned my neck and saw that the mailbox I'd installed that morning was still standing. Imagine that. Maybe I should be hosting one of those trendy home-improvement shows.

I looked in the other direction. Didn't see any bad guys parked at the curb, watching the house. Then again, I didn't expect any.

I was fidgety.

I knew what was bothering me. The tracker. I couldn't remember the last time one had simply stopped working abruptly. Sure, I'd seen the battery power slowly dwindle, but they didn't drop from a 50% charge to nothing in a matter of 24 hours.

I set the bottle of beer on the counter and opened the Waze traffic app on my phone. It's a handy navigation system that also shows user-reported wrecks, traffic jams, speed traps, and so on, all in real time.

Sure enough, there was a wreck at MoPac and Parmer Lane.

I closed Waze and opened a police scanner app. Tuned in to the Austin Police Department frequency. Immediately heard a tense voice saying extraction was going to be required. Several units were on the scene. Two vehicles involved. EMS was en route. All northbound lanes were closed. Never a good sign when all lanes were closed. Obviously a major wreck.

At this point I assumed Lennox Armbruster was involved, and the crash was severe enough that the GPS tracker had been destroyed.

I listened to more chatter back and forth, but I didn't learn anything else.

It was almost two hours later before any video from the scene made it on to the local news channels. But when it did, the footage included various shots from the wreck itself. Cops directing traffic. Long lines of cars backed up as far as the camera could see. Witnesses standing on the median, waiting, arms crossed, anxious. An ambulance rushing to the hospital.

A Ford Excursion with a damaged front end.

And a crumpled Alfa Romeo.

I was tempted to call Mia and tell her what had happened. Get a fresh perspective on the entire case. But she didn't need me bugging her.

I continued checking news reports, social media, and various online sources, and it wasn't long before I had a more complete picture of the wreck, although they weren't naming the victims yet.

According to witnesses, a dark-colored truck—which was possibly a Chevy or a GMC or even a Toyota—had swerved into the Alfa Romeo's lane, as if the truck driver hadn't seen the much smaller vehicle, and that caused the driver of the Alfa Romeo to swerve, too. He lost control and careened to the right, and then back to the left, and ended up perpendicular to the lanes of traffic, and was then T-boned by the Excursion, which was moving at roughly 75 miles per hour.

The driver of the truck hadn't stopped.

Interesting.

Maybe he hadn't seen the wreck he'd caused. Maybe he thought he'd be charged with something. Maybe he was drunk or stoned or texting. Maybe he simply hadn't had a chance to stop because of the traffic coming up behind him.

I'm saying "him," but I don't even know if that's accurate, because nobody had gotten a look at the driver. One witness said the truck had some writing on the passenger-side door, possibly a business logo and phone number. Other witnesses said it did not. A different witness said the truck had a dented rear fender, but, again, nobody else could corroborate that.

A reporter said one driver was transported to Brackenridge Hospital with life-threatening injuries. The other suffered minor injuries. Which was which?

I spent another hour pondering ways to proceed, and I got nowhere. Sometimes you can't just wait around. Sometimes you have to rattle the bushes and make things happen.

So I came up with a plan.

12

A plan? Sure.

I've said it before and I'll say it again. Everybody has a plan until they get punched in the mouth. That's a quote from Mike Tyson, and I'm sure it applies in the boxing ring, but it also applies figuratively, to life itself.

I took a punch to the mouth the next morning when I walked into the offices of JMJ Construction for the third time.

My plan—wise or not—was to confront Joe Jankowksi and see what I could get him to say in response. Tell him I knew he'd sent Damon Tate after me and that I'd seen them together yesterday. Tell him I knew he'd had a dash cam in his SUV when he'd hit Lennox Armbruster. Prod him about the fact he didn't stop right away after the accident, until he noticed there was a witness nearby. Try to piss him off. Make him blurt something out.

Meanwhile, I would be wearing a hidden camera, of course. In my hat. Compact, but the video quality was damn good, and the audio was crisp. I might not get very far, though. He might kick me out after the first question. Or he might be the type who wants to hear everything I know. Who thinks he's smarter than everybody else. In that case, I'd push him as far as possible.

That was my plan, for what it was worth.

But then I walked into the offices and saw a different young lady sitting at the reception desk.

"Brandi, you've changed," I said.

The young woman smiled. "I'm Cindy. Brandi isn't here today."

"Oh, yeah? She sick?"

"Well, we're not sure. We haven't heard from her yet, which is totally unlike her. Anyway, I'm filling in."

Doesn't happen often, but I was at a loss for words.

"You okay?" Cindy asked.

I probably had a stunned look on my face. Sometimes that is unavoidable, despite my attempts to roll with the unexpected.

"You bet," I said. "Uh, but I just remembered that I have a pedicure this morning. Where is my head today? Not on my feet apparently. I'll have to come back later."

Cindy emitted a laugh, but I could tell she didn't know if I was kidding or not.

I started to turn for the door, but I couldn't leave it at that. I said, "Not that it's any of my business, but has anyone tried to call Brandi?"

"I did, several times."

"Has anyone called the cops?"

"Somebody said they couldn't do anything for 48 hours, I think," Cindy said.

"That's not exactly true," I said. "An officer can swing by her house and see if everything's okay. But somebody needs to call and explain the situation, and then ask for a welfare check."

She looked at me, uncertain how to respond.

"Will you call?" I asked.

"Yes."

"Promise? You don't need your boss or anyone else to give you approval."

"I will, really. Right now."

"A welfare check," I repeated. "Insist on it. Tell them how reliable she normally is."

She lifted the phone and held it to her ear. I gave her a wave and exited the office.

That news scuttled my plan, for now. I wouldn't confront Jankowski until I'd thought this through.

I sat in the van, dumbfounded, quite frankly. Another rarity. I'd seen a lot in my years working fraud cases, but occasionally I still heard or saw something that shook me up pretty good.

This was one of those cases.

Brandi Sloan was missing.

Had she taken off? Had something happened to her? Was she simply sick and had her phone turned off? Seemed unlikely, but it was possible. I might be overreacting.

I started the engine. Made my way over to Interstate 35 and went north. Waded through heavy traffic until the MLK exit and went east to E.M. Franklin Avenue. Drove slowly past Brandi Sloan's house—my first time seeing it—and was impressed. The place appeared to have been recently renovated—fresh paint, new metal roof, extensive landscaping. A Land Rover Discovery was parked in the driveway. Not a cheap vehicle. All of this raised new questions. How did a receptionist afford all this stuff? Family money?

There was no sign of a patrol officer yet, so I pulled to the curb. Waited.

Ten minutes passed. Not a single car, bike, or pedestrian, went by.

I decided I would wait another thirty minutes, and if an officer hadn't arrived by then, I'd go check it out myself. At least knock on the door and peek through any open windows.

Finally, just as I was about to get out of the van, a patrol unit showed up and parked at the curb. I stayed where I was. Watched as the cop climbed out and walked up the sidewalk to the front door. He knocked and waited. Knocked again and called out. Repeated several more times. He keyed the microphone attached to his collar and spoke to dispatch.

Then he tried the front doorknob and found it unlocked. He swung the door open, called out again, and then went inside.

I realized my entire body was tense.

Five minutes passed.

Then the cop came back outside and closed the door behind him. He tucked a note or business card into the crack between the door and the frame, then returned to his unit and drove away.

Simple as that.

He'd found nothing. Had seen nothing that concerned him.

Brandi wasn't inside.

But she was still missing, wasn't she? For the moment, yes, she was.

It occurred to me that Brandi was now the second person connected to Joe Jankowski who'd gone missing. What was the name of the first person? Took me a moment to recall.

Brent Donovan. The construction worker who had tried to orchestrate a fake injury on a Jankowski job site. Then he'd fled town to avoid criminal prosecution.

I was starting to wonder about that.

"Mrs. Donovan?"

"Yes?"

"I'm hoping I can speak to you for a few minutes about your son Brent."

"Who is this?"

Doris Donovan sounded fifty years old, but I knew she was really 84 from looking her up in online records. She'd given birth to Brent when she was 47 years old.

"My name is Roy Ballard and I'm a legal videographer. It's a long story, but I am currently working on a case that has made me aware of Brent's disappearance."

"I'm sorry, you're a what?"

"A legal videographer," I said.

"I'm not sure what that is," she said.

I'd read the newspaper articles that had been published in the days after Brent allegedly fled town to avoid prosecution, and that's where I'd learned his mother was the only family he had left. I figured if anyone could shed any light on this at all, it would be her.

"Normally I investigate insurance fraud," I said. "And before you hang up on me, please hear me out. Do you happen to remember when a little girl named Tracy Turner went missing?"

"Why, I do remember that. The whole city was looking for her."

"I'm the man who found her."

I paused to let that sink in. I was shamelessly using that accomplishment to gain her trust.

"Bless your soul," she said. "What was your name again?"

"Roy Ballard," I said.

"Hang on a sec," she said.

I waited. Didn't know what she was doing.

"Ma'am?" I said.

"I'm just googling you," she said.

I had to laugh. She was googling me. Teach me to make assumptions.

"Smart," I said. "Make sure I'm telling you the truth."

"Damn right," she said. Twenty seconds later, she said, "Well, I guess you are a genuine hero."

"I wouldn't say that...even if it's true."

"And humble," she said.

"Absolutely," I said. "That's one of my most admirable traits, my humility."

Now she laughed, and then she abruptly went quiet again. I knew she was continuing to read the article. She was learning more about my past. A long moment passed, and then she said, "Oh. I see that your own little girl went missing."

"She did, yes, many years ago. Her name is Hannah."

"She was abducted."

"She was, but a smart cop found her."

It was my fault, I wanted to add. *I wasn't watching her closely enough. Even two minutes was too long to leave her unattended. I failed. My marriage failed. My ex remarried, and now my daughter lives two thousand miles away. We talk now and then, but she isn't much interested in her dad. Too busy being a teenager—or that's what I tell myself. Harder to face the fact that we simply don't have a close relationship.*

Doris Donovan said, "I live in Westwood. You know that neighborhood?"

"Yes, ma'am. Very well."

"Why don't you come over and we'll talk?"

"What time would work for you?" I asked.

13

Westwood was an upper middle-class neighborhood in the city of Westlake Hills that had been built in the sixties and seventies. Doris Donovan's home was on the north end of Blueridge Trail. The lawn was immaculate. An iron gate opened onto a flat stone patio that led me to a bright red front door. I was pleased to see a security camera hanging from the eaves.

The door opened before I reached it and there stood Doris Donovan. She was short and slender, with ramrod-straight posture. Her short hair was as white as a duck's feathers. She wore round, rimless eyeglasses.

"Well," she said, "you're more handsome than that horrible photo in the newspaper."

"I think they captured my worst side," I said. "My front."

She laughed and shook my hand with a firm grip. "Please come in. I made coffee."

Five minutes later, we were seated in her living room, which featured a wall of east-facing windows that provided a breathtaking view of the Austin skyline. I'd done some snooping and learned that Doris had lived in this house for nearly fifty years. Her husband had passed away nineteen years earlier. She hadn't remarried. Brent was her only child.

"Beautiful place," I said.

It was one o'clock in the afternoon.

"It's old enough now that things are starting to fall apart. Just like me."

She laughed, so I did, too. "You seem like you're in great shape," I said.

"I walk the mall nearly every day," she said. "Barton Creek Mall. Sometimes on nice days, I walk the trail around Town Lake."

I noticed she didn't refer to the lake by its newer name, Lady Bird

Lake. Hard to drop the old name after all these years.

"How far do you walk?"

"Three or four miles, at least. Sometimes farther if I'm up for it."

"Thanks again for seeing me," I said.

"Would you like some cookies with your coffee?" she asked.

It was possibly the most grandmotherly thing I'd ever heard, which was ironic, since she was not a grandmother.

I nearly declined reflexively, but I caught myself and said I'd love some. She went into the kitchen and came back a minute later with half a dozen cookies on a small plate, which she placed gently on the coffee table.

"Thank you," I said. I grabbed one. It appeared to be oatmeal and chocolate chip.

"I'm still not sure what you're after, to be honest, but you didn't sound like a cop or a reporter, so that got you through." She looked at me skeptically. "At least for the moment."

"I'll do my best to behave myself," I said.

"Make sure you do," she said.

I liked her, and I think she liked me.

I took a bite of the cookie, and wow, it was fantastic.

"These are incredible. Did you make them?"

"I did. My mother's recipe."

"Your mother was some sort of wizard," I said, "and she must've passed the gene along."

"I'm glad you like them."

I took another bite, then said, "Let me explain why I'm here."

"That would be a good start," she said.

So I gave her an overview, without too much detail. Explained what a legal videographer was, and told her I was working on a case that was connected to Joe Jankowski. Then I told her someone involved in this current case seemed to have disappeared—although it was too early to know where she had gone, or why. She might pop back up at any minute. But it made me wonder about her son Brent.

She was ahead of me. "I've been trying to tell the police for months that Brent didn't just take off," she said. "He disappeared."

"And what have they told you?"

"Well, I don't think they believe anything I say, because they think I'm protecting him. They haven't come right out and said that, but it seems obvious to me. When I push back, they say they have no way of finding him unless he uses his credit cards, or unless someone spots him. Or if someone finds his body. I hate to think it will come to that, but I've prepared myself for it."

"What about his cell phone?" I asked.

"They found it in his apartment. Wherever he went, he didn't take it with him. Makes me wonder if he left in a hurry."

My reason for coming here was simple: to determine if Doris Donovan had heard from her son anytime after he disappeared. I didn't even need to ask outright. It was obvious she had not, or that she was a hell of an actor.

"What kind of son was Brent?" I asked, just to keep the conversation going.

"He had his problems, no doubt about that," Doris said. "I tried to help him on dozens of different occasions, and then it reached a point where he had to help himself. Tough love. I'm sure you've heard that phrase."

"Yes, ma'am."

"At the same time, he had a lot of good qualities. He was very friendly and you couldn't help but like him. Always joking around and laughing. He made friends easily, and many of his friends he's known since he was just a boy—going all the way back to first grade."

"That's rare nowadays," I said.

"I've talked to all of them several times, but if they know where Brent is, they aren't saying. Being loyal, I guess."

I nodded slowly and took another nibble on the cookie.

She said, "Once he started working regularly at that construction job, I was hoping he'd turned things around. But then he came up with that nonsense about the cement mixer." She was shaking her head, and then she let out a sad laugh. "That was really an idiotic scam, wasn't it? How on earth did he think that was going to work?"

"Did he admit to you that he'd set the whole thing up?"

"Not really, but I'm his mom. I could tell from the things he said. And then that other man he worked with came forward and spilled the beans. Just such a mess. I offered to hire an attorney for him—for Brent—after Joe Jankowski started pushing so hard for criminal charges. See, I don't think Brent even understood he could get in serious trouble for that kind of fraud. He thought he'd get fired and that would be the end of it. And Brent said he didn't need an attorney because he had a way to straighten everything out. He said Jankowski would drop the whole thing."

"He thought he had a way out of it?" I asked.

"That's what he said."

"What was the way out?"

"I don't know. He never told me. He disappeared just a few days later."

She looked toward the windows—the skyline in the distance—and I could see that she was getting emotional.

"I'm sorry," I said.

She took a moment, then said, "I'm not naïve enough to think I'll see him again, but I'm hoping to find out what happened to him. I think that's reasonable, don't you?"

"Absolutely," I said.

"And you seem to have a knack for this sort of thing, which means I'll help you however I can."

Driving. Just driving. Heading west on Bee Caves Road. Sometimes just getting out and cruising could help me think.

What I knew so far:

Joe Jankowski had struck Lennox Armbruster with his SUV—allegedly an accident—and he'd had a dash cam installed at the time, even though he'd said he hadn't.

Based on what little I'd seen, Armbruster had not been faking his injuries. I couldn't ascertain whether or not Armbruster had stepped in front of the vehicle on purpose.

Damon Tate, the man who'd accosted me on my porch, was an employee of JMJ Construction. He'd carried a gun that had been stolen from Claudia Klein, who used to be Lennox Armbruster's neighbor.

There was no indication that Armbruster had any association with Jankowski or Damon Tate prior to the accident. Didn't mean there wasn't a connection, just that I hadn't found one.

I hit Highway 71 and took a right, then drove for a couple of minutes and took a left on Hamilton Pool Road.

Brent Donovan was almost certainly dead. A guy like him—a bumbler without a lot of common sense—couldn't disappear for any length of time without leaving an electronic trail or getting spotted. It just wasn't feasible. I was a believer in Occam's razor, the philosophical and scientific principle that the simplest explanation was usually correct. Not always. Usually. Was Brent alive and somehow managing to avoid detection and capture, despite the fact that technology today makes that damn near impossible? Or was he dead and buried in a shallow grave somewhere? Occam's razor said it was the grave. The only other scenario I could envision was Brent being kidnapped and held somewhere. But why? And by whom?

Doris Donovan had given me a short list of names and phone numbers—Brent's friends and a few coworkers. She'd also sent me along with a plastic bag of cookies, and I had already eaten five. Shame on me.

I turned left, heading south, on Ranch Road 12. The little town of Dripping Springs was eight miles ahead, but before I got there, I took another left on Fitzhugh Road. By now I had a destination in mind.

Ten minutes later, I turned on a caliche driveway between two cedar posts. Drove fifty feet and parked in a flat, grassy area.

Not long ago, I'd bought a nice little piece of land out here. Nine acres with one hundred feet of Barton Creek frontage. Gorgeous place. Heavily wooded with oaks, cedars, and a few madrones. I'd planned to build a home here, near the pristine waters of the creek, but then things had changed—for the better. Mia and me.

I got out of the van and walked down to the creek. The recent rain had it flowing well. I simply stood there on the bank and enjoyed a quiet moment.

It was right here that I'd told Mia I loved her, and now this spot would forever hold a place in my heart. That's why it was so difficult to come to terms with the idea of selling it. But it made sense. Mia and I were getting married, and we planned to remain in the Tarrytown house afterward, and I was all for it. So why keep this tract of land? If I sold it, I would make a nice little profit, too.

Because we were getting married.

Right?

What if we weren't?

Letting that thought take root in my head brought a wave of melancholy over me as palpable as the leading gusts of an unexpected cold front.

It was too much to take. What if Mia couldn't live with the news I needed to share with her?

Worse, what if she decided she could live with it, and we moved forward, and she ended up terribly unhappy as a result? I couldn't bear to think about that.

But come on. Not so fast.

I was getting ahead of myself. Maybe the problem wasn't a problem after all. I wouldn't know for sure until I spoke to the specialist. I'd called his office this morning and scheduled an appointment in three days.

But I would talk to Mia before then. Probably as soon as she got back home. She deserved to know what was at stake.

I walked up the hill and got into the van.

Normally I left the Barton Creek property feeling recharged and a little less stressed, but this time I simply felt down. Sad and anxious.

I got back onto Fitzhugh and turned left on Highway 290, and my mood did not improve when I began to suspect that I was being tailed by a black GMC truck.

After two miles, I pulled into a gas station. The black GMC continued down the highway. As the tank filled, I got back inside the van and retrieved my Glock nine-millimeter semi-automatic from a secret hiding compartment under the rear bench.

Five minutes later, I got back on the road, and before I reached the Y—a busy intersection in Oak Hill—the black truck was behind me again.

14

The truck's front license plate was missing. That's illegal in Texas, but some people—even those who weren't tailing someone—liked to remove the front plate. This was especially true for owners of expensive vehicles who didn't like the plate ruining the slick look of a high-dollar sports car. Cops might pull you over for it occasionally, but it wasn't high on their list.

I took a right on William Cannon Drive and the truck followed, staying eighty or ninety feet back, with a small coupe between us.

I turned right on Escarpment Boulevard, left on Convict Hill, and right on Beckett Road. The truck followed, but still hanging back. This shows you the level of skill I was dealing with, which wasn't much. The GMC truck thought I still hadn't spotted him. What was his plan? It could be something as ill-conceived as pulling up next to me and opening fire. That's the kind of thing an amateur would do. Sloppy, sure, but I could wind up just as dead. So I had no intention of letting him catch up. Good thing I knew this neighborhood.

I hung a quick left on Hitcher Bend, a quiet road that provides a shortcut to Davis Lane, a busy thoroughfare with a median in the center. A privacy fence at the intersection of Hitcher Bend and Davis was blocking the truck's view of me for the moment, which was handy. Instead of staying on Hitcher Bend, as most people do when using it as a cut-through, I took a right on Neider Drive, then a left on Fulbright Lane, and then I eased to the curb and waited.

From here I could see Hitcher Bend again, and I would easily spot the black truck. It was doubtful he would look to his right and see me, because he would be turning left toward Davis. Basically I was pulling the same trick Steve McQueen pulled in *Bullitt*. One minute the truck was following me, the next I would be following him.

A few seconds later, the black truck appeared, moving slowly, and sure enough, he hung a left and continued to the stop sign at Davis Lane. By then I had eased away from the curb and followed behind him.

The rear window of the truck was tinted fairly dark, but as I pulled up behind the truck, I could see two silhouettes inside, both of them looking left and then right—looking for me. Wondering where I'd gone. How had I disappeared from view so quickly?

I noticed the truck had no rear license plate, either. That was a major red flag. You don't remove your rear plate unless you're planning to commit a crime and don't want anyone to ID your vehicle.

The truck still hadn't budged from the stop sign, and now the person in the driver's seat froze, plainly looking at the rearview mirror. I'd been spotted. I gave him a dainty wave, fluttering my fingertips. The passenger turned and looked directly at me. Wish I could've gotten a better look at him and the driver, but the tint was just too dark. Was one of the men Damon Tate? Impossible to tell.

I gave them a shrug, like, *Well, it's your move. How are you going to play this now?*

Frankly, I was having a good time.

But I would be ready with the Glock, too, if I needed to be. Right now I had it cradled between my thighs, muzzle pointing downward, chamber empty.

Finally, there was a break in the traffic on Davis, but the black truck didn't move. No other vehicles had pulled up behind me. I put the van's transmission in park, just in case. I could see the men inside the truck talking. Arguing, even. The passenger looked back at me again.

I racked the slide on the Glock, popped my seatbelt loose, then gripped the door handle with my left hand, ready for action. If either man started to exit the truck, I'd hop out and wait just long enough to see a weapon. Then I'd do whatever I needed to do. I was glad my dash cam was recording all of this.

By now my heart was pounding in my chest, palms getting warm and moist. I tried to breathe deeply and slowly.

I knew I should just back the van up and leave, but I couldn't resist the temptation to stay and fight. If something happened—if one or both of them stepped out of the truck—there was a good chance I would learn something from the ensuing confrontation.

The passenger door opened about ten inches.

Now a garbage collection truck was coming down Davis Lane from the right.

The passenger door of the truck closed, and now the driver mashed the accelerator and took a hard left, tires squealing, pulling in front of the garbage truck, which had to hit the brakes.

Not a bad move.

I pulled into the center of the road, to the break in the median, but I was stuck waiting for the garbage truck to pass, and then there was a car behind it, and a motorcycle after that, and by the time I was able to make the left, the truck had a sizeable head start.

The van isn't any rocket ship, but it moves along a little more quickly than most people would suspect. Still, most vehicles were faster, and by the time I passed the garbage truck and had a view of the road ahead, the truck was leading me by at least a hundred yards. I could see it blowing through a stop sign and then pulling into the left lane to turn onto the expressway—but several cars were waiting there at a yield sign. So the driver changed his mind and swung back into the middle lane, passing under the expressway and picking up speed quickly.

I was in the left-hand lane. Just as I began to give it some gas, an SUV took a right out of an apartment complex and pulled straight into my lane. I couldn't switch to the right-hand lane because the motorcyclist I'd passed earlier was coming up quick from behind.

Stuck again for the moment.

But the SUV drifted into the left-turn lane and now I had open road ahead. The black truck was now just a speck, but I gunned it hard and tried to catch up. The speed limit was 40 through here, but I was hitting 75.

Blew past Copano Drive.

Blew past Corran Ferry Drive.

Now I was going 85 miles per hour and was gaining on the truck. Less than forty yards ahead.

Stupid, yeah. Risky. But I had open road. I saw no pedestrians. No joggers. No bicyclists.

Then I approached Ovalla Drive, which intersected from the right, and a large panel van—a repair vehicle of some kind—started to make a left from Ovalla, crossing in front of me, a T-bone collision waiting to happen.

I had to stomp the brakes hard. I mean *hard*.

The driver of the repair vehicle saw me and panicked, also hitting his brakes, which made the situation worse, stopping directly in my path. His eyes were wide and fearful as my van bore down on him. My wheels were locked and my tires were smoking.

And my front bumper stopped two feet from the terrified man's door.

After my nerves settled, I pulled into a convenience store parking lot and called JMJ Construction.

"Brandi Sloan, please."

"I'm sorry, she's not available right now. May I take a message?"

"Cindy?"

"Yes?"

"This is Roy Ballard. The guy who was in there this morning? Handsome and charismatic?"

"Oh, hi!"

"I'm just wondering about Brandi. Any word from her?"

Cindy lowered her voice. "Not yet. I called the police, like you said I should, but they said she wasn't home. They said there wasn't a lot they could do right now, and that I should check with her friends and family members, which I did."

"Nobody has heard from her at all?" I said.

"Not that I know of. It's kind of scary, but everyone up here is acting like it's no big deal."

"Does Mr. Jankowski know what's going on?"

"I haven't seen him today."

"He hasn't been in?"

"I don't think so, but he doesn't come in every day. Sometimes he has meetings, or he visits the construction sites."

"Hands on kind of guy, huh?"

I was talking just to hear her tone of voice or hope she might say something useful. You just never know.

"I'm sorry," she said, "I don't think I ever got the company you're with."

For the first time, she was wondering why I was asking so many questions and had an interest in Brandi's whereabouts.

"I'm just a subcontractor," I said, which was true, in a sense. "I had a meeting with Joe three days ago. That's when I met Brandi, and she seemed so nice, and that's why I'm a little worried about her. Hey, does the name Lennox Armbruster ring any bells?"

"I'm afraid not."

"How about Damon Tate?"

"Oh, I remember him calling for Mr. Jankowski a couple of times last week. He works for us, I think, but I'm not sure what he does. I have to ask…are you like a cop or something?"

Not suspicious, just curious.

"No, I'm looking into a case of insurance fraud. That's all I can share with you, but I do appreciate your help so far."

"Oh, no problem. Will you let me know if you find Brandi?"

"Absolutely."

Man cannot live on cookies alone, so I stopped at a little Tex-Mex joint called Casa Arandinas, on Brodie Lane, just south of Davis. It was nearly three o'clock and I was ravenous. The place was fairly quiet at this time of day, so I got seated right away. Didn't bother with a menu, but instead went with the beef enchiladas. Always a good test meal at a new Tex-Mex place.

The décor was about what you'd expect. The walls were faux stucco. Arched niches—recessed no more than six or eight inches—were painted with kitschy murals, such as a sombrero-wearing gentleman dancing with his señorita. Heavy wooden tables were surrounded by barrel chairs made from red pleather and brass studs.

Members of the wait staff wore crisp pink button-down shirts with the restaurant's logo over the left breast. A full bar on one side of the room had dozens of glasses hanging upside-down from overhead racks. Guessing they would serve up a damn tasty margarita.

And, of course, half a dozen TVs hung at evenly spaced intervals around the room. Most of them had the volume off, or so low I couldn't hear, except for the one TV closest to my table.

It was tuned to a local channel, and before I could get the first tortilla chip into my mouth, I heard a short promo for the upcoming news at five.

New information on the major crash on MoPac last night, said the anchor, a perky blond woman with extremely white teeth. *More at five.*

New information was always promising. What would it be? More details about the cause of the accident? An update on the injured driver's condition?

I pulled my phone out and went to the website for the station that had just aired the promo. Found the relevant article and clicked on it.

And I finally learned that Lennox Armbruster was the driver who'd been taken to Brackenridge. His injuries were no longer considered life threatening.

Witnesses said that in the minutes leading up to the crash, Armbruster had been the victim of an apparent road rage incident. The truck in question had been following him closely, then pulling around him and swerving into his lane, or getting in front and hitting the brakes. Trying to intimidate him, at a minimum, or hoping to make him lose control and crash. Which is exactly what had happened. One woman claimed that the passenger had pointed a gun at Armbruster.

What kind of vehicle? Witnesses said it was a black GMC truck with tinted windows.

Of course it was.

And a few witnesses mentioned that it had no license plates.

Of course it didn't.

15

I still wasn't ready to share everything I'd learned with the cops. Part of that was ego—me thinking it was better to look into things on my own—and part of it was apprehension that the cops would interview Damon Tate and perhaps Joe Jankowski, and learn nothing, but alert them both that I knew that Tate was the man from my porch.

I'd asked Doris Donovan to put a star on the list beside the names of Brent's five closest friends, and when I got home, I called them. None of them answered, which was not a surprise. Unfamiliar phone number. I left a similar message each time.

My name is Roy Ballard and I'm trying to find your friend Brent. I'm not a cop. Actually, I work for an insurance company as a legal videographer. I learned about Brent through a different case involving someone Brent knows and, quite frankly, it just seems weird to me that the police aren't making more of an effort to find him. If you have a minute, please call me back and let's talk about it. I spoke to his mother Doris today and she'd love to know where her son is. Thanks. Call anytime.

My theory was the same as it had been when meeting with Doris: If these five people knew that Brent was alive and well and maybe even knew where he was, they would not call me back. But if they were concerned about him and hoping someone would do something to find him—something more than the cops had done—they would return my call. They would be grateful that someone was looking into it more deeply.

So I sat. I waited. I got up and grabbed a beer from the refrigerator. Sat back down again.

Checked the time. Wondered what Mia was doing right now.

The weather had gotten cooler in the past few hours and the heater had been running. I made a mental note to check the filter.

Then my phone rang.

One of Brent's friends, Raul Ablanedo.

"Dude, I am so glad somebody is finally doing something about this," he said. "He, like, disappeared, and I know it looked like he probably just took off, but there ain't no way. He's the kind of guy who would face the music—know what I mean? He's not a runner. He wouldn't run. That's not his style. He's got friends, you know? And his mom. No way would he just take off."

All I had said so far was, "Hey, thanks for calling me back." He hadn't even asked me to explain in greater detail who I was and why I was interested in the case.

"How long have you known Brent?" I asked.

"Since middle school," he said. "Sixth grade. He's my bro."

Raul struck me as the laidback stoner type.

"And you haven't heard from him?" I said.

"No, man. Not a word. He, like, vanished. I'm telling you, he would serve a couple of years in jail instead of running away forever. He's a mellow guy. If he did run away—which he wouldn't—he'd let me know he's okay. He'd email me or something. Or get a new phone and send a text."

"How often did you see him?" I asked.

"In person? Maybe every two months or so. Life's busy, you know? But we were texting all the time."

"Did he tell you anything about the incident at the job site?"

Raul laughed. "The incident? You mean the scam he was trying to pull? Yeah, he told me a little, but not much. Just that he accidentally got hurt, and then one of his coworkers ratted him out, and then his boss was doing every damn thing he could to make sure Brent went to jail for it."

"When was the last time you texted or talked to him?"

"Well, the last time he replied was the day before he went missing. It was on a Friday. Of course, nobody knew he was missing right then, until it became obvious he was gone, and the cops figured out a few days later that the last time anybody saw him was that Saturday. I texted him Sunday, the day after, but he never got back to me. It wasn't a big deal, because I was only asking if he wanted to come over and drink a couple of beers."

"You don't think there's any chance he just decided to haul ass?"

I asked. I used a tone of voice that said, hey, this is just between you and me. I won't tell anyone. Promise.

"Zero chance of that," Raul said. "None at all. Where would he go? All his friends are here. Besides, if I thought he was hiding out, I wouldn't be talking to you."

"And I wouldn't blame you. Friends stick together."

"Damn right."

"Did he ever mention anyone who was mad at him? Anybody who might want to harm him or get back at him for anything?"

"Nah, man, except for his boss, obviously." Raul said. "Jablonkski or whatever it is."

"Jankowski."

"Yeah, that's it. He's the one you should be looking at. He probably had somebody do it."

"I talked to his mom earlier today and she said Brent talked about having some kind of way out of his troubles with Jankowski—something that would make Jankowski drop the charges. You happen to know what that might've meant?"

"You mean after he got injured in the scam?"

Of course I did. Why would Brent be talking about a way out *before* his scam went south?

"That's right," I said. "After the scam. Jankowski was coming after him hard, but Brent assured his mother he had a way to make all of his troubles go away."

"But he didn't say what it was?" Raul asked.

"I'm sure you can figure out the answer to that one, Raul," I said, maybe a little too sharply.

"Dude, I'm, like, trying to help."

"I'm sorry."

"Be patient with me."

"Of course."

"The answer is no, I don't know anything about that. He was probably just saying that to make his mom feel better. That's the type of thing he would do."

So Brent Donovan had disappeared. So what? How did that help me with the Lennox Armbruster case? Who's to say it was connected?

My thoughts turned again to Brandi Sloan. Had she reappeared?

I knew from my years working in offices, such as the news station, that the receptionist always knows *everything* that is going on with the employees. Affairs. Divorces. Medical issues. Legal problems. Drug use. Who's about to quit or get fired. The receptionist either hears about these things outright or can piece it together from incoming phone calls, mail, and overheard conversations. They are the eyes and ears of the organization.

Had Brandi Sloan learned something she wasn't supposed to know? If so, had something happened to her, or had she had the sense to get the hell out of there?

Surely the police were looking into this by now. They had the authority to monitor her cell phone and bank cards. Should I tell them I suspected a connection between the Brent Donovan case and her disappearance—and, hey, by the way, maybe it had something to do with Lennox Armbruster, too?

Yeah, right. I needed more than that. I wasn't even convinced myself.

Start at the beginning...

Brent Donovan came up with a stupid scam and got exposed. Subsequently, Joe Jankowski wanted him prosecuted to the fullest extent of the law. Then Brent disappeared. No warning. No traces left behind. Just gone. And the consensus from his mother and friends was that Brent had not gone on the run, and something had happened to him.

Why? By whom?

I couldn't answer the first part, but I could guess the second part.

But why would Jankowski harm Brent Donovan when it appeared Donovan was going to be prosecuted for his scam? To make an example out of him? Maybe it was simply because Jankowski was an ill-tempered asshole. He got angry and did something rash. Or had someone do it for him.

How did Lennox Armbruster fit in? No frigging idea.

I was too tired to think straight.

I woke at 2:23 in the morning. Didn't need to take a leak. So what had stirred me?

I lay quietly and listened. Five minutes passed. Nothing.

Started to doze off again, but then I heard something. Just a soft, unidentifiable sound, like any old house makes many times in the night. Nothing unusual about it. Could be floorboards contracting, or the wind gently pushing against the siding, or the weight of water in the pipes in the walls.

Damn it.

I climbed from bed, slowly and quietly, and put on some sweatpants that I'd draped over a chair. Then I went to my dresser and opened the second drawer. There, nestled under some sweaters, was a Mossberg pistol-grip pump-action 12-gauge I'd bought for home protection. This particular model had only recently become legal in Texas. Loaded with double-ought buckshot—one in the chamber, five in the tube. Less than thirty inches long.

I stood there in the semi-darkness, the Mossberg cradled in my hands, and listened. Five more minutes passed. Still, nothing. I retreated quietly to my nightstand and grabbed my phone with my left hand, still holding the Mossberg in my right.

Opened the app for my security cameras. Clicked the window for the camera on the front porch. Started with a live view. Nobody out there. Scrolled through the timeline, looking for activity in the past several hours. Nothing unusual. Cars passing on the street every now and then. An occasional moth flying past.

Clicked the window for the camera on the back porch. Live view showed nothing there, either. So I scrolled through the timeline and saw a man in a ski mask on the porch seven minutes earlier. He had approached the back door, tried the knob, found it locked, then disappeared to the left side of the camera, moving counter-clockwise around the house, toward Regina's house. When he walked away, I could see a handgun dangling from his right hand.

Call the cops. Call 911.

Nope. I wanted to handle this one myself.

I slipped my phone into the pocket of my sweatpants and moved slowly from the bedroom into the hallway, shotgun aimed ahead of me. The alarm system would alert me if the guy had breached a door or window. It was top dollar. Hard to get around, especially for anyone who doesn't circumvent alarm systems regularly.

I stopped in the short hallway and listened some more. The heater shut off and the place was quiet.

Think like him. What would he do after he found the back door locked?

Go around the perimeter of the house and check the windows. They'd all be locked. Okay, what next?

If his job was to kill me, he couldn't just give up and leave. Breaking in would be too noisy. I would hear him coming. So what would he do?

Try to lure me out. Or to a window. Make me show myself and present a target. He'd make a noise. Something that would make me curious, but not suspicious.

I waited some more. There was no value in moving around the house. I wasn't going to peek out any windows or open any doors, so it was better to stay put. Wait for him to make his move.

I checked the cameras again. Nothing. Made a mental note to add even more cameras to the perimeter of the house, including the sides. Should've done that already. Stupid. Needed to cover every possible angle.

A few minutes later, the heater kicked on again. That would mask any soft, subtle sounds. Stupid of me, because I was standing right beside the thermostat. I reached over and lowered the target temperature several degrees. In thirty seconds or so, the unit would shut down again.

Still waiting. Maybe the intruder had called it off. Lost his nerve. Good chance of that, unless he was a pro. Pros don't just give up and go away without good reason.

The heater shut down again.

It was now 2:34.

Checked the cameras again. Nobody in front, nobody in back. That I could see.

Maybe he really had gone away.

Then I heard the sound—very loud—and I'll admit it made me jump.

Cats fighting just outside my bedroom window, between my house and Regina's. For maybe a quarter of a second, I bought into it. That's how realistic it sounded. Yowling like you wouldn't believe.

I let ten seconds pass.

I took a deep breath.

Then walked back to the bedroom doorway and turned on the light. That's what I would normally do if cats actually were having a fight outside my window.

Then I moved quickly but quietly down the hallway, through the living room, still in darkness, and eased the back door open. I stepped outside onto the back porch. Slowly. So glad it was concrete and not a wooden deck that might squeak or groan under my weight.

The catfight was even louder now—and it didn't sound quite right. Out here, without the walls as a buffer, it was more obvious that the sounds were artificial—coming from the man's phone, most likely.

I wanted to give my eyes time to adjust, but I couldn't afford to wait. I stepped from the porch onto the cool grass, the Mossberg extended in front of me, and made my way toward the corner of the house.

The yowling stopped.

I reached the corner and paused. Then very slowly peeked around.

The man in the ski mask was ten feet from my window, the handgun extended in front of him, gripping it with both hands. Waiting for me to show. The light from the window was washing over him, even through the curtains. What an idiot. It also meant he had light in his eyes—not a lot, but enough to prevent him from seeing me, should he look this way. Which he would, real soon.

I had been in situations like this before, and it makes the adrenaline flow, but this time, I was oddly calm. Confident. I had him. No question.

Staying where I was, the corner of the house providing protection, I pointed the shotgun at his midsection and said, very firmly, "Don't move!"

Know what he did? He moved.

He swung toward me with his revolver and I had no choice.

I pulled the trigger.

16

Helpful tip: Don't shoot anyone if you need to be anywhere soon, because your next four or five hours are going to be occupied, at a minimum. Maybe several years or even decades, if the cops and the DA decide the shooting wasn't justified.

The detective assigned to the case was named Randy Wolfe. I'd never met him, but that might've been the point. Give the case to someone who'd had no dealings with me before, positive or negative.

"So what happened tonight?" Wolfe asked. "Walk me through it."

We were seated in a small, windowless interview room inside Austin Police Department headquarters. Obviously, I'd already told my story—the highlights, anyway—to several people, including the 911 dispatcher and the initial responding officer, who had turned out to be Ursula Broward. Of course, she was followed by several more, because that's what happens when you shoot someone. Then the crime scene techs arrive, and several members of upper brass, and sometimes the medical examiner.

"Is he dead?" I asked. I was feeling nauseous. Somewhat lightheaded. Still adrenalized.

"We'll get to that," Wolfe said.

"That means he's dead, right?" I said. "Who was it?"

I knew it wasn't Damon Tate. The guy I'd shot had been shorter than Tate. Smaller.

"Go ahead and tell me what happened," Wolfe said. Easygoing demeanor. Not pushy.

He was in his mid-forties. Thinning hair, with a goatee. Maybe six feet tall. Dressed in jeans and a blue polo shirt, with his badge and revolver clipped to his belt. Slender, but well muscled, like a triathlete or distance runner. I'd gotten the sense, in just a few minutes, that he was keenly intelligent and competent. Could be wrong.

I said, "I woke up—still don't know why, maybe a noise—around two-twenty or so. Checked my security cameras and saw that a man wearing a ski mask and carrying a gun had been on my back porch a few minutes earlier."

I was expecting him to ask a very obvious question right here, but he didn't ask it. He let me keep talking.

I said, "So I grabbed my Mossberg and waited to see what might happen next. I kept watching the cameras, but I didn't see him again. I don't have cameras on the sides of the house—just front and back."

"Where were you at this point?"

"In the hallway just outside the master bedroom. I shut off the heater so I could hear better."

He nodded, as if he thought that was a smart move.

I said, "Nothing happened for probably six or eight more minutes, and then I heard the sound of cats fighting just outside the bedroom window."

"The master bedroom?"

"Right. But I knew it wasn't really cats. He was playing a recording on his phone—trying to get me to part the curtains and look out."

"How did you know this?"

"Gut instinct. It just didn't sound real."

"What did you do?"

"I turned the bedroom light on, because that's what he would expect, and then I hustled down the hallway and out the back door. When I peeked around the corner, he was waiting there with the gun fully extended, aiming at the window. He was waiting there to shoot me. I yelled—told him not to move—but he swung around with the gun and I had no choice. I shot once and that was enough. He dropped his gun immediately and fell to the ground."

"It's a twelve gauge?"

"Right."

"Buckshot?"

"Yes."

He nodded again. "Why didn't you call 911 before you went outside?"

There it was. The obvious question. Could be a legal minefield.

"I wanted to handle it myself. I'm within my rights to respond to an armed man on my property. Standing my ground, right? He was a danger to me, and if I'd waited for an officer to arrive, he could've been gone by then, at which point he might've been a danger to my neighbors, too. Or he could've come back later. I had the element of surprise, knowing he was there, so I wanted to take advantage of it. But I didn't want to kill him."

Wolfe didn't argue the point.

"Do your security cameras record to a DVR or stream to the cloud?"

"The cloud."

Smart question. Video on a DVR could be deleted fairly easily and quickly, whereas video on the cloud, not so much.

"We'll need that video," he said.

"Absolutely. I'll get you a copy."

See how cooperative I was?

"Tell me what was going through your mind as you made your way outside," he said.

Trying to get me to say the wrong thing. That was his job, to some extent.

"I just wanted to catch him and hold him until the police arrived. I would've much rather had it happen that way. I didn't want to shoot him, but he forced the situation."

Which was all true.

"How much time elapsed between the time you told him to drop his gun and your shot?"

"It was immediate. He spun toward me and I shot."

"Could there have been some other explanation for his sudden move? Maybe he was simply surprised."

"No. No way. He was turning to shoot me. No question about it. He led with the barrel."

"It was pretty dark on that side of the house," Wolfe said. "Are you sure you could see what—"

"I saw the gun in his hand," I said. "I don't mean to interrupt, but there was plenty of light for me to see the gun. There was no question in my mind about that. And you'll see the gun clearly on the video from the porch."

I didn't want a prosecutor to claim later that I'd seen the gun *after* I'd shot the guy.

"What happened after the shot?" Wolfe said.

"He dropped his weapon and fell to the ground. I stayed at the corner of the house, watching, to make sure he didn't reach for the gun again. There was a little bit of movement, and some unpleasant sounds, and then nothing else."

"What kinds of unpleasant sounds?"

"Coughing. Gurgling. He sang part of a Barry Manilow song."

He raised an eyebrow at me.

"Just trying to lighten the mood," I said. "I'm kind of shaken up, to be honest."

"Understandable. So he didn't actually say anything?"

"He did not."

Right now, as we were having this conversation, I knew my house was cordoned off with yellow tape and crawling with police personnel. The curb in front of our house would be crowded with marked and unmarked vehicles. All the commotion would wake the neighbors on both sides of the street. I'd sent Mia a lengthy text earlier, explaining the situation, so she wouldn't hear it first from someone else and wonder if I was even alive. I'd stressed that I was fine and she shouldn't worry and I'd be in touch ASAP.

"Did you approach him?" Wolfe asked.

I noticed he didn't say "the body." Might mean something. Or not.

"No, I stayed right where I was at the corner of the house and called 911."

"You had your phone with you?"

"I did."

"Were you holding it and the shotgun at the same time?"

"It was in the pocket of my sweatpants. I was wearing sweatpants. No shirt, no shoes."

In these interviews, no detail is too small. That's how they determine if you are telling a consistent story. Would I mention the sweatpants later, or say I was wearing something else?

"So you shot him and then called 911?"

"Right."

"How quickly after the shot?"

"Within thirty seconds. After it appeared he wasn't going to move."

"You didn't attempt to render any first aid?"

"Nope. He could've been bluffing. The gun was within his reach."

"You didn't touch the weapon?"

See? Questions designed to make you contradict yourself.

"Didn't get anywhere close to it. Like I said, I stayed where I was, at the corner."

He paused for a moment. Trying to decide what angle to take next.

"Any idea where your neighbor is?" he asked.

"Which one?"

"The one on the side where you shot the guy. We knocked on the door several times and nobody answered."

He was hoping to find a witness—someone who could confirm or counter my story. He wasn't going to find one.

"That's Regina," I said. "She's out in Big Bend right now."

"She live alone?"

"Yes."

"What about you?"

"My girlfriend—my fiancé—and I live together. She's in Miami Beach."

He nodded slowly. He was a very deliberate man who chose his words and questions carefully.

"Any idea who the man tonight was?" he asked.

"None. You got an ID on him?"

"We're working on it. Can't even speculate who it was?"

He might've already identified the man. He wouldn't necessarily share that with me.

"I'm not a fan of making wild guesses," I said.

"Humor me."

"No offense, but I'd rather not."

He continued to ask questions, many of them similar to questions he'd already asked, for another thirty minutes. All of the questions were specific to the shooting itself and the minutes before and after it. At one point I checked my watch and saw that it was nearly five in the morning, and by then I was tempted to get up and leave. After all, I was free to go whenever I wanted. But, again, it was better for me to cooperate in this situation, in order to cultivate a decent ongoing relationship with the police.

He finally widened the scope of his questioning. "You think this guy tonight had anything to do with the armed man you encountered on your porch a few nights ago?"

So he'd been filled in on that. He'd probably had a conversation with Billy Chang, the detective assigned to that case, before this interview. Woke Chang up in the middle of the night and got the lowdown.

"Possibly," I said, "although 'encountered' doesn't quite do it justice. I prefer the word 'accosted.'"

He grinned for my benefit. "What's the story on that?"

"Well, that's a good question, Randy, but that's a long story, so before I start, you mind if I take a leak?"

17

I was buying myself a few minutes to make a decision.

If the armed man tonight was connected to the Jankowski/Armbruster case—and he probably was—how much should I tell Wolfe? I decided the answer was all of it. Time to dump it into his lap and let him take it from there. Meanwhile, I could move on with my life. In fact, by moving on, perhaps Jankowski would stop sending armed men after me. If I wasn't poking around in his business, he wouldn't see me as a threat. Right?

So, when we both returned to the interview room, I spent a solid thirty minutes telling Wolfe everything, starting with a more detailed explanation of what I did for a living and why some of the people I put under surveillance might want to harm me.

Then I gave him the specifics of the Armbruster case and the questions it raised:

Where was Armbruster going when he was struck by Jankowski's vehicle?

Where did Armbruster get the money for the new Alfa Romeo?

Why didn't Jankowski want to admit he'd had a dash cam in his SUV? Had the camera simply failed to record the accident, or was there more to it? Had he hit Armbruster on purpose?

What was the significance of Armbruster's visit to Brandi Sloan's house? Did they know each other? Were they scamming Jankowski together?

When I reached the part about hearing a familiar voice outside of Jankowski's office and identifying that person as Damon Tate, I fudged a bit. I said Tate *sounded* like the man who'd pulled a gun on me, but I couldn't be sure, and maybe I was letting my imagination get the best of me. I waffled because if I'd *known* Tate was the man from my porch, the cops could give me some serious grief for failing to report what I'd learned.

Likewise, I made no mention of having attached a GPS tracker to Armbruster's car, because I don't like sharing information that implicates me in a crime. I'm funny that way.

Wolfe was taking notes, but he hadn't asked any questions yet.

So I continued, telling him about my interview with Claudia Klein, the woman whose stolen gun had been used against me by the man on my porch, and I revealed that Lennox Armbruster had lived next door to her. Coincidence? No way.

It also wasn't a coincidence that Armbruster had nearly been killed two days ago in a wreck.

Or that a black GMC truck had been harassing him. Or that I'd been tailed by two men in a black GMC truck yesterday.

Wolfe listened and took detailed notes, and that indicated that the prowler tonight was probably, or at least possibly, tied into the Armbruster case. If he were unconnected—if he were simply a random burglar or psychopath, for instance—Wolfe wouldn't concern himself with any of this stuff. A detective couldn't afford to be distracted or sidetracked by unrelated cases.

So I asked him, "Know the name Brent Donovan?"

"Not off the top of my head," Wolfe said.

"He was a construction worker for JMJ who went missing after he tried to stage an accident on a job site. He still hasn't been found. I think the official APD conclusion is that he's fleeing prosecution, but from what I know, he's not smart enough to pull that off. Even his mother agrees. I talked to her yesterday."

I could tell this was news to Wolfe, but obviously he couldn't be familiar with every case APD handled.

"You think Jankowski did something to him?" Wolfe asked.

"I think *somebody* did," I said. "And Jankowski had a pretty good motive."

"What was the motive, if Donovan's scam had been exposed?"

"Revenge," I said. "Jankowski is a hothead. Talk to him and that becomes obvious in about five minutes. He's the kind of guy who would want to teach Donovan a lesson."

"And you're thinking the same thing is true with Armbruster? Jankowski thought it was a scam—Armbruster jumped in front of his SUV on purpose—and Jankowski decided to have him killed?"

I couldn't tell if Wolfe was buying into my theory or not. He was probably still gauging my credibility.

"Seems like a reasonable possibility," I said, "depending on who was driving the black GMC truck. And this may be unrelated, but that receptionist I mentioned earlier, Brandi Sloan—the last I knew, nobody could find her. She didn't show up for work yesterday morning. Dispatch sent an officer out to her place for a welfare check and she wasn't home. Armbruster was over at her place three nights ago, and now he's in the hospital and she's missing. What would you conclude from that?"

It was a rhetorical question, but even if it weren't, Wolfe wouldn't have answered.

Instead, he said, "Excuse me for a minute." He got up and left the interview room, closing the door behind him.

I waited patiently. Mia had not called or texted me back, but it was still early in Miami and she was probably sleeping.

Wolfe came back six minutes later. I'm guessing he had used that time to instruct someone to look into the Brandi Sloan situation. See if she had been located. He had two cans of Dr Pepper with him, one of which he set in front of me. I popped the top and took a long drink as Wolfe got settled into his chair.

"Let's say you're right about all this," Wolfe said. "If you're trying to help Jankowksi out of a fraud situation, why is he sending men after you with guns? That's your theory, right?"

He knew the answer, but he wanted to hear it from me—to have it on record.

"Because he's afraid I'll find out what really happened to Brent Donovan and Lennox Armbruster and perhaps Brandi Sloan. If he did anything to any of those people, he doesn't want anyone looking into it. At this point, hitting Armbruster with his car is the least of his worries, even if he did it on purpose."

"Do you have evidence for anything you're suggesting?" he asked.

"Just my razor-sharp instincts," I said.

"It's all circumstantial at this point," he said.

"Want me to beat a confession out of someone?" I asked.

"What I want you to do is tell me more about hearing Damon Tate outside Jankowski's office."

"What would you like to know?"

"How certain were you that he was the man who tried to abduct you on your front porch?"

"Not certain at all. I just noted that the voice sounded very similar, but I knew I'd need more to determine if it was him or not."

That's known as fudging.

"So what else did you do to find out?"

"Like I said earlier, I got his license plate and identified him, and then I followed him to a job site on Burnet Road, which is how I confirmed that he was a JMJ employee. Beyond that, I did nothing."

I was positive the man I'd shot a few hours earlier was not Damon Tate, but maybe my perceptions had been altered by fear and adrenaline. Maybe it *had* been him, which would explain Wolfe's focused interest.

"You never approached him. Never talked to him?" Wolfe asked.

"Nope."

"Never did anything to let him know you knew what he'd done?"

"I didn't *know* he'd done anything," I said.

"Any idea if he saw you tailing him?"

"I don't think he did, but I guess anything is possible."

"Did you confront Joe Jankowski about his connection to Damon Tate?"

"Actually, I went to his office yesterday morning to do exactly that, but I discovered Brandi Sloan was missing and decided to hold off. Why all this interest in Tate? Was it him that I shot?"

I could tell Wolfe was wavering. Some investigators would withhold that information until they'd done their best to verify my statements and determine if I was being totally forthcoming. I believe I had earned Wolfe's trust by this point, or perhaps he wanted to see my reaction. Seasoned investigators could learn a lot from expressions and body language.

He stared at me for a long moment, then said, "His name is Nathaniel Tate. Damon Tate's younger brother."

Oof. A punch to the stomach. I let that sink in for a moment. "I can tell you right now that I had no interaction with him whatsoever. I never even knew he existed until now."

Wolfe didn't need me to lead him to the obvious conclusion—that Damon Tate had sent his brother after me.

"I assume you checked Damon's record at some point?" Wolfe asked.

"Of course I did. Needed to know who I was dealing with—if it was him on my front porch."

"Then you won't be surprised to know that that kind of behavior runs in the family. Nathaniel is even worse, actually. Both of them are bad dudes."

"You said *is* and *are*," I pointed out.

"He's alive. But you did some serious damage to him."

"How bad? Is he going to live?"

"Probably. He might be paralyzed from the waist down. Piece of buckshot grazed his spinal cord. The doctors don't know yet how it will affect him."

I felt more relief than I expected. Don't know why. Nathaniel Tate had been trying to murder me, but I was glad I hadn't killed him. Not just because he could be questioned and perhaps become a witness, but because I didn't want a death on my hands. Even a justified one. And if he survived, perhaps Damon Tate wouldn't come after me seeking an eye for an eye.

Or maybe he would anyway. Maybe I couldn't move on with my life just yet after all.

18

At 4:17 that afternoon, Mia exited the secure area on the second floor and came down the escalator toward baggage claim. I could hardly contain myself, waiting on the lower floor by a stone pillar, but I have to admit the anticipation was half the fun. Her eyes were searching for me, jumping from person to person, and when she was halfway down, she spotted me and began to smile. I grinned back as my heart melted. Damn. I hoped that I would always appreciate how she made me feel and never take moments like this for granted.

We had agreed earlier, on the phone, that we wouldn't discuss Joe Jankowski or the Tate brothers or any of that stuff until tomorrow. I'd already updated her by phone after my interview with Wolfe, but we still needed to discuss how—and if—we were going to respond to the situation. But that could come later. Tomorrow.

She reached the bottom of the escalator and began to stride across the marble floor. I stayed right where I was, knowing the pillar would give us a tiny bit of privacy.

"Wow," I said as she got close. "Check the tan. If it's possible, you're even hotter than—"

She pressed her lips against mine and kissed me hard, wrapping her arms around my neck. I encircled her waist and kissed her right back.

It was intense. Almost too much.

Finally she stopped for a moment and said, "I missed you so much."

"I missed you, too," I said. "But if you keep that up, I'm gonna have to hide behind this pole for a while."

"Which pole are you talking about?" she whispered into my ear.

"Oh, man," I said. "We'd better grab your luggage and get out of here before there's an incident."

We went home, straight to the bedroom, and spent the next two hours doing many of the things I'd been daydreaming about in her absence. Yet again, I found myself reveling in the fact that such a beautiful woman—such a caring, giving woman—was willing to hop into bed with a guy like me.

Now we were lying quietly, enjoying the late afternoon. She had one arm draped over my chest, with her head resting on my shoulder.

"At the risk of repeating myself," I said, "your body is ridiculous."

"Thank you."

"I mean, seriously. Do you realize what you look like? Ever seen yourself in a mirror?"

She nuzzled in closer. "You're sweet. You have a few physical attributes of your own that I happen to appreciate."

"Stop it. I'm swooning."

"Your elbows, for instance. They are totally hot."

"I exfoliate. And I use cocoa butter."

"It shows."

"It's a strict regimen invented by George Clooney."

"He never said a word about it the last time we were in bed together," she said.

"Well, if he experienced what I just experienced, he was probably speechless."

"Nice," she said.

The weather outside was gorgeous, but I didn't risk opening the bedroom window—not solely because I'd dealt with two armed intruders on the property in the past few days, but because I didn't want Mia to start thinking about what had happened right outside that window. There was probably still blood on the grass.

"So I take it you enjoyed Miami Beach," I said. "Did you young ladies behave yourselves?"

"More or less.

"More or less?"

"Well, *I* did."

"But the others?"

"Let's just say we all had a great time."

"Some hijinks going on?"

"I'll never tell. Nobody did anything they shouldn't have done."

"Then how did you have fun?"

"We are mature adults. You should try it."

"Somebody must've gotten wild. I bet it was Dianne, that little harlot."

"Dianne is dating Clint, and they're serious. And she's not a harlot!"

"Then it was Cheryl, the strumpet."

"Nobody hooked up with anybody. Sorry to disappoint you."

"I'm crushed."

"Cheryl did meet a guy from Dallas she really liked. This was by the pool. He was staying at the hotel."

"Did anyone warn him that she's a strumpet?"

"You know how shy Cheryl is. She was too nervous to even talk to the guy."

"So you pumped her full of booze?"

"We tried to boost her confidence and then gently encouraged her to say hello, as good friends do in these types of situations."

"And then you bought her a couple of margaritas?" I asked.

"And then she had a respectful adult conversation with a man who turned out to be a true gentleman."

"Right before she tore her top off and cannonballed into the pool?"

"Exactly," Mia said. "That's exactly how it all happened."

"I figured as much."

"Other than the obvious, did anything exciting happen while I was gone?" she asked.

"Let me think. I won three dollars on a scratch-off card, so we can afford to remodel the kitchen now. Oh, and the fat squirrel in the backyard continues to raid the bird feeder shamelessly. I worry about his cholesterol."

We fell into silence again for a long moment.

Now was the time to tell her—to share the secret I'd been holding in. Surely I'd been worrying too much. Everything would be fine. It would all work itself out one way or another, right?

But, of course, now that I'd worked up the nerve, I could tell from her breathing that she'd dozed off. It was not even eight o'clock, but I had a suspicion Mia would be out until the morning. That was fine. The conversation could wait.

19

He'd had a bad dream, but it was all too real.

Waking in a haze, unsure of his surroundings. In a bed. Dim light. Staring at a window to his right, but his eyes wouldn't focus. Near sunrise? Near sunset?

Where the fuck was he? What the hell had happened?

Was it a hospital? Sure smelled like one. Fucking gross.

He rotated his head to the left and something popped. Jesus effing Christ, that hurt. Sore as hell. Moving was not a wise idea.

But now he could see a door. Partially open to a hallway. Hospital for sure. Late at night? Where were the retards who ran this place?

Still couldn't focus.

His neck hurt like a son of a bitch, so he straightened it again and stared at the ceiling.

He tried to call out, but something was wrong with his mouth. It wouldn't move. He couldn't open it. His teeth were clenched. Something wrong with his jaw. He tried to raise his right hand to probe his face, but he couldn't lift his arm. Too heavy. Same with his left. He could shift both of his legs an inch or two, which was great news, but he couldn't move them any more than that.

Out of the corner of his left eye he could see some kind of tall electronic machine near the bed, not far from his left elbow. It had various gauges and digital readouts, but that's all he could tell.

There was a TV mounted high on the wall in front of him, but it was not turned on.

Was it a car wreck? He seemed to remember a crash. Couple of men in a black truck hassling him—pointing a gun?—and then a crash.

Then this. Being here.

He wished he could focus and look at his phone. He might be able to figure things out. Wait, where was his phone? What had these retards done with his phone? Morons. No telling where it was right now. Or his wallet. Or his clothes. Maybe the ambulance driver stole it. Or some nurse in the emergency room. What about his frigging brand new car? Those fuckers at his insurance company better not give him any trouble.

He must've dozed off, because suddenly a nurse was standing beside the bed. Or maybe a doctor. Somebody. A visitor?

Lennox tried to turn his head toward the person, but the pain was too sharp. Whoever it was, they'd closed the door after they'd entered.

Then the person leaned in close, smelling of whiskey and garlic and body odor, and whispered into Lennox's ear from an inch away.

"Listen up, fuckhead. I'm done screwing around. Time to stop playing your silly games, you got me? Or next time you ain't gonna be so lucky."

Fucking Jankowski. That retard. "This is lucky?" Lennox wanted to say, but he could only grunt.

"I'm a reasonable guy, but if you keep it up, you're gonna force my hand, know what I mean? Make me get creative—like maybe paying a visit to Kerri and Jack. You understand what I'm saying?"

Lennox wanted to scream, to jump from the bed and beat Joe Jankowski to a bloody pulp, but he could only lie there. He couldn't even yell for help. He could only nod.

"You change your mind later or try to warn your sister, Jack'll disappear one day. Poof. They won't find a single hair. Same thing if you talk to the cops. You know by now that I mean what I say. Am I making myself crystal clear?"

Lennox nodded again and the pain was nearly unbearable, but he wanted to make sure Jankowski saw that he was ready to cooperate.

20

I prefer to have Mia beside me in bed when I wake up, but if she isn't there, that disappointment fades a tiny bit when I smell the aroma of bacon in the air, as I did the morning after she'd gotten back from Miami.

I got out of bed, and as I made my way down the hallway, I could hear music playing lightly from the living room stereo. I had to grin when I realized it was "Rhythm is Gonna Get You" by Gloria Estefan and Miami Sound Machine—one of their early singles in the mid 1980s. Old school.

I found Mia in the kitchen, wearing a red satin kimono and cracking eggs into a tall glass. And dancing. She saw me coming and put on a show, moving her hips and arms and shoulders and thighs in a very smooth and practiced salsa dance, which is possibly the sexiest dance ever invented. Did I mention she was wearing a red kimono?

"Looks like you picked up a few moves," I said, watching from the other side of the pass-through bar.

"I practiced for hours, just so I could come back home and give you a show," she said.

"Liar," I said. "But I'm not complaining."

"I think I heard more Miami Sound Machine by the pool at our hotel than I did in the preceding twenty years," she said. "And I heard that song 'Despacito' about a thousand times."

She finished her dance and leaned over to give me a kiss.

"How do you want your eggs?"

"Over easy—just like last night."

"As you wish," she said, and she poured the glass of eggs into a skillet heating on the stovetop.

"I woke up early this morning and began to think about this mess with Jankowski," she said.

"I'm sorry."

"Part of the job," she said. "Anyway, I came to the conclusion that there are only a couple of options."

"I'm listening," I said.

"First, we could simply talk to him, tell him what we suspect, and then mention that we have no intention of probing any further—as long as he leaves you alone."

"He'll deny everything," I said.

She grabbed a carton of orange juice from the refrigerator.

"Of course he will. But if he has any sense, he'll leave you alone."

"What if he doesn't have any sense?" I said. "He may think he needs to take us both off the board."

She looked at me. "Did you just say 'Take us both off the board'?"

"I've been reading a lot of James Lee Burke lately."

"He can get away with it. You can't."

"Fair enough."

"Anyway, that brings up option number two, which is probably the way we need to go."

"Let's hear it."

She filled two glasses with juice and set one on the bar for me.

"We dig up enough evidence to get him charged with something and thrown into prison. Whatever we find will almost certainly implicate Damon Tate, too, and so we'll be killing two bad guys with one stone."

The smell of the bacon was making me salivate. She was baking it in the oven on a cookie sheet lined with foil—a cleaner, easier method that I'd somehow never discovered until I'd met Mia.

I said, "My first reaction, off the top of my head, totally going with my gut, is that we should choose option number three."

"Which is?"

"Well, it's exactly like option two, except we eat breakfast and then take a shower together first."

She pointed the spatula at me with approval. "You are nothing short of a genius."

So much of what we do is rooted in research.

Learn as much as you possibly can about your subjects before you take action. It's boring, tedious, and time-consuming, but it almost always pays off in one way or another.

I'd already researched Joe Jankowski, Lennox Armbruster, and Brent Donovan extensively, but now Mia took a shot, intending to dig up anything interesting or relevant I might've missed.

Meanwhile, I looked into Nathaniel Tate—and I was immediately unsettled by what I found. Randy Wolfe hadn't been kidding about this lunatic.

His first arrest as an adult had come on his 17th birthday. That was literally the first day he could commit a crime and have it reflected in his adult records. In fact, if he'd committed the crime just three hours earlier, he would've been considered a juvenile.

That arrest—the first of many—was for aggravated assault against his own father. I managed to find enough court records and newspaper articles to piece it together. Young Nathaniel glued shards of a broken Mountain Dew bottle all along the barrel of a wooden baseball bat. Not large shards that might puncture an eye or lacerate a major neck artery, but smaller shards designed to puncture and tear flesh and leave a bloody mess, but without being fatal. Then he approached his dad, who was watching a football game, and clubbed him all over the head and face with it.

Just for grins, I checked the father's record and discovered that he had been arrested twice for domestic abuse against his wife and four children, including one daughter. I guess Nathaniel had decided enough was enough. If he'd only committed the crime a little earlier, perhaps he wouldn't have served a year for it. There was no word on how badly his father had been injured in the attack.

Other arrests followed, of course, as you would expect for a kid raised in those conditions.

Drunk driving.

Possession of a controlled substance several times.

Terroristic threat.

Aggravated assault.

Passing a bad check for more than $500.

Criminal mischief several times.

Most of the charges had been dismissed or lowered in a plea deal, which explains how punks like Nathaniel Tate manage to return to the street time and time again.

On one hand, it's easy to feel empathy for someone like Nathaniel Tate, who likely never had a decent role model or any incentive to behave like a rational, respectable person. On the other hand, he had free will and the ability to make his own decisions.

Plus, he'd intended to kill me, which always earned a negative mark in my book.

If he'd ever held a job for longer than a year, I couldn't find any evidence of it. He didn't own any real estate. He'd been married at the age of 23, divorced after ten months, with the wife alleging verbal and physical abuse. His credit was terrible. He was four months behind on the loan for the truck he drove. It was a black GMC Sierra. No big surprise.

Mia, seated at the kitchen table with her laptop, said, "Did you ever find Lennox Armbruster's Instagram account?"

"I did not."

"It appears he uses the same screen name for all of his social media, and he posted a photo of his Alfa on Instagram with the caption, 'Just drove this sweet ride off the lot.' And he added a hashtag 'better than the lottery.'"

"What's better?" I was seated on the couch, working on my own laptop.

"He didn't say. Let me keep looking."

A minute passed.

Then she said, "You know those really obnoxious rich kids who spend all day posting status symbols showing how wealthy they are? Yachts, private jets, jewelry—stuff like that? Armbruster started doing the same kind of thing, but on a much smaller scale, obviously. I'm looking at a photo he posted of a pile of cash."

"How much cash?"

"Looks like at least ten or fifteen grand, or maybe more, depending on whether all of these bills are actually hundreds. He could be staging it—putting some singles underneath the hundreds. Hey, counterfeiting could be better than the lottery, if you didn't get caught. Maybe that's what he was talking about."

I was skeptical.

Mia added, "Then again, there's nothing in his background to suggest he'd have the talents for that, and it would be very difficult for a guy like him to launder large sums of cash."

I was still researching Nathaniel Tate, but I figured I'd found everything useful I was going to find.

"You know what else could explain a wad of cash like this?" Mia asked.

"Bank robbery. Armored truck heist. Kidnapping. Being a really good gigolo."

"Be serious."

"Some other low-end scam," I said. "Armbruster seemed to like fraud. Say he does a good old-fashioned slip-and-fall routine inside a mom-and-pop store, and they decide to pay him under the table instead of getting sued."

"Possibly," Mia said.

"But not what you were thinking," I said.

"No, I was thinking blackmail."

"Okay, but who's he blackmailing?"

"Don't know."

"And for what?"

"Don't know. Maybe Joe Jankowski. He seems to be the troublemaker lately. Everything seems to lead back to him."

I stopped what I was doing on the laptop and focused my attention fully on this potential scenario.

I said, "If Armbruster was blackmailing Jankowski, that would mean Jankowski hit him with his SUV on purpose...right?"

"I would think so, yeah. He didn't just happen to run Armbruster down by sheer chance."

"You know what? I like this idea."

"Thank you."

"It explains a lot. Well, maybe not a lot, but more than I figured out so far on my own. Well done."

"My mind is rested," she said.

"And your body is tan, and it has some very—"

She waggled a finger back and forth at me. *Don't get sidetracked.*

I said, "If Armbruster was blackmailing Jankowski for some as-yet-unknown reason, and then Jankowksi ran him down—ostensibly to end the blackmailing—it would make sense that Armbruster wouldn't tell the cops what had actually happened, because he'd be exposing himself to a felony charge in the process and giving up any future payments. So, instead, he just kept his mouth shut."

Mia was nodding. She said, "And then Jankowski remembered he had a dash cam in his SUV, so he lied about it. Otherwise, that video would've been evidence against him, because I'm betting he sped up or swerved to hit Armbruster."

"And he was going to take off afterward, except he saw Sarah Gerstenberger on the side of the road and realized there was a witness. So he pulled over."

"We need to figure out where Armbruster was going that night," Mia said. "And did Jankowski know Armbruster was going to be in that particular location? Maybe he was waiting in his vehicle for Armbruster to show up and cross that street in that exact spot."

"Maybe, but what would—" I stopped talking for a moment.

"What?" Mia said.

"It just occurred to me that a golf course, especially at night, would make a great drop spot for a bag of cash from a blackmail victim. And then Jankowski could look at a map and figure out where the blackmailer was likely to park and cross the street. Is that a stretch?"

"I don't think so," Mia said. "But in order for Jankowski to run Armbruster down, he—Jankowski—would have to know who Armbruster is and what he looks like. Which means Armbruster never worried about concealing his identity—pretty damn stupid—or Jankowski figured out who he is. You agree?"

"I do, and Armbruster must not have known that Jankowski had identified him or he wouldn't have needed a drop spot. He could've just met him face to face. But Jankowksi identified Armbruster without Armbruster knowing it."

Maybe all of this was wrong. We knew that. But brainstorming had value, because it could help us see possibilities we'd overlooked before.

"Could've been as simple as tailing him after a money drop," Mia said.

"Or tracking his IP address, if they were exchanging emails," I said. "I'm guessing Jankowksi has some IT guys on his payroll."

Neither of us needed to mention that fraudsters like Armbruster weren't typically Rhodes Scholars. They were the type of people who made mistakes and got caught.

Mia said, "Maybe we should go look around the golf course and see where it takes us."

I said, "Good idea, but we'll stay off the fairways so the golfers won't get…teed off."

She looked at me and shook her head.

"Hey, will you be my driver?" I asked.

She groaned.

"You have no sense of humor. That's your handicap," I said.

"Well, don't let it drive a wedge between us," she said.

"Oh, you've outdone me again," I said.

"Par for the course," she said.

"I've created a monster."

It was a nice moment. I had no idea that two hours later I would open my big mouth and ruin the day, and perhaps the rest of my life.

21

We parked in the lot outside the Randall's grocery store, which is the same place Lennox Armbruster had parked the night he'd gotten hit.

The intersection of the two roads—Lake Austin Boulevard and Exposition—formed a V that pointed due south. Nestled inside the lowest point of that V was the green for the second hole of Lions Municipal Golf Course. I'd lived here all my life, and until now, after having checked a course map online, I couldn't have told you it was the second hole that ran parallel to Lake Austin Boulevard. It was the second hole that made drivers clench up a bit when driving past, hoping some duffer didn't shank a shot high and wide and crack a windshield. A little higher in the V, just above the second green, was the tee box for the eighth hole, and just above that, the green for the seventh hole.

"If Armbruster was using the course as a drop spot," I said as we waited to cross Exposition, "I think he'd want the money fairly close to the street—someplace where he could just hop the fence, grab the cash, and then get the hell out of there."

"Sounds reasonable," Mia said.

We crossed the street and began to walk northeasterly on the sidewalk along Exposition. Here there was a four-foot chain-link fence surrounding the golf course, but it would've been easy for Armbruster, or anyone else, to vault the fence. The first one hundred feet of fence was lined with thick shrubs and trees, making it difficult to see the golf course on the other side.

We got to an opening in the trees, far enough north that we were now gazing across the fence to the tee box for hole number eight, where a threesome was waiting for some golfers well down the fairway to move along. But between us and the tee box was a small limestone building with a metal roof. Couldn't have been more than ten feet square.

"Wonder what that is," I said.

"Bathroom?" Mia said.

"That's what I was thinking at first, but there's no sidewalk or cart path leading up to it. Thinking more like an equipment shed or something. Hop the fence or walk all the way around to the entrance?"

"Oh, no question," Mia said, and before I could offer her a hand, she was hoisting herself over the fence.

"You're pretty graceful for a gangly girl," I said.

"I prefer 'spindly,'" she said. "You coming?"

She began to walk toward the small building, so I climbed over the fence, perhaps not quite as smoothly as she did, and followed after her.

As we got closer, I could see that the shed wasn't actually a shed, nor was it even enclosed. It had two stone columns in front, and the back half was a semi-enclosed space similar in size and shape to a bus stop.

"Oh, I know what this is," Mia said. "A lightning hut."

The description was self-explanatory. I started to ask how she knew that, but I remembered that her former boyfriend Garlen, the sociopath, was a golfer, and she had probably gone with him a few times.

We stepped into the hut and looked around. I didn't see any obvious hiding places.

"I guess you could stash a bundle of cash in here just for an hour or two, especially at night," I said.

"Yeah, but would you? What if some kids stopped in here to party? What if a homeless person came in here to sleep? Chances are slim, but why take the risk when there are probably better hiding spots?"

She was right. I took a seat on the bench and opened my phone to look at the golf course map again.

Mia remained standing near the two stone columns at the front of the hut.

I found the little hut on the satellite view. I tried to place myself in Lennox Armbruster's position. Where would I tell Joe Jankowski or one of his errand boys to leave the money? Behind a tree? Under a bush? Inside a golf hole? I was baffled. There were plenty of places a person could leave a small bundle of cash, but none were better or more obvious than the others. None were particularly good choices. I was losing confidence in our theory.

"I think we have way too many guesses stacked on top of each other," I said.

Mia didn't reply.

"It's one thing to brainstorm a little, but we let our imaginations run wild," I said.

Mia was watching a golfer line up a putt on the seventh green. It had turned into a gorgeous day.

"I tried to play golf a few times," I said. "It has to be the worst—"

"In a sand trap," Mia said abruptly. "He could've buried the money in a sand trap, then raked over it."

I had to smile. She turned to face me.

"What do you think?" she asked.

"It's perfect," I said.

"Thank you."

"You're spindly, yet brilliant," I said.

"Problem is, we'll never know if I'm right. How can we prove any of this is accurate?"

I put my phone away and stood up. I wasn't ready to give up yet.

"Do we agree that Jankowski could've looked at a map, same as we did, and figured out where Armbruster would've parked and where he would've crossed the street?"

"Definitely. There are no other logical choices."

"So Jankowski probably would've also parked in the Randall's lot and waited for Armbruster to show up. Then he nailed him. All planned out."

"That I'm not so sure about," Mia said.

"What's the alternative?"

"Maybe Jankowski came out that night simply to let Armbruster know he'd been identified—to tell him his little blackmail scheme was over. Intimidate him. Threaten him. Make him stop. But not to hit him with his car. That's not the best way to take care of a blackmailer."

"You are harshing my buzz," I said.

"But…" she said.

"Yes?"

"Maybe Armbruster told him to screw off. Jankowski got mad and ran him down. Spontaneous, not planned."

"Damn, you're good," I said.

"Thanks. But we still can't prove any of this is right."

She came over and sat beside me. We both were quiet for a long moment. It was peaceful out here.

"Here's a thought," I said. "Jankowski would've put the money in the sand trap, just in case Armbruster approached from a different direction and Jankowski never saw him."

"In that case, why wouldn't Jankowski just hang out by the sand trap?"

"Fear of getting shot," I said. "It's dark out there. Armbruster might've been armed. A Randall's parking lot is a safer place to confront him."

"Okay, true."

"So my point is, I think Jankowski would've put the money in place anyway, just in case he didn't get a chance to deliver his threat to Armbruster."

"Why?"

"So Armbruster wouldn't arrive at the drop spot and get suspicious when the money wasn't there."

"I guess that makes sense."

"You *guess*? Work with me, people," I said.

"Okay, it makes total sense, and you are a genius."

"Attagirl. So Jankowski puts the money in place, then waits at Randall's. He sees Armbruster and delivers the threat. But Armbruster tells him to take a walk. So then Jankowski loses his cool and hits Armbruster with his SUV. Then what?"

"He had to hang around and deal with the cops."

"Right. And would he risk going back to the golf course later to recover the money? What if a cop or security guard saw him wandering around out there? It was probably just a few thousand dollars. Wouldn't he just write that off as a loss and move on?"

"How do you know it was just a few thousand dollars?"

"If Armbruster was a smart blackmailer, he started by asking for a small amount and promising that would be the only payment. And then he went back again and again, until Jankowski had had enough and wanted to put a stop to it. So he figured out who Armbruster was and the rest is history."

I stood now, getting excited.

"So many what-ifs," Mia said.

"But where's the weakness in it?" I asked. "It all fits."

"Maybe," Mia said.

"And I think that money is either still in that bunker or, more likely, someone found it. If Jankowski didn't go to retrieve that money, somebody got it."

"Okay, but who?" Mia asked. "Some golfer who hit into the trap and got lucky? What's that look on your face?"

"Are you Tad?" I asked a young man twenty minutes later. We'd gotten his name and location from a woman working at the clubhouse. She'd checked in with him via a walkie-talkie clipped to his belt.

"Yeah?" Tad said. He was in his early twenties. Slender. Extremely blond hair. Had a tan from working outdoors all the time. He was working on what appeared to be some sort of pump that was part of the sprinkler system.

I said, "If I left a club in a sand trap last night, right before dark, I understand you would've been the person to find it, right?"

"Yeah, but I didn't find anything this morning."

"That's because I didn't actually lose a club. I just wondered who would've found it if I *had* lost one."

He looked at me, puzzled. "Well, that's weird, but okay."

"The point is, you tend the traps every morning, right?"

"I do, yeah."

"That includes raking them?"

"Yes, sir."

"How long have you been doing that?"

"About four years. I'm not sure what this is about. Did you really lose something?"

"I lost my sense of wonder years ago, if that counts. But let's not worry about that right now. Instead, I need to ask you one more question, and if you answer it honestly, no matter what the answer is, I promise we'll leave and you'll never see us again. No cops, either. Just tell the truth and we're gone. You understand what I'm saying?"

"Not really."

"But if you lie, things will not go well."
"Lie about what? Dude, I've got no idea what you're even—"
"The cash you found in the sand trap."
He looked at me for a long moment, then said, "Oh."

22

"Good man," I said. "You've chosen to be honest. And we'll stay true to our part of the deal. How much was there?"

"You said just one more question," Tad said.

"Exactly. Just one more question. How much was there?"

Tad let out a sigh and glanced around, as if to make sure nobody else would overhear.

"Four thousand dollars. All in hundreds. Are y'all cops?"

"You worried about cops?" I said.

"Where was the money, exactly?" Mia asked. "Which bunker?"

"God, how many questions are you people gonna ask?" Tad said.

"Come on, Tad," Mia said. "Don't be like that. We promise not to tell."

Tad looked at her. I could see the resistance in his eyes fading.

"It was near the seventh green," he said.

The map had shown me that there were two bunkers on that par-three hole—one just before the green and one just past it. I knew which bunker it would be.

"There are two over there," I said. "Which one?"

"The one more to the east," Tad said.

Bingo.

Just so there was no confusion or mistake, I said, "The one closer to Exposition, right?"

"Right."

"Not far from that little lightning hut," I said.

"Yeah," Tad said.

Easy access for Lennox Armbruster. Just hop the fence and trot over to the bunker. Probably in and out in less than a minute—unless you get hit by a car.

"What was the money in?" Mia asked. "A sack or what?"

"It was loose in a white envelope," Tad said. "Somebody had obviously put it there for some reason. It wasn't like they lost it. They hid it. Buried it."

He was rationalizing—insinuating that he would've turned it in if someone had lost it.

"And you never told anybody you found it?" I asked.

"No, and nobody ever came looking for it. Plus, there's no law that says I had to report that money."

"Actually, yeah, there is," I said.

"Well, there shouldn't be. What about finders keepers? I figured it was like drug money or something like that. Or from a robbery or something. Who buries money in a sand trap?"

"You never saw anyone hanging around that green, looking like they lost something?"

"Nope."

"Never saw any evidence that anyone was digging around in that trap?"

"Never."

"Was the envelope sealed?" Mia asked.

"Yeah."

"Did you save it, by chance?" I asked.

"The envelope? Why would I?"

Bummer. There would be no DNA to test, if it ever came to that.

"You have any of the bills left?" Mia asked.

Tad shook his head. "I blew it all pretty quick. It was found money, you know? So I went down to Port Aransas and had a blast. Partied for a week. First real vacation I've ever had."

Tad was kind of a weasel, so I couldn't resist giving him a hard time. Just a little.

"Are you planning to report the money on your tax return?" I asked.

"Uh…what?"

"You are legally obligated to report it and pay any taxes that are due," I said. "You think the feds are gonna miss a chance to take a slice?"

"Fuck," he said. Then, glancing at Mia, "Excuse my language."

"And then there's the question of it being found on City property," I said. "That will make things even more complicated. Wouldn't surprise me if you lost your job for keeping it."

"Shit!" Tad said. "Fuck! Sorry."

"A little advice for you, Tad," Mia said. "If the police come around someday and ask the same questions we're asking, tell them everything and make sure it's the truth—but get an attorney first."

Tad was looking queasy.

A few minutes later, we reached the stretch of fence we'd crossed earlier. Once again, Mia vaulted it like a practiced athlete. I followed, but it wouldn't have been as satisfying for any bystanders to watch. We walked to the corner and crossed Exposition.

"I'd say, at this point, our entire theory—*your* theory—is spot on," I said. "It explains everything perfectly. Lennox Armbruster was blackmailing Joe Jankowski."

"But for what?" Mia asked.

"Don't know yet, but we'll get there," I said. "Enjoy the moment!"

We'd reached Mia's 1968 Mustang fastback—a head-turning classic—and she unlocked the passenger-side door for me. No remote unlocking for this car. I climbed inside, then reached over to unlock her door.

Mia fired up the engine and the throaty rumble of the V8 gave me chills, as it usually did.

It was a good day to be alive. We had the windows down and some ZZ Top on the stereo.

You wouldn't believe the mood-lifting rush you experience when you suddenly make big strides in a case like this one. You get downright giddy. The day suddenly improves. All of your problems seem much less significant.

Like the secret I'd been keeping. I was less than one minute from revealing it—and ruining everything.

Mia pulled out of the Randall's parking lot and went south on MoPac expressway. We'd agreed earlier to stop at Best Buy for several more security cameras to install around the perimeter of the house.

That's when it happened. When I blurted it out. I wasn't planning it, and I didn't think about it or agonize over it. I simply started talking.

"I need to tell you something I've never mentioned before," I said.

"What?"

"I had a vasectomy."

If this had been a movie, viewers would've heard the sound effect of a needle scratching across a record and coming to an abrupt stop.

Mia looked over at me, and I could tell she didn't know what to think.

So I said, "I know I joke around a lot, but this isn't a joke. I wouldn't joke about this."

"I don't know what to say," she said.

"It was years ago, after the nightmare with Hannah," I said. "You already know I wasn't doing real well at that point, from a psychological aspect. Dealing with the guilt and all that."

She nodded.

"I felt like a failure as a father, so I got a vasectomy a few months later. I figured it would be better if I didn't have any more kids."

She looked at me, then at the road again. I had been hoping she would allay my concerns right away—maybe laugh about it or say it was fine with her—but that wasn't happening.

"How come you've never told me?" she asked. Her expression was hard to read.

"I didn't intentionally keep it from you," I said. "It's just that I didn't tell many people. It isn't something that comes up much in conversation. If we'd ever had a discussion about birth control—which we didn't, beyond you being on the pill—I would've mentioned it then."

A long silence followed. Traffic was somewhat heavy, but still moving along at about fifty miles per hour.

I said, "There's another topic we haven't discussed, and that's having kids."

"I want kids, Roy," she said quickly. "I've definitely brought that up before, because I wanted to see how you'd react."

"You did?" I said.

She nodded.

"When was this?"

"When I was working at the bar," she said.

Long time ago. I didn't remember it.

She'd revealed to me not long after we'd finally gotten together that she'd been attracted to me back then, when I was her regular customer, after she'd gotten to know me and realized I wasn't as obnoxious as I appeared. I, on the other hand, had had a crush on her from the first time we'd met. It had taken us both a good while to address those feelings.

"What I mean is, we haven't talked about it, you know, as a couple," I said.

"I've made references to it," she said, "and you never gave me any indication that it might not happen, or that you were opposed to it in any way."

"I'm sorry."

"Are you saying you don't want any more kids, even now?" she asked.

"Maybe. I don't know. I still think about Hannah. I left her alone in the car. I never should have done that. I wasn't a good father."

"You were, Roy. You made one mistake that could happen to any parent."

"But it happened to me, and it was my fault."

Mia didn't argue further. That wasn't her style. She simply repeated her question. "So you don't want any more kids?"

We were approaching our exit.

"I'm closing in on forty years old, Mia," I said.

"You're only thirty-eight, but that doesn't really answer the question. A vasectomy can be reversed."

"I know," I said. "I talked to my doctor about it last week, and I'm going to see a urologist tomorrow. The problem is, the more years that have passed since the original surgery, the lower the chances I'd be able to get you pregnant. It might not happen, even if we both want it to."

My procedure had been more than ten years earlier. From what I'd read, Mia and I had roughly a one-in-four chance of having a child together, but there were many variables that could affect the outcome—including the skill of the surgeon. The chances could be higher, or almost nil.

"I can't believe you've been looking into all this and haven't even talked to me about it," she said. "You haven't said a word. That's not how couples work."

"I wanted to know what I was dealing with," I said. "I wanted to see what our options were."

"Yes, *our* options," she said. "You should've included me."

"I know. I'm sorry."

She pulled into the parking lot at Best Buy and found an isolated spot.

Then she began to cry, and it just about tore my heart in two.

I reached over and grasped her hand. "Let's not worry too much until my appointment, okay?"

She nodded but didn't look at me.

I said, "I know there have been some advancements. We just need all the facts."

She didn't say anything. Just stared down at her lap.

Did I want more kids? That was hard to answer.

There was another question I couldn't bring myself to ponder: If Mia and I couldn't have kids together, would she stay with me? Who could blame her if the answer was no?

"Mia?" I said.

"I don't want to talk about it anymore right now," she said. "Let's just go inside."

23

I tried not to obsess about it, but our conversation had been a train wreck.

I lay awake that night convinced Mia and I were done. She was asleep beside me, but it felt like she was on another continent. We hadn't actually fought, but it felt like we had. She wasn't mad at me, exactly, but all was not right in our world, plainly. She hadn't raised the issue for the remainder of the evening, and she'd gone to bed at 8:45. The goodnight kiss she'd given me was perfunctory, at best.

Thirty minutes later, I was tempted to go into the bedroom and check on her, but I was afraid I would find her crying, and I just couldn't handle it. Probably better to let her process what I'd told her and then let me know when she was ready to talk.

Fortunately, my mind would wander on occasion and I would stop dwelling on the way I had mishandled this situation.

I had seen a report on the ten o'clock news that the police were taking a fresh look at the disappearance of Brent Donovan, thanks to "some new information that had been received by investigators this week." That would be my conversation with Randy Wolfe. Nice to see he was taking me seriously. According to the reporter, the police were asking anyone with information about the disappearance of Brent Donovan to call the Austin Police Department.

Then they launched right into a report about Brandi Sloan, "who worked for the same company that had employed Brent Donovan." Police were saying there was no indication of foul play, but they couldn't rule it out, either. She had simply disappeared. Family members and friends were concerned.

My mind kept going to Armbruster's visit to Brandi Sloan's house on E.M. Franklin Avenue. What did it mean? What was the purpose? What was the connection between those two? What had happened to

Brandi?

And what kind of damaging information did Armbruster have on Jankowski? I couldn't think of a way to figure that out. In fact, there was no indication whatsoever that the men had had any kind of interaction prior to the night of the "accident" on Exposition Boulevard—but they must've, obviously.

How did they know each other?

How did Armbruster get dirty laundry on Jankowski?

I was stumped. My normally vivid imagination was not playing along. I was too stressed by my conversation with Mia. Had I blown the best thing that had ever happened to me?

Then, at 4:42, I heard a noise.

Damn it.

Just a nondescript sound. Muffled. A thump, sort of. Car door closing? Something bumping against a wall? A compressor inside an appliance shutting off? It was hard to tell where it had come from— distance or direction. Was it from inside or outside the house?

Now, of course, my imagination was running wild.

I forced myself to lie quietly and wait.

Three or four minutes passed and I heard nothing more.

We had new cameras on the sides of the house now, plus alarms on the doors. I'd installed all of it when we'd gotten home from Best Buy. Didn't take long. Plug and play.

The good news was, this old pier-and-beam house made all kinds of noises when someone walked from one room to another. Not very noticeable during the day, with a TV or stereo playing, but in the dead of the night, when everything was still and quiet, the creaks and groans seemed ridiculously loud. If anyone managed to get inside, which was virtually impossible, I would hear him coming.

I grabbed my phone off the nightstand and opened the app to check the cameras. Nothing out there that I could see. No indications of any recent activity.

"What's going on?" Mia said.

She was lying on her side, facing me.

"Sorry, but I heard a noise," I said. "Just checking the cameras. Don't see anything."

"What kind of noise?"

"Just sort of a thump or a bump."

"Where?"

"I couldn't tell. It's probably nothing. Possums having a party."

She yawned, then rolled onto her back.

Fifteen minutes passed and I thought she was asleep again, when she said, "You awake?"

"Yeah."

"It occurs to me that maybe we're overlooking a simple solution."

I didn't know which topic she was talking about—us or the case.

"Let's hear it," I said.

She said, "If Lennox Armbruster is blackmailing Joe Jankowski, couldn't we use that against him?"

I waited for her to say more, but she didn't.

"Use it against who?"

"Armbruster."

"And use it how?"

"Tell him we figured out what's going on, and force him to tell us more or we'll take it to the cops."

"So we'd blackmail the blackmailer?" I said.

"Pretty much, yeah."

"Hmm," I said. "I like it, but won't he just deny that he's doing it?"

"Well, sure."

"And without Jankowski willing to confirm what's been going on, why would Armbruster tell us anything?"

"Roy, you're forgetting one of the key points you made sure I understood when you first trained me for this job."

"Which was?"

"That most criminals aren't all that smart."

"That's true," I said. "It's a very keen and astute observation. I should listen to myself more often."

24

On one hand, I always marvel that the security in most hospitals is fairly lax. On the other hand, despite what you might see in the movies, how often are patients in hospitals really threatened or assaulted? I'd say you're in much greater danger in a church, school, or theater.

We were able to obtain Lennox Armbruster's room number at the information desk and then walk right in without clearing it with anyone.

He was awake, watching an episode of *Veronica Mars* on the wall-mounted TV.

"Some witty writers on that show," I said.

Armbruster moved his eyes in our direction, but not his head, because he was wearing a neck brace that prevented movement.

"Who is it?" he said.

We walked to the foot of the bed so he could see us.

"Hi there," I said.

"Oh, great. I told that retard nurse I didn't want to deal with this today."

"Deal with what?" Mia said.

"The paperwork and all the crap," he said. "You're with the billing department?"

"I'm thrilled to tell you we are not," I said.

"Well, that's good," he said, "because that's not gonna be a pleasant conversation. Is it my fault I don't got health insurance? They want me to fill out some kind of form promising I'll pay for all this shit."

"The nerve," Mia said.

"I know, right? I'm guessing aspirin is ten dollars a pop. Meanwhile, you wouldn't believe how quickly they're trying to get me out the front door now that they can't milk some insurance company for all kinds of bullshit."

He had a sallow complexion and a week's worth of razor stubble, but he was in better shape than I had anticipated. Then again, he'd had four days to recover from the wreck. He had an IV in his arm and one of those oxygen-level gizmos clipped to the end of one finger. A big machine next to the bed monitored his vital stats.

"How bad were your injuries?" Mia asked.

Armbruster opened his mouth to reply, but hesitated, then said, "Who are you?"

Mia said, "My name is Mia and he's Roy."

As if that explained it all.

"Okay," Armbruster said. "And?"

Mia looked at me.

I said, "Joe Jankowski's goons have tried to kill me twice. Well, okay, just once for sure, and probably twice. That puts you and me on even ground, doesn't it?"

He appeared somewhat amused and intrigued.

"I'm gonna need to know more than that," he said. "Who are you, and I don't mean just your name. Why are you here?"

I said, "When you got hit by Jankowski's SUV, his insurance company hired us to determine whether or not you were committing fraud. It occurred to them that perhaps you had jumped in front of that vehicle on purpose, especially given your colorful past."

"What the hell do you retards know about my past?" Armbruster asked.

Mia pointed a finger and glared at him. "Don't use that word. It's ugly."

"Whatever," he said.

"Everything is online nowadays, Lennox," I said. "Criminal records, lawsuits, bankruptcies, and just about everything else. It's easy to find, especially if you know where to look."

"And we know where to look," Mia said.

"We came to the conclusion that you weren't faking your injuries," I said. "Which made us think it really was an accident, or maybe you did jump in front of the SUV on purpose, but you weren't as graceful as you'd hoped to be."

"That's stupid. You people are stupid."

"And you're a ray of sunshine," Mia said.

"We didn't consider the idea that maybe Jankowski hit you on purpose," I said.

"Where do y'all get your dumb ideas?" Armbruster asked.

I said, "And then we discovered that you owned a brand-new Alfa Romeo, and that seems kind of weird for a guy who doesn't work all that much. How can you afford that?"

"How is that your business?"

We remained standing at the foot of the bed, because if we sat down in the chairs to the side of the bed, he wouldn't be able to see us, and I wanted to maintain eye contact.

I said, "Even if you financed the car, you probably had to pony up a big down payment, and then the monthly payment on a high-dollar vehicle like that has to be five or six hundred, at a minimum. It's curious, you know?"

"But it finally made sense when we figured out what was really happening between you and Jankowski," Mia said.

"Y'all should leave before I ask a nurse to get security," he said.

"See, we started wondering where you were going that night," I said. "Why were you crossing Exposition? There's nothing over there except the golf course. Then my partner here came up with a brilliant theory, and all the pieces fit. Mia, would you like to do the honors?"

Armbruster said, "Yeah, please, tell me all about this crazy theory, and then maybe you can give me a sponge bath."

It takes restraint not to react to a jerk like him, but we both ignored his remark. However, I could tell Mia was losing her patience, because she cut right to the heart of the matter.

"You're blackmailing him," she said.

We both stared at him, and he made a "pfftt" sound.

Mia said, "The golf course was the drop spot for the payment that night. You might be too slow to figure this out, but Jankowski had identified you by then, so he guessed where you would park—the Randall's, obviously—and waited for you to show. Then I'm guessing the two of you had an argument, and then he decided to hit you with his car. He has a temper."

Armbruster was making an expression meant to say, *What a bunch of nonsense.*

I said, "I'm guessing you don't want to admit to committing a felony—not just because you might get prosecuted, but you don't want to give up your cash cow, even after they've tried to kill you twice. You've had a lot of time to think about it, lying there in that bed, and

I'm guessing you've decided you simply need to tighten up your scheme to stop him from making more attempts on your life. Am I right? Maybe arrange it so that the information is shared with the police if anything happens to you. That's how they do it in the movies."

Armbruster was about to respond, but a nurse entered the room right then. She was all bubbly and friendly and asked how Lennox was doing. He said he was doing okay—and made no mention of calling security. She checked his IV and his vitals, nodded at us, then left.

"You people are morons," Armbruster said. "Think you're smart, but you ain't got shit."

"Exactly how dense are you?" Mia asked. "Can't you see what's about to happen?"

"Why don't you tell me, smart lady?"

"We'll tell the cops everything we just told you."

"There's nothing to tell."

"And the thing about the cops is, they can dig much deeper than public records. For instance, they can get a warrant for Jankowski's phone records, and that'll be a problem for you, won't it?"

"Nope."

"Did you use a burner phone to contact him? Even if you paid cash, there was probably a security camera wherever you bought it."

"Didn't buy one."

"Plus, the cops can get location data for that phone that will lead right to your apartment, because you're dumb enough to make those calls from home. So, no matter what you do from here on out, your blackmail scheme is over and done with. You might as well come to grips with that."

"You're friggin' delusional, you know that?"

"Then why were you crossing Exposition that night?" Mia said. "Where were you going?"

He was stumped. I could see it on his face. He'd had plenty of time to prepare for that question, yet he'd never thought about it or devised a reasonable answer. Finally he said, "I like to go there and look for golf balls. Then I sell them online."

"Oh, Lennox," Mia said. "You don't think the cops will check to see if that's true?"

Finally, Armbruster sputtered, "I don't have to explain myself to you."

Mia let out a sigh. I drummed my fingers on my thigh. Was the blackmailing theory off target? Maybe there was an equally plausible explanation. But what about the money in the sand trap? Maybe our theory was close, but far off enough that Armbruster didn't feel compelled to cooperate.

Time for one last attempt to shock him into talking.

"What were you doing over at Brandi Sloan's place five nights ago? I asked.

"What the fuck?" he said. "The hell've you been doing?"

"Part of our job is to follow fraud suspects around and see what they do. I followed you over to her house. Ever since, I've been wondering what the two of you were talking about."

He had nothing to say.

"Were you and Brandi working together to scam Jankowski?" Mia asked.

"No, of course not," he said. "And who says I was scamming the guy?"

Then Mia got smart and realized there was an obvious pressure point we'd overlooked.

"Did you know Brandi has gone missing?" she asked. "That's something else the cops will be interested in figuring out—whether you had anything to do with her disappearance."

Suddenly he looked less cocky.

"Were you carrying your cell phone when you went over there?" Mia asked. "Because if you were, that'll be a big red flag to the cops. You won't be able to deny meeting with her."

"And I'll be sure to tell them I saw you over there," I said. "Here's what you need to do. Tell us what you've got on Jankowski. Then we'll go away and keep it to ourselves. You've got my word. I just want to stop Jankowski from coming after me."

I was lying, of course. If we needed to tell the police what we learned, we would. Eventually.

I could tell that Armbruster was contemplating the offer. He wasn't wasting time with denials anymore.

Mia said, "He'll keep trying to kill you. Despite what you're thinking, he is obviously intent on it, and he thinks if it looks like an accident, he'll get away with it. He almost succeeded last time, didn't he? That's why you're here. You're lucky you're alive. You're not going to be safe until he's in jail."

We gave him a moment to think about it.

"I could just tell him I won't be bothering him anymore," Armbruster said.

Finally. He was ready to spill.

"Meaning you won't extort any more money from him?" Mia asked.

"Right. Yeah."

"That won't be enough," I said. "You know something incriminating about him, and he'll always worry about that. Hell, he's sent men with guns after me twice simply because he thinks we'll figure it out. He's worried about what we'll dig up. I need to know what you know, and then we—Mia and me—can take him down."

He let out a long sigh.

"You don't even need to be involved after this," Mia said. "But if you don't come clean, you're going to be in danger as long as he's free, and it won't be long before the cops come around asking about Brandi Sloan."

"Damn it," Armbruster said. "This sucks."

We waited. Then he broke.

"What do you want to know?" he said.

"Just start at the beginning," Mia said.

"Okay. Shit. Whatever. The thing is, I had no idea who Joe Jankowski was until I stole a bunch of shit from his car."

"When was this and what did you steal?"

"Couple of months ago," he said. "His SUV was unlocked, sitting there in his driveway. What kind of retard—I mean idiot—leaves his vehicle unlocked?"

"What did you get?" I asked.

"A GPS unit. A dash cam. An iPad. And his wallet was in there. What a moron. I took the cash and left the rest. I'm not into using hot credit cards, because that's a good way to get busted. Oh, he had a gun in the glove compartment, so I took that, too."

That made me think of Armbruster's former neighbor, Claudia Klein, who suspected that Lennox had burglarized her duplex and stolen a gun. She was obviously right, and it made me wonder how that gun ended up with Damon Tate, but that part of the story would have to wait.

Mia said, "Okay, but how did you end up blackmailing him? Did you find something in the SUV?"

"It was the dash cam," he said. "I thought I might keep it instead of selling it, so I was fooling around with it, seeing how it works and all that. It had video files on there from being in Jankowski's car."

"And you saw something on one of those files?" I asked.

"It wasn't what I saw. It was what I heard."

Damn. I'd been so focused on what might've been recorded on video, I'd never considered audio.

"What did you hear?" I asked.

"You should close the door," he said.

I did what he asked.

Then he quietly said, "The sound wasn't real great—lots of road noise—but Jankowski was talking to somebody on the phone about a body."

Now my adrenaline was really pumping. It took effort to keep my voice calm and quiet. I'd learned it was better if you didn't let a guy like Lennox Armbruster understand that he was providing enormously valuable information.

"Who was he talking to?" I asked.

"I don't know. I couldn't hear the other person."

"He never said a name?"

"Not that I could hear."

Later, when the time came, the cops would be able to figure out the date and time of the phone call, then review Jankowski's phone records to determine who he'd been talking to.

"So what did he say about a body?" I asked. "What did he say exactly?"

"I can remember it mostly word for word, because the call didn't last long. He answered, then he said, 'I've been wondering if you need to move the body, or whatever's left of it.' Then there was a pause, and he said, 'You sure about that?' Then he said, 'How deep?' And that was pretty much it."

How deep? How deep was it buried? How deep was the water? Could mean either one.

"Did he say whose body it was?" I asked.

"Nope."

"And what came next?" Mia asked.

Armbruster said, "He hung up and said, 'That guy is almost fucking worthless.'

"Talking to himself?"

"No, to Brandi Sloan."

"What? On the phone?"

"No, she was in the SUV with him."

25

I was momentarily speechless. I had not expected that answer, because I had never considered that scenario—that Brandi Sloan was working with Joe Jankowski, not with Armbruster.

I eventually said, "How did she reply? How did you know it was her?"

"Well, at that point, I didn't know who it was, but she said, 'Do you think you can trust him in the long term?'"

The subtext in that question was chilling. *Do you think you'll have to kill him, too?*

"What did he say?" Mia asked.

"They stopped at a light right next to a loud motorcycle and I couldn't understand what they were saying for about two minutes. When they pulled away, they weren't talking anymore."

"They didn't say anything else relevant?" I asked.

"Nope, although she did call him 'baby' at one point, so it's obvious what's going on there."

How had I missed this?

"Did you review every file on the camera?" I asked.

I could see on the bedside monitor that Armbruster's heart rate and blood pressure had gone up. I'm sure mine had, too.

He said, "Yep. There wasn't anything else good. That was it—the part about the body. I did some poking around online and found out that one of his employees had gone missing, and that dude had been trying to pull a workers' comp scam, and Jankowski got real upset about it, so I figured it was probably that guy they were talking about."

Mia and I had questions, of course. Many questions. And he answered them all. Mia and I learned that our theory was basically spot on, and we were also able to fill in the blank spots.

"How did you go about blackmailing Jankowski? How did you

contact him?" Mia asked.

As we'd guessed, Armbruster had bought a burner phone and called JMJ Construction. Brandi answered. He recognized her voice and realized she was the woman in the SUV with Jankowski. She wanted to know what Armbruster was calling about, so he said he had something that used to belong to Jankowski and wanted to give it back. It went from there.

Armbruster told Jankowski what he'd heard on the dash cam and asked for $20,000 in cash to keep quiet, promising it would be a one-time payment. He was lying and I'm sure Jankowski knew that. Jankowski gave him the $20,000, then more cash in smaller increments, because what choice did he have? Armbruster specified several different drop spots, with the last one being the golf course.

Armbruster didn't realize that Jankowski was cooperating only until he could figure out a way to identify the blackmailer. He—Armbruster—hadn't taken as many precautions as he should have to conceal his identity. Jankowski, or one of his minions, had apparently staked out one of the drop points and then followed Armbruster home. An amateur mistake on Armbruster's part. The kind of mistake a first-time blackmailer makes.

"Do you know if Brandi Sloan knew what you were doing?" Mia asked.

"At first, no, I don't think so, but then, on later calls, I could tell from her voice that she wasn't happy to hear from me. Either she knew what was going on or Jankowski told her I was a deadbeat client or something. Who knows?"

"You never got Jankowski's cell phone number to call him directly?"

"I didn't ask and he didn't give it. I figured why make things complicated?"

I wanted him to explain why he'd gone over to Brandi Sloan's house that night, but all in good time. One thing at a time.

"Tell us what happened on the night Jankowski hit you with his SUV," I said.

Armbruster said he had parked at Randall's and was immediately approached by Jankowski, and now it was clear that Armbruster had been identified.

"It probably shoulda freaked me out a little more than it did,"

Armbruster said, "because this was a guy who'd already killed one dude, apparently. But I'd been drinking vodka that night and was feeling kinda ballsy. He told me this was gonna be the last payment or I was gonna regret it, and I said like hell it was. I was thinking, like, what's he gonna do right here in the parking lot of a grocery store? He made some vague threats, like how he could make me disappear, too, and then he left."

Armbruster thought that was the end of it—until a few minutes later, when he began to cross the street and suddenly Jankowski's vehicle was bearing down on him.

"That's when I knew the dude was serious," Armbruster said without any hint of irony. "And then it got even worse when I got out of the hospital and went back to my apartment."

"What happened?" I asked.

"They had broken in and took a bunch of my shit. That included the dash cam and my laptop. I guess they figured I would've downloaded the file from the dash cam to my laptop, which was right."

I said, "Please...tell me you had it backed up on something else."

Before I was even done talking, Armbruster was shaking his head slightly, neck brace and all, and then cringing from the pain.

"Oh, jeez," I said.

"I didn't expect to get ripped off, you know?" Armbruster said.

"How stupid do you have to—"

"How was I supposed to know that would happen?"

"You could've just emailed the file to yourself," I said, the exasperation plain in my voice. "Or put it on a flash drive. Then you would've had a—"

"Too late now, bro," he said.

It was incredibly stupid on his part, but shouldn't I have expected that? Obviously, Jankowski had taken the gamble that Lennox hadn't backed up the file, and that gamble had paid off.

"When did they break in?" Mia asked. Being pragmatic. Wanting to learn everything we could learn.

"Sometime while I was in the hospital. I don't know for sure, because technically they didn't break in. They must've picked the lock, because they didn't kick the door in or break a window or anything like that."

"Or you left the door unlocked," I said.

Armbruster glared at me. "Whatever. There was no sign of them being there, except for the shit that was missing."

"How about the gun you took from Jankowski's SUV?" I asked. "Did the burglar get that, too?"

"Yeah."

"And what about the gun you stole from Claudia Klein?" I asked.

"Who's that?"

"Your old neighbor in the duplex off South Lamar," I said.

He appeared puzzled for half a second, then grinned with guilt when he realized who I was talking about. "I'd forgotten about her. Y'all are pretty thorough."

"Remember when I said Jankowski tried to kill me, too? The man he sent was carrying her gun, a forty-caliber Ruger. When I talked to her, she said she figured you were the one who stole it."

"Well, that wasn't very nice of her."

"But she was right," I said.

"Yeah, but she didn't know that for sure."

I glanced at Mia, and her amused eyes said, *Why bother?*

"Back to the question," I said. "Did the burglar take that Ruger, too?"

"Yeah."

Now I knew how Damon Tate had ended up with it.

"I'm assuming you didn't report the burglary," I said.

"Hell, no. I don't want the cops in my life if I can avoid it. And what would I tell them—that a bunch of stuff I'd stolen had been stolen?"

"So what happened the next time you tried to get money from Jankowski?" I asked.

"He wouldn't take my calls at first. Finally I pestered him enough and he talked to me, and I said I was about to send the video clip to the cops. Then he agreed to pay me."

"How much in total did you get?" I asked.

"None of your business," he said.

That left just one question.

"What were you doing at Brandi Sloan's house that night?" I asked.

"Well, when Jankowski finally refused to pay me any more, I decided I'd work on her a little. Tell her I'd testify against her if it came to it. Try to scare her."

"Scare her into what?" Mia asked.

"Coming up with some cash," he said.

"You were trying to milk some cash out of a receptionist?" I asked. What a total sleaze.

"Yeah, but she has a nice house, so I figured she has some money. And even if she didn't, I figured she'd turn around and put the squeeze on Jankowski, considering that they're sleeping together. She'd get the money from him."

"Did you contact her first or just go over there unannounced?" Mia asked.

"I just showed up," Armbruster said.

"And what did you tell her?"

"I said I had audio of her and Jankowski talking about a dead body, and man, I could tell he hadn't said a word about it to her. She turned totally white, like a damn ghost. But she denied everything, and she told me to get the hell out. I kept pushing her, and then she got up and went into another room, so I hauled ass. I figured she might be coming back with a gun or calling the cops or something. She could say I forced my way in or that I threatened her or whatever. I bailed before she came back."

His heart rate had climbed even higher—now at 122 beats per minute—as he recounted his experience that evening.

"Did you talk to her anytime after that?" Mia asked.

"No. Why would I? It was a dumb idea to begin with. If I hadn't gone over there that night, I probably wouldn't be lying here right now. But I kept pushing, so Jankowski pushed back. She must've told him I'd been over there."

That explained why she'd gone missing two days later. The visit from Lennox freaked her out and she decided to take off.

"Did you get a good look at the men in the truck on MoPac?" Mia asked.

"The passenger, kinda, but it wasn't anybody I'd seen before. He was wearing sunglasses and needed a shave."

"Ever hear the name Damon Tate?" I asked.

"No."

"How about Nathaniel Tate?"

"No. Who are these people?"

I said, "Damon Tate works for Joe Jankowski. He came after me with Claudia Klein's gun on my porch last week and tried to make me leave with him. I think he was planning an intimate trip for two to Barbados, but I could be wrong."

"Roy opted to knock one of his teeth out and take the gun away from him," Mia said.

"Which is how the cops knew where it came from," I said. "But I didn't know until now how Damon Tate got ahold of it."

"Then there's Nathaniel Tate, Damon's brother," Mia said. "He showed up at the house, too, and tried to shoot Roy through a bedroom window. Roy shot him with a twelve gauge."

"Fuck," Armbruster said, looking at me with new respect.

"He's clinging to life in this very hospital right now," Mia said. "Which brings up a question: Whose side do you want to be on? Ours or theirs? The people who walk away unscathed or the people who wind up in the hospital?"

"I don't want to be on anybody's side," Armbruster said. "Leave me out of it. I don't want to choose sides. I'm done."

"Too late for that," I said.

"I was having a pretty good day until you people showed up," he said. "Maybe it's time for you to leave."

"First I'm going to tell you what you need to do now, Lennox," I said.

"Oh, goody. Can't wait."

"You need to tell the police everything you've told us."

"Not gonna happen. No way. Not a chance in hell."

"Why not? You could make a deal with the prosecutor. I bet you wouldn't serve a single—"

"Forget it," he said loudly.

Mia said, "We have some connections, and we'd stick by your side to make sure—"

"I said no!"

The bedside monitor began to sound a beeping alarm. His face was bright red.

"What's the problem?" I said. "So far, you haven't done a very good job of—"

"Stop!" he said. "Just stop for a second, okay?"

I shut up. The monitor continued to beep.

Then Armbruster said, "I've got a nephew named Jack. Eight years old. My sister's kid. Jankowski came in here two days ago and said Jack could disappear, too. So he can't know I told you anything, you understand? This was between you and me and now you've got to leave me out of it. If you tell anybody what I said, and if something happens to Jack, so help me God, I'm not a violent guy, but I'll come after you and—"

He went silent as the door swung open and the same nurse came into the room, saying, "Everything okay in here?"

26

It wasn't even eleven o'clock in the morning, but I had no idea what we would do with the rest of the day. We'd learned a lot, but now what?

If Armbruster was willing to talk to the police, we'd simply turn everything over to them, as I'd done during my interview with Randy Wolfe after I'd shot Nathaniel Tate. But Armbruster wasn't willing to talk, so it was a moot point for now.

"You were great in there," I said. "That was smart to use the Brandi Sloan situation against him."

"Thanks," Mia said.

"Think we can believe him?" I asked.

"Don't know."

We were in the car again, moving slowly in MoPac traffic.

"The part about Jankowski threatening his nephew seemed real, and he might be making all the rest up because of it. Then again, in that case, why would he make up a story that still implicated Jankowski?"

Mia didn't say anything.

I said, "Or maybe the part about the threat is a lie."

We both knew that we had to assume Jankowski had made the threat. He had probably been at the hospital to visit Nathaniel Tate—who'd been taken there after I'd shot him—and Jankowski decided to visit Armbruster on the same trip. One-stop shopping. And if the threat was real, we couldn't tell the cops what we'd learned from Armbruster without placing the nephew at risk.

I said, "If he's telling the truth, I figure there's about a fifty-fifty chance Brandi Sloan is okay, but hiding out, and it was probably Jankowski who insisted she take off."

Mia nodded. I didn't need to say what the other fifty percent was. If Jankowski had had Brent Donovan killed, and he'd also tried to kill

Lennox Armbruster and me, why not add one more person to the list? Sure, Brandi Sloan had been his lover, but that didn't mean he'd be willing to go to prison for her.

"If she's alive and we can find her, we can probably break this one open," I said. "I think she'll be smart enough to understand her choices are limited if she wants to live a normal life from here on out."

Mia took the Enfield exit.

"Of course, that depends on how much she participated," I said.

I'm no idiot, and by now I'd noticed Mia wasn't actively participating in this conversation.

"Want to grab an early lunch?" I asked.

"I'm not very hungry, and I've had a headache all morning that won't go away."

"I'm sorry," I said.

"I feel like I just need to go home and lie down," she said.

"I have that doctor's appointment at one o'clock," I said.

I'd been wondering if she might want to come with me, to ask questions and understand exactly what we were facing. But she hadn't raised the idea and I hadn't asked. I didn't want to ask. I wanted her to come up with the idea herself, which would indicate that she wasn't completely defeated by what I'd told her.

She didn't reply.

"As far as the surgery itself, it's minor—an outpatient procedure. Recovery is quick and there are rarely any complications."

I liked this guy. He seemed intelligent and competent. His reputation, from what I could gather online, was immaculate. He had lots of experience, the latest technology, and an excellent support staff. His success rate was very good. He even *looked* like a doctor, which was meaningless and yet somehow comforting. I judged him to be nearly sixty. He had silver hair and wore wire-rimmed glasses.

He asked, "Do you have a partner right now? A significant other?"

"Yes. A fiancée. Mia."

"When are you getting married?"

"Next year."

"I assume Mia wants children, which is why you're here."

"She does, yes."

"How many?"

"I'm not sure. At least one. Probably more if they're running a special."

He chuckled. "That's something the two of you should discuss, because the answer to that question could impact your decision."

"How so?"

"Have the two of you talked about in vitro fertilization?"

"We have not," I said.

"For some couples who want a single child—some—that can be a better alternative to a vasectomy reversal. Not always, but sometimes. Have you done any research about IVF?"

"A little bit, but not much," I said, feeling less and less prepared for this appointment.

"It can have a higher success rate, but it's also more expensive. Quite a bit more. You'll want to see if your insurance covers it. Another potential drawback is that the sperm-retrieval techniques can limit the chance of success for a reversal if IVF doesn't work out. I'll give you some materials that discuss all of these factors and might help you decide how you want to proceed."

"That would be great."

"How old is Mia?"

"Thirty-three."

"Is she on birth control?"

"The pill, yes."

"How long has she been on it?"

"I'm not sure. Pretty long."

"How is her reproductive health?"

"No problems. All good."

"No fertility problems that you're aware of?"

"Nope."

"And her health in general?"

"Excellent."

"Has she ever been pregnant?"

"Not as far as I know."

He grinned. "You'd be surprised what some people learn about their partners when they come to see me, but I'll take that as a no. Have either of you ever had an STD—as far as you know? It can affect fertility."

"No, but not for lack of trying. I mean on my part, not Mia's."

"I gathered as much."

"Frankly, I couldn't tell you if she's ever had, uh, anything or not," I said. "I guess she could have a long time ago. I doubt she'd tell me about that if it wasn't, you know, contagious. Why would she want to talk about that?"

"Oh, I understand. Many people don't. These are just general questions that allow me to get a sense of the situation."

"And it's not like it's something to be ashamed of."

"Of course not."

"I'm babbling, aren't I?"

"You're not the first person in this room to do that," he said. "If I tell you there's no reason to be nervous, will that help?"

"Probably not."

"I didn't think so," he said. "But it was worth a shot."

"Mind if I ask how many reversals you've done? That might soothe my nerves a bit."

"At this point, thousands," he said. "More than many surgeons, but not quite enough to make the Guinness book of records."

"Still, that's a lot," I said.

"I've been doing this for a long time," he said. "Since you were a teenager, or thereabouts. If you're having second thoughts about the procedure, you could always—"

"No, I'm good," I said. "No second thoughts."

"How is Mia's state of mind right now?"

I think he somehow sensed he wasn't getting the full story.

"Well, honestly, not so great, because she only learned about all of this yesterday afternoon."

He tried to keep a poker face, but I could tell that he was surprised.

I said, "That was stupid, huh? Keeping it from her?"

"Well, I always encourage partners to be totally open and honest with each other," he said. "That starts with deciding whether you both want to have children, how many, a timeframe, and then how to go about it. The process is a lot less stressful when you're working together as a team and have a plan. Going forward, you and Mia should probably focus on communicating as much as possible."

"Meaning me, specifically," I said.

"It wouldn't hurt. May I ask why you didn't discuss it earlier with her?"

"That's a good question," I said. "So good that I'm not even sure I know the answer."

In the parking lot, I called Randy Wolfe and had to leave a voicemail.

"Hey, it's Roy Ballard. Just wondering where your investigation stands. Hoping you aren't planning to arrest me anytime soon for shooting Nathaniel Tate, because I have tickets to *Hamilton* next week and I'd be totally bummed to miss it. Also, any sign of Brandi Sloan? In all seriousness, I would appreciate any news on her. Thanks."

I hung up and sat quietly in the van for a moment.

Mia was at home, possibly still sleeping. Or maybe she was awake and wasn't in the mood to have me home. Good chance of that, seeing as how she hadn't texted to see how the appointment went. Instead of waiting, I texted her.

How's your head?

Waited five minutes for a response, but didn't get one.

I drove to a nearby mall and parked in a remote area of the lot, with no other vehicles within fifty feet. Then I sat right there in the van and spent a solid hour online with my laptop. The subject of my research: Brandi Sloan. My objective, of course, was to figure out where she might be. Or, worst case, where her body might be. Mia had come up with the brilliant and correct blackmail theory, and now I felt it was up to me to bring this thing home.

I started with family and friends on Facebook.

Think some otherwise honest people won't deceive the police and go to great lengths to protect a loved one? Imagine that your daughter comes to you, crying, and says she accidentally got mixed up with some bad people. It wasn't her fault, you understand, but now she thinks she's in danger and doesn't know what to do or where to go. The worst part is, the police might come looking for her and she doesn't think they'll believe the truth about what really happened. That's because the bad people—powerful people—might try to frame her. They'll blame everything on her. What would you do to protect your little girl? How much would you spend? How many lies would you tell? I had no idea if this type of scenario explained Brandi's disappearance, but it was worth exploring.

Her younger sister owned an art gallery in Ruidoso, and her older brother was a software designer in Georgetown, about an hour north of Austin. Her parents lived in Spicewood, a small community northwest of town, along the south banks of Lake Travis, well upstream from the main basin.

The brother, sister, and father were not on Facebook, as far as I could tell, but her mother was. Her name was Lucinda Sloan, a nice-looking, athletic, blond woman in her mid-fifties. It appeared that most or all of Lucinda's posts were set to Public, meaning they were viewable by people who were not her friends. She posted frequently and received many comments from a wide circle of friends. She was a runner and a yoga enthusiast, and she liked to post photos from her workouts, with messages encouraging a healthy lifestyle. The photos were tasteful and not at all the "look at me" type, but I couldn't help noticing she had the physique you would expect of a person decades younger.

But as I scanned her posts, I immediately noticed that something wasn't right.

Lucinda Sloan hadn't posted about her daughter's disappearance. Not one word. Several of Lucinda's friends had written pleas for assistance in tracking down Brandi, and Lucinda had shared those posts and thanked them profusely for their efforts, but she hadn't posted about it herself.

I guess there was a small chance Lucinda had created a post and forgotten to make it Public, but frankly I was skeptical. One of her Facebook-savvy friends would have reminded her to change the setting so it could be shared and viewed widely. Was Lucinda just too distraught or otherwise distracted to have thought of it? Did it mean anything? Did she know where Brandi was? If she did, I could assume that it might not have occurred to her that she needed to behave exactly as she would if Brandi had truly gone missing.

Or maybe it meant nothing.

I sent her a friend request from my fake Linda Patterson Facebook profile, which I used for instances exactly like this, and moved on.

I had reviewed Brandi's social media accounts four days ago, after Lennox Armbruster had stopped at her house the night before. Now I took a fresh look at her Facebook account. I didn't see anything new from her, of course, but she'd been tagged by friends in several posts and those showed up on her profile page. Those friends' posts were similar to the ones written by Lucinda's friends—pleas to help find Brandi. I checked those friends' profiles and from what I could see, all of them were genuinely concerned about Brandi and desperate to find her. I sent Brandi a friend request, too.

Next, I jumped over to the county tax records website for a moment. When Tracy Turner had gone missing, I'd managed to find her by checking properties her father owned. During an ugly divorce, he'd hidden Tracy with his brother in an unoccupied house. Maybe something similar was happening here. Maybe Brandi was hiding in a property owned by her parents. Except I learned there was nothing on the tax rolls other than the home they owned in Spicewood. I checked several surrounding counties and found nothing.

While I was on that site, I checked to see if Damon Tate owned any property. He did: A house in south Austin, in a neighborhood off Stassney Lane, near Garrison Park. I noted the address and tried not to think about him anymore right now. It wasn't easy, knowing that he might seek revenge at any moment.

Forget about him. Focus.

What about Brandi's sister in Ruidoso? Ingrid, the art gallery owner. She presented an intriguing possibility. Could it be that obvious? Brandi could have hopped a bus and been in Ruidoso less than 12 hours later. Just hang out at sis's place until everything blows over. Talk to an attorney. Figure out the best way to proceed.

But wait a second. Ingrid would have to come to Austin, right? How would it look if her sister was missing and she didn't come to town? So I needed to find out if she had or not. If she had, Brandi would have Ingrid's house to herself while Ingrid was in Texas, pretending to look for her sister.

I clicked over to a subscription-based telephone directory that was helpful on occasion. Most phone directories were riddled with inaccurate or outdated information, but I'd found one in particular that was correct maybe half of the time. That was about as good as they got. And it even included cell phone numbers, which was a must nowadays.

In less than five seconds, I had a number for Ingrid Sloan. Was it the right number? Should I call it now or wait? While I was trying to decide, I got a text from Mia.

Still at the doctor?

Strange that I experienced so much joy from a simple text, but that was the current state of affairs. She wasn't ignoring me. She was showing some interest in the situation.

No, sitting in a parking lot, doing research. Didn't want to wake you. How is your headache?

She replied: *All gone. How was the doc?*

I said: *Fine. We have a lot to talk about.*

She said, *k.*

Not very enthusiastic. I said: *Ready to give up on me yet?*

A minute later: *Of course not. You know better.*

I'll admit it: There are times when I'm a sensitive guy. Right now, I was tearing up. Not sure why.

I should have told you sooner, I said.

True, she said.

I had to laugh.

I sent: *xo.*

She said: *Coming home soon?*

Not yet. There's something else I need to do.

27

The home was on a street called Turtle Creek Boulevard, which was way too cute of an address for a man like Damon Tate. The house needed paint and a new roof, just for starters. This guy was in construction? He owned the most neglected home on the block, by far. Maybe that's why he was willing to do Jankowski's dirty work; he needed the money. Should've simply asked for a raise.

I was relieved to see that his dirty Chevy truck was parked in the driveway. Made sense, though. He wouldn't be at work while his brother was in the ICU, but he wouldn't want to hang out at the hospital all day.

I drove past, then turned around at the end of the block and parked in front of a home that looked quiet, with no vehicles in the driveway. There were quite a few vehicles parked along the curb on this block, so the van blended in just fine.

I waited. It was 3:14 in the afternoon. I knew he might not go anywhere. No problem. I had plenty of patience when so much was on the line. Worst case, the sun would set and then I could take action.

But I got lucky. Forty-seven minutes after I'd parked, Damon Tate emerged from his house, climbed into his truck, and drove away.

I followed discreetly.

East on Turtle Creek.

North on Emerald Forest.

East on Stassney.

Then a left into a retail center, where he parked in an angled spot in front of a place called the Rusty Cannon Pub.

Perfect. I parked closer to the Rite-Away Pharmacy and watched. Tate got out of his truck and went inside. I gave it five minutes, then I got out of the van and walked casually in the direction of his truck. Fortunately, there were vehicles on both sides of the Chevy to shield me from view.

A few more steps and I reached the tailgate of his truck. I'd learned over the years to always act like you know exactly what you're doing and you have every right to do it. I squatted down, rolled onto my back, and shimmied underneath the rear of the truck. It took me less than five seconds to find a good out-of-the-way spot to slap a magnetic GPS tracker. Then I was back on my feet, returning to the van. Quick. Smooth. Nobody saw a thing.

But, out of pure caution, I sat in the van for five minutes and watched, just to be sure Damon Tate didn't emerge from the restaurant to see what I'd been doing under his truck. Nope. All good.

I opened the GPS app on my phone and created a custom setting. Now if Tate came within one hundred yards of our house in Tarrytown, I'd get a real-time alert.

But I wasn't done yet.

As I opened the door to JMJ Construction at five o'clock, I realized it would be quite a twist if I found Brandi Sloan seated behind the reception desk, going about business as usual. But, no, it was Cindy, the woman who'd been filling in when I'd been here three days ago.

"How was your pedicure?" she asked.

It took me a second to remember what I'd said last time.

"Not bad, but they charged me extra because I have cloven hooves," I said.

She laughed sharply and said, "You are so weird. But, like, in a good way."

A little flirtatious, but I have to admit it felt good, given my mood for the past day or so.

I said, "Not to be a total downer, but any sign of Brandi?"

Her smile slowly disappeared. "Actually, no, and we're all pretty upset about it. The police told us to call if we hear anything from her at all."

"It's a sad situation," I said.

I was taking a calculated risk being here in this office. What if

Jankowski spotted me? On the other hand, so what if he did? What would he do? What could he do? He might not know that I knew the connection between him and the Tate brothers, so he would be forced to play it cool. Pretend that everything was fine. Even if Cindy happened to mention later that I'd been there, so what?

"It sure is," she said. Then she added, "Uh, are you here to see Mr. Jankowski? He's in a meeting right now."

"Actually, I was just driving by and I just thought I'd stop to see if Brandi had been found."

"Aw, that's very sweet of you. But I tell you what—if you'll give me your phone number, I'll call you if we hear anything."

"That would be outstanding," I said.

She slid a notepad across the desk and I jotted my number down.

"Guard that with your life," I said, sliding the pad back to her. "People would pay good money for that number."

"I'm sure that's true," she said. "Mostly women. I might auction it off to the highest bidder."

"You could retire early," I said.

It was harmless for me to flirt back, right?

"That's what I was thinking," she said. "Or I might just keep it for myself."

Oops. Had I pushed it too far? I got back to the topic at hand by saying, "Well, I hope Brandi turns up real soon."

"If you had to guess," Cindy said, her voice lowered, "what would you say happened to her? I mean, it just seems so…grim. Like we're not going to be hearing any good news, that's for sure."

I could tell Cindy was genuinely concerned and distressed.

"I really wouldn't even want to speculate," I said. "And I'd say it's way too early to give up hope. Just keep a positive thought until the police learn more."

That seemed to buoy her spirits, and I wondered if I was setting her up for disappointment later. Maybe.

I gave her a wave and headed out the door to the central atrium of the building.

Before I'd gone inside, I'd spotted Jankowski's Land Rover SUV parked in a reserved spot near the entrance to the building. How convenient. And I knew that the view of that particular spot from the atrium was limited.

I exited to the outside, descended the steps, and veered toward the SUV. I began tossing my keys a few inches in the air and catching them, just as casual as could be, until I was beside the SUV. Then— oops—I dropped the keys. Bent down to get them, and on my way up, I slapped a tracker under the rear passenger wheel well. It wasn't as well hidden as the one on Damon Tate's truck, but it would do for now.

I walked to the van, fired it up, and took off.

Now if Jankowski and Tate got together in person to make more plans against me or Lennox Armbruster, I'd know. Ain't technology great?

I decided it was time to call Ingrid Sloan—assuming it was the right phone number—and see what I could learn. A woman answered on the second ring.

I said, "This is Tony with American Parcel Service trying to reach Ingrid Sloan."

"This is she."

Wow. Not only had I reached her, she was good with grammar.

"We have a package for you, but we've been unsuccessful in delivering it," I said. "We've left a couple of notices, so we're wondering if the address is correct."

"What address do you have?" she asked.

Smart. Better than giving out her address to some random dude on the phone.

I read off her home address, which I'd found in the tax rolls, but I changed an 8 to a 3. She corrected me, and I said, "Sorry for the mix-up. At this point, we want to do everything we can to make up for the delay and the inconvenience, but I also see here that the package is going to require a signature, per the shipper's instructions. So I just—"

"Who is the shipper?" She sounded impatient, and who could blame her, under the circumstances?

"Uh…Old West Mercantile," I said.

"Never heard of them," she said.

"Somebody might have sent something to you from them," I said. "Maybe a gift."

"If they did, I'm going to chew their ass out, because this is a hassle."

I laughed. "Would you like to decline the delivery?"

She let out a sigh. "No, that's fine. Just, uh, when can you bring it?"

"We will be happy to accommodate your schedule," I said. "So whatever works. Really, anytime, including evenings."

"Can you deliver it to my business instead?"

That told me she was still in Ruidoso, and possibly that she wanted to keep people away from her house.

"Yes, ma'am, if that would work better for you. What's that address?"

28

The next day and a half passed without any additional progress or news on the case. I had most of the puzzle put together, but I didn't know what to do with it or where to go with it. Tell the cops? Neither Billy Chang nor Randy Wolfe, the APD investigators, had shared anything with me, so why should I share anything more with them?

This case wasn't the only topic for me to worry about.

I'd told Mia about my appointment with the urologist, and I left the materials on the living room table for her to read. She'd seemed neither interested nor indifferent. This was a side of her I'd never experienced before, and that in itself was disquieting. What were we waiting for? Didn't we need to talk about this and figure out what we were going to do?

She was at the gym for a mid-morning workout when the doorbell rang. I checked the camera on the porch and saw a youngish gentleman waiting harmlessly, hands in pockets, for me to answer the door, so I did.

He had a slight build and closely cropped red hair with a matching goatee.

"Hi, I'm your neighbor right down the street," he said. "Blane Benson?"

Oh, right. Now I recognized him. We shook hands.

"Hi, Blane," I said. "I'm Roy Ballard."

"Right, and you replaced my mailbox last week?" he said.

"Yep, that was me, and I hope the note made sense," I said.

"Well, yeah, I guess it did, and I kind of wanted to talk to you about that. First, I wanted to say thanks, I guess."

I guess?

"Is there a problem with the mailbox?" I asked.

"No, it's fine. It's more with the situation that led to the mailbox being destroyed."

He seemed somewhat nervous.

"What situation is that?" I asked.

"What I mean is, we talked to the cop that night when she knocked on our door, but to be honest, we didn't really understand what had happened. Or why. We just knew that somebody had driven over our mailbox and left the scene. Not exactly the crime of the century, right? But I started getting curious, and I read the police report from that night, and then you actually shot a man right outside your home, and that made me—well, I started doing some research about you."

"About me?"

"Yeah, and what you do for a living."

"I'm a legal videographer."

"I'd never heard of that profession before," he said, "and it sounds so...I don't know. Innocuous? Is that the right word?"

Blane was beginning to annoy me.

"I don't know, Blane. You tell me."

"I'm not explaining why I'm here very well," he said. "It's just that, given what you do and the kind of people you bring into our neighborhood, I was just wondering if you might consider moving. You and your wife."

I almost laughed, because I didn't know what else to do.

"You want Mia and me to move out?" I said. "Her family has owned this place for nearly a hundred years."

"I'm not sure what that has to do with it."

"How long have you lived here?"

"Five months."

"Why don't you move instead?"

"Because I'm not the problem," he said.

"So you want us to move," I said. "That's the solution you propose?"

"I don't think it's an unreasonable idea," he said. "There are a lot of families in this neighborhood."

"There are a lot of families in most neighborhoods," I said, feeling the heat rising in my cheeks and the back of my neck.

"I'm not trying to agitate you," Blane said. "I just feel that you present a certain danger to everyone else on the street. Do you disagree?"

"I don't even know where to start, Blane, to be honest. What if I was a cop or a judge or a prosecutor? The situation would be similar.

Would you still ask me to move?"

"You had to *shoot* a man," Blane said. "What if you'd missed? Where might those bullets have gone? What about a ricochet? Have you not thought about these possibilities? And how do you know it won't happen again?"

Honestly, I didn't have a good answer for his questions.

"I'll have to get back with you on that, Blane. Thanks for coming by."

When Mia came home from the gym, I didn't say anything about his visit.

Later that day, a client called with a new case—a fairly straightforward slip-and-fall accident—and we agreed that Mia would tackle it solo for the time being. She got right on it, too. After reviewing the file, she headed out in her Chevy Tahoe to put the subject under surveillance. Was it just my imagination, or was she looking for excuses to get out of the house lately?

I sat down in the living room with a notepad on my lap.

Some things I knew:

Nathaniel Tate had not died and I assumed, at this point, he was going to survive.

I had not heard from Randy Wolfe or anyone else at APD, so I also assumed there was a strong chance I was not going to be charged for the shooting, which was as it should be.

Neither Damon Tate nor Joe Jankowski had driven anywhere near our house, and they had not gotten together in person—at least, not in the two vehicles carrying my GPS trackers. Likewise, neither of them had gone anywhere that seemed suspicious or out of place, unless you consider the Yellow Rose, a strip joint, out of place. Damon Tate had gone there a few hours after his late lunch at the Rusty Cannon.

Blane Benson was weighing on my mind. Should he? Did he have a valid point? Or did he simply have a stick up his butt because his parents had named him Blane?

I absentmindedly drew an elephant on the notepad, but it looked more like a deformed donkey.

Lennox Armbruster had been released from the hospital, and although he had answered when I'd called yesterday, he still wasn't interested in talking to the cops. His sister and nephew were fine.

Brandi Sloan was still missing.

Her mother, Lucinda Sloan, had accepted the friend request from my fake profile, Linda Patterson, yesterday. When I visited her timeline, I didn't see any posts that I hadn't been able to see previously, which meant she had never written a post about her daughter's disappearance.

I'd been thinking about Brandi a lot, and it had become crystal clear that she was the key to closing this case. She was in it up to her neck. She'd talked to Joe Jankowski about a body. If she knew about that, she probably knew every detail. Every player. Depending on the extent of her involvement—assuming she didn't kill Brent Donovan herself—she could probably cop a plea and bring Jankowski and Damon Tate down, and possibly Nathaniel Tate, too. She wouldn't skate totally, but she might be able to stop this fiasco from ruining the rest of her life.

If she was still alive.

The police would have gotten warrants for her cell phone and bank cards in order to monitor for any activity. If she or anyone else was out there using them, they would know that by now, and they would have most likely found that person. Hence nobody was using them. Had she planned ahead and stockpiled a bunch of cash before she took off? If so, why? Why had she run?

I remembered that her Land Rover had been parked in the driveway when I'd parked on her street during the welfare check, so how had she left town? Airplane? Bus? Rental car? Gotten a ride from a friend? Simply walked away? Or been carried, lifeless, perhaps rolled in a tarp or squeezed into a large suitcase?

I'm not a big believer in, like, cosmic alignment or the idea that there are no coincidences, but my phone rang right then with a call from Randy Wolfe.

"I finally had a chance to interview Nathaniel Tate in the hospital, and I'd say you're in the clear," he said. "Figured you'd want to know."

"Let me guess…he gave conflicting stories, threw in some obvious lies, and somehow couldn't remember a whole bunch of details. And the reason he was playing a recording of a catfight on his phone—well, that was just a prank, because that kind of thing is hysterical."

"I can neither confirm nor deny any of that," he said.

"I'm surprised he agreed to an interview. Have you charged him?"

"It's coming."

"Attempted murder?"

"Don't know," he said. "That's up to the prosecutor."

"I'm sure you can understand why I would be rightfully upset if it's anything less than attempted murder, seeing as how he intentionally tried to lure me to a window while he waited with his gun drawn."

"You know how these things work," he said.

"Unfortunately, yeah, I do. Have you warned Damon Tate about the idea of, you know, trying to kill me for revenge?"

"Not my job," Wolfe said. "But I called him anyway. Left a message. He didn't call me back."

"Thanks for trying," I said. "Have you processed Brandi Sloan's place?"

Best to try to get as much out of him as I could before he was ready to end the call.

"Can't get a warrant. We have no evidence she's been the victim of a crime or an accident, and nobody else has the legal right to let us search her house or her vehicle. Her name is the only one on the deed."

"When that deputy did a welfare check—"

"How did you know about that?"

"I was watching. I see all, know all."

He didn't say anything, because he didn't like my flippant attitude.

So I said, "Okay, I encouraged the other receptionist at JMJ Construction to ask for a deputy to be sent over, and then I went over to watch. I was concerned about Brandi and I wanted to know if the deputy saw anything weird or out of place. I assume the answer is no."

"That is correct. Obviously. Which is one reason we can't get a warrant."

"What about the parents?"

"What about them?"

"I'm betting they have a key to the place and are free to go inside if they want, and they already have."

"They do, and they went inside the same day as the welfare check. They didn't see anything that concerned them. Same with the vehicle."

"Speaking of which," I said, "any idea how she managed to afford a Land Rover on a receptionist's salary?"

"If I had access to any of her financial records, I might know the answer to that, but, again, can't get a warrant."

Since he was sharing information with me, I was tempted to tell him everything I'd learned from Lennox Armbruster, but I resisted. Armbruster would deny all of it, and Wolfe would be left with nothing but my secondhand account. He wouldn't be able to verify anything Armbruster had said. And, most important, it could put Armbruster's nephew Jack in danger. Would Jankowski follow through on that threat? If he did, I'd never forgive myself.

"You think something happened to her or she took off on her own?" I asked.

"I'm not a fan of making wild guesses," he said.

Which was clever, because it was the same thing I'd said to him when he'd interviewed me about shooting Nathaniel Tate.

"Awfully wise of you," I said. "You're aware she has a sister in New Mexico?"

"Of course I am. I've talked to her a couple of times and she knows nothing about it."

"Or that's what she says."

"You want to stop beating around the bush?"

"Has the sister come to town?" I asked.

"She has not. So what?"

"Do you have a sister?" I asked.

"As a matter of fact, I have two," he said.

"How far would you go, and how quickly would you get there, if one of them went missing?"

"That's an appeal to emotion, not facts or evidence," he said.

"Exactly. Did it work?"

"It did not. Do you have some special information you need to share about the situation? Something that indicates Brandi is in New Mexico and her sister is covering for her?"

"None whatsoever, unfortunately. It's just something that should be checked, in my opinion."

"I've heard that you sometimes like to tell cops how to do their jobs, but I hadn't seen it until now."

"I like to think of these ideas as friendly suggestions."

"Here's a suggestion: Don't do that anymore."

He hung up. I sat in silence for ten minutes, pondering what I'd learned.

I wished Wolfe could get warrants for Brandi's home, vehicle, cell phone, and bank data, but at the same time, I doubted he would learn anything from any of it, regardless of what had become of her.

Going on the run without leaving a trace was extremely difficult nowadays. Almost impossible, especially if you were talking about dropping out for good, never to be seen again. But could someone disappear for a short period of time, like a month or two, or maybe even a few years? Still a long shot, but I couldn't rule it out. Brandi seemed like an intelligent woman, and, unlike most older folks, she would be more likely to understand the technology traps that would leave a digital trail showing where she'd gone. If that's what had happened, she likely did her best to make a clean getaway.

If someone had killed her or simply abducted her, that person had likely been Joe Jankowski or one of his lackeys. The fact that they'd managed to make Brent Donovan vanish without getting caught left me thinking they could've done it again with Brandi.

Which was more likely? I would've said it was a toss-up—except for the behavior of Brandi's parents and sister. They weren't doing the things one would expect them to do. That tilted me toward Brandi running away. Total hunch, admittedly.

But so what?

I clicked over to the website for Southwest Airlines and checked the route map. Closest destinations were El Paso and Albuquerque. El Paso was slightly closer, but I chose Albuquerque because it would be a nicer drive. The flight I selected departed at 6:40 the next morning.

29

Did I really need to go to Ruidoso, or was I just giving myself an excuse to get out of town? Temporarily running away from Mia? Or, to put a positive spin on it, taking a well-deserved break to handle stress and anxiety more effectively?

Nonsense. It wasn't going to be a break. I would be working.

Early this morning, as I gave Mia a goodbye hug while she lay in bed, I admitted that I was worried about leaving her home alone.

"I know you can take care of yourself," I said, "but still."

She rubbed my back and said, "You know as well as I do that the odds of Damon Tate coming over here again are virtually nil, especially after you shot his brother. They've tried it twice, so how obvious would it be to try it in the same location a third time?"

"I agree, unless he's smart enough to think we reached that conclusion, which would then make a third attempt at the house all the more surprising."

"You know these guys never give anything that much thought," she said. "He'd try to get to you somewhere else. Maybe steal a car, then pull up beside you at a red light and open fire."

"I'm glad you haven't been giving this any thought," I said.

"Or maybe he'll drop a giant anvil on your head."

"At least that would be quick," I said. "Just be careful while I'm gone."

"You worry about me too much," she said.

It was true, and although I would never reveal this to her, there were times I wished I'd never asked her to be my partner. It was a dangerous job. What if something happened to her? In this case, however, involving Damon Tate, I was confident she was right. If he did try anything, he wouldn't do it at the house. He'd try to kill me in a manner exactly as she described, where there would be no reliable

witnesses and very little evidence. Even better if he could make it look
like road rage or a random street killing during a robbery.

"I worry just the right amount," I said.

I let my hand drift under the sheets and—

"Stop that," she said. "You'll miss your flight."

"But when I get back?" I asked.

"I'll be here," she said.

Progress?

The flight landed on time and I got my rental car—a plain-vanilla
sedan with gray paint and tinted windows—without any issues.

I stopped for some outstanding huevos rancheros at Standard
Diner—a busy place housed in a remodeled 1930s Texaco station—
then went south on Interstate 25.

Google Maps estimated that it was a three-hour drive to Ruidoso,
and that's roughly what it took. Gorgeous scenery all the way. High-
desert terrain at first, with gentle hills and junipers, then the road began
to climb into forests thick with Ponderosa pines. Mountains in the
distance. Rough country. The weather was downright heavenly.
Seventy degrees with no humidity whatsoever. I drove with the
windows down.

I came into Ruidoso from the north on Highway 48 and drove from
one end of town to the other, just to get my bearings. It wasn't a big
place. The bulk of the town, or at least the retail district, was situated
along two streets—Sudderth Drive and Mechem Drive, which formed
an upside-down T intersection on the south side.

The streets were lined with dozens and dozens of small shops,
galleries, inns, cabins, and restaurants, but it wasn't garish or tacky.
The town had a welcoming and laidback feel to it. Eclectic. Artsy. With
a Native American theme to many of the names and signs.

Heading west on Sudderth Drive again, I spotted Chaparral Arts,
which was Ingrid Sloan's place. I'd done a little more research via
overpriced Wi-Fi on the plane, and even though Chaparral Arts was
classified as an art gallery, it was more of a gift shop that included arts

and crafts on consignment from various local artists.

I glanced through the double glass doors as I cruised past, and I saw a few people inside, but I couldn't make out any faces. It was tempting to pull over and go in, and I could just imagine the thrill of locating Brandi mere minutes into my mission, if she happened to be there. But what were the odds? I figured I'd better plan something a little more organized than just wandering inside and seeing who was there.

I knew from googling that there were some chain motels on the edge of town—Comfort Inn, Motel 6, Super 8, and a few more—but those were outnumbered by quaint little properties that featured collections of individual cabins tucked among the pine trees. Many of them were flashing a neon VACANCY sign, so I had my pick. After all, despite the great weather, it wasn't yet ski season, when this little town would be packed.

I spotted a place called Apache Village Cabins and swung into the drive. Apache Village consisted of maybe a dozen small cabins in three neat rows, with one cabin acting as the front office. I parked and went inside. There, I found a friendly older gentleman who took my information, charged me a reasonable fee for a two-night stay, and said I could almost certainly extend that stay if necessary, because it wasn't like he was expecting a big rush at any moment.

"We don't get many drop-ins without a reservation," he said. "What brings you to town?"

"Just needed a break," I said. "I was overcome by ennui."

"On what?" he said.

"Ennui," I said. "I was restless."

"Sign right here," he said.

I could tell that my one-bedroom cabin had been built some time ago—maybe in the forties or fifties—but it had been well maintained. It had character—and a fireplace, complete with a supply of pine logs. The living room had pine walls, a pine ceiling, and a pine coffee table and entertainment center. I found pine cabinets and countertops in the kitchen. All of the bedroom furniture was built from—wait for it—pine. Everything smelled a little musty and smoky, but in a good way, if that makes sense. It smelled like a cabin in ski country, and that's hard to beat.

I put my small suitcase on the bed and went out to the living room.

It was 3:18 in the afternoon, one hour earlier than it was back home.

I backed into a corner, took a photo, and texted it to Mia.

Thirty seconds later, she said, *Cute. Is this toilet also made of pine?*

I said, *I hadn't noticed, but that explains the splinters in my butt.*

She said, *Keep me posted. xo.*

I sat on the couch and tried to make a choice. Go into Ingrid Sloan's shop as a customer and see what I could learn, or wait outside and follow her when she left?

If I went into the store, I would immediately give something away—my appearance. She would see me face to face and might remember me later. That may or may not be a problem.

I opted for Plan B, but first I took a quick nap.

I got lucky and found a primo parking spot in a large lot between two curio shops, and directly across the street from Chaparral Arts, which would close at 5:00, according to the website. Right now it was 4:48.

As far as I could tell from my online snooping, Ingrid didn't have any employees. She opened and closed the place every day of the week except Mondays, which she took off. So she was in there right now, just waiting for one last customer to leave. I was using a small super-zoom camera I'd packed in my suitcase to check things out from a distance, and it looked like the customer was a lone older woman with white hair.

I knew what Ingrid Sloan looked like from photos on Lucinda Sloan's Facebook page, and there was a more recent photo on the website for her shop: Ingrid smiling invitingly from behind a glass-topped jewelry case, with some oil paintings on the wall behind her. Nice looking lady. Probably 30 years old. So I wouldn't have any trouble recognizing her. I knew from driving behind the shop earlier that there was a back door, but there weren't any vehicles parked in the back. She would leave from the front entrance and walk to her vehicle, probably that green Subaru Outback parked forty feet from the door, because the only other nearby vehicle was a boring late-model sedan, which screamed rental car, which most likely meant the white-haired woman was driving it. A tourist.

So I waited patiently.

I would follow Ingrid Sloan from a discreet distance, and with any luck she would go straight home. Then I'd decide what to do next. Figure out a way to determine if Brandi was holed up inside. Maybe wait until tomorrow and stake the place out, waiting for Brandi to go somewhere. Or attempt to get a look through a window—without being arrested for peeping. It would all depend on where Ingrid lived—house, condo, apartment?

Now it was 4:57. I could see the back of the customer's head, and she appeared to be talking to someone—had to be Ingrid—I couldn't see.

I hoped Ingrid didn't have some long list of tasks she completed daily before closing down the shop for the night. Balancing the books? Sweeping the floors? Making calls or returning emails?

The white-haired lady was still talking, and then she gave a wave and turned for the door, and now my camera was zoomed right into the face.

Holy mother.

It's not often that I'm totally stunned by something I see, but in this case…wow. Never expected it.

The white-haired lady was Doris Donovan. Brent Donovan's mother. Not someone who looked like her, but absolutely her. No doubt.

What the hell was she doing in Ruidoso, New Mexico, talking to Brandi Sloan's sister?

30

I followed her, of course.

She went west on Sudderth and turned north on Mechem.

I'd already made up my mind that I was going to confront her. I had to know what was happening here. I needed answers.

She slowed as she neared the Apache Village Cabins, and for one strange moment, I thought she was going to take a left into the same drive I'd used earlier. But she took a right instead on Terrace Drive, then kept left on Lower Terrace Drive and turned right into a place called Idle Hours Lodge. She pulled up to a cabin very similar to my own and parked her rental car.

I pulled in behind her, but I could tell she hadn't noticed me yet. I stepped from my car and waited for her to get out of hers. When she did, I said, "Hi, Doris."

She was a bit startled by my voice, and she looked at me, and for a brief moment, I could tell that she recognized me, but she didn't remember from where. Then she got it. Her eyes widened and she said, "Good Lord, what are you doing here?"

"Excuse the trite reply," I said, "but I was going to ask you the same thing."

I was ready for a lie. *I'm just here on vacation.* Something like that. She'd be nervous, stammering, because I'd caught her at…something. Was she somehow involved with Brandi Sloan and Joe Jankowski? Had she taken part in her own son's disappearance and apparent murder? That sounded downright insane, but I'd dealt with enough evil scumbags over the years to know that they sometimes had a talent for masking their true selves. You see it on *Dateline* all the time.

But Doris Donovan didn't appear guilty or worried. Instead, she grinned.

In a low voice, she said, "I'm here looking for Brandi Sloan." She looked particularly tickled when she added, "And I found her yesterday."

"This is all new to me," she said. "I don't know what to do in a situation like this. Do I just go up and knock on the door? Do I call the police?" She touched my forearm. "It's so great that you're here, because now you can tell me what to do!"

She had invited me inside and now we were seated at the dinette table in the cabin's small kitchen.

"Absolutely," I said, doing my best to keep my excitement in check. She may or may not have found Brandi Sloan. She could be mistaken. Might've seen someone who *looked* like Brandi Sloan, somebody she really wanted to *be* Brandi Sloan. I've done the same thing myself many times. So I said, "Can you start at the beginning and tell me why you're here?"

"Oh, you bet," she said. "After our meeting—excuse me, would you like something to drink?"

"Sure."

"Bourbon and Coke on the rocks?"

Didn't expect that.

"Great."

She got up and went to the fridge, where she retrieved a liter-sized bottle of Coke. Pulled a bottle of Jim Beam from the cabinet.

As she mixed the drinks, she said, "After we talked, I started thinking about Brandi Sloan and the fact that she'd gone missing, just like Brent. And maybe I've read too many Helen Haught Fanick novels, but it made me start wondering if I could figure out what had really happened."

She came back to the table with the two drinks in short glasses and sat down.

"Thank you," I said. I took a sip of the drink and it was damn strong.

She said, "I figured it was one of two things—same as with Brent. She's dead, God rest her soul, or she ran away. And I wondered—if she did run away, was it because she knew something about Brent?"

"Makes sense," I said.

"So I got on Facebook and managed to find some of her family members. I saw that she had a sister out here, and I thought Ruidoso would be a wonderful place for Brandi to hide out."

This was either a remarkably savvy lady, or my job was a lot easier than I'd led myself to believe.

"That's why I'm here," I said.

"I figured as much," she said. "Oh, hang on."

She got up again, went to the pantry, and came back with a metal tin filled with her amazing cookies. "I've always liked something to nibble with my bourbon," she said. "Help yourself."

I took a cookie but didn't eat it just yet.

"So you just decided to launch your own investigation?" I asked.

She chuckled. "I don't think I'd call it that, but I knew the police wouldn't come all the way over here to look into things, and I'm retired, so I figured why not? I used to come to Ruidoso years ago with my husband and I thought it would be nice to visit again. If I didn't find her, it would just be a vacation."

"When did you get here?"

"Three days ago," she said. "I waited a couple days after we talked to see if anyone found her."

"And, like, how…what have you done so far?"

"Well, on the first afternoon, I parked outside of Ingrid's studio and waited until she left, and then I followed her home."

Good God. We shared a brain.

"Did she see you?"

"I don't think so. I stayed far back. She lives on Carrizo Creek, on the way out to Inn of the Mountain Gods. You know where that is?"

"Not really."

"It's about three miles due south of here, but it takes about ten minutes to get there. It looks like she has a couple of acres and a horse. Nice place."

"So you followed her out there and then what?"

"Well, then I knew where she lived, and when she was working the next day, I went back out there and parked along the shoulder where I could see the house. Sure enough, I saw a light come on in a room up front, and then a woman passed by, just for an instant, and I'm fairly certain it was Brandi Sloan."

Fairly certain. She was sharp, but "fairly certain" wasn't good enough.

"How far away would you say you were from the window?"

"Oh, it's probably at least fifty yards, but I was using binoculars. I bought some that morning."

"Okay, and then what happened?"

"You're not eating your cookie," she said. "You should eat your cookie."

I took a bite just to appease her, but damn, that was a tasty cookie, and I'm sure I made a face that showed how much I enjoyed it.

She nodded, satisfied, and said, "Well, as I said before, I wasn't sure what I should do, so I thought about it for a while, and then I parked in the driveway and marched right up to the door and knocked. Nobody answered, so I knocked again, and then again, but whoever was inside wouldn't answer. That says something right there, doesn't it? And when I left, I noticed that the blinds were drawn in the window where I'd seen the woman before. They were open when I went up to knock." I was shaking my head, amazed, so she said, "What?"

"You are incredible," I said. Which was true, even if the woman in the house wasn't Brandi Sloan.

"So I did okay?"

"Okay? You did better than a lot of cops I know. But go on. Tell me what happened next. Did you see the woman again?"

"I knew that my one sighting wasn't actual confirmation—I didn't *know* it was her—so, again, I wasn't sure what to do. Then I decided I needed to think like Brandi Sloan. Would she come out of the house at some point? I didn't think there was much chance of that—unless I could make her nervous enough to move. So I—"

She suddenly began to giggle. I waited with all the patience I could muster.

She said, "So I went up to the door and knocked again, and I began to call out for Mildred. I knew Brandi—or the woman inside—could hear me, but she didn't answer, of course. So then I went back to my car and waited for Ingrid to get home, and as she pulled into the driveway, I followed her."

"You are actually making my palms sweat, Doris," I said.

"Then I must be telling the story well," she said. "Shall I continue?"

"Please do."

"I greeted Ingrid when she got out of her car, and then I pretended to be a dotty old woman who was looking for her sister Mildred. I told her I was positive I'd seen Mildred through one of the windows."

"Oh, man," I said.

"She said nobody else lived there, but I was very persistent about it, and I asked if I could go inside, knowing full well the answer would be no, which it was."

Her ruse reminded me of some of the tricks Mia and I pulled when necessary. The beauty of it was that if Brandi was inside the home, Ingrid Sloan wouldn't risk calling the police or any sort of social service agency.

"How did she react?" I said.

"I have no doubt she thoroughly bought my little act, and she was patient, but ultimately she asked me to run along and not come back. But I did go back the next day—that was yesterday—when Ingrid was gone. I knocked on the door and shouted for Mildred. That appears to have done the trick, because Ingrid closed up shop early and came home within the hour. She asked me to leave again, and I did. Well, to make a long story short, although it's too late for that, I found a good hiding spot down the road a ways and then waited for Ingrid to leave again. She did, just thirty minutes later. I followed at a distance and I was glad I was driving such a common type of car. I couldn't see anyone else in Ingrid's car, but my theory was that Brandi was lying down on the back seat, and Ingrid was taking her to a motel or somewhere else to stay for a few days until the nutty woman stopped coming around."

"Where did they go?" I asked.

"Here," Doris said quite simply.

"Here?" I said.

"Brandi Sloan is staying in the cabin behind this one."

31

I had to resist the urge to get up and peek out the rear windows.

"Have you seen her?" I asked.

"Oh, yes," Doris said. "When she got out of Ingrid's car, just as I suspected, and made a dash for the cabin. But I wasn't able to get a good photo."

"But you did get a photo?"

"Several, on burst mode," she said as she pulled her phone from her pocket. She found the photos and passed the phone to me. They were all blurry and the woman in them, wearing sunglasses and a baseball cap, may or may not have been Brandi Sloan. But who else would Ingrid Sloan be hustling from her house to a rented cabin?

"Did they see you?" I asked.

"I was very careful," Doris said.

"But did they see you?" I said.

"I can't guarantee they didn't, but I saw no indication that they did."

"So after Ingrid moved her over here, what? You rented a cabin?"

"Exactly. And I said I liked the look of number five, because I didn't want them to put me right next door or in a cabin with a clear view from mine to hers. There are a lot of trees behind this cabin that separate it from Brandi's cabin, but I can see her porch fairly well from the window in the kitchen."

"And she hasn't come out since yesterday?"

"Not that I've seen."

"Has Ingrid come back? Or anyone else?"

"Not that I've seen. If a car parked in front, I'd be able to see that, too, and probably hear the doors closing."

She munched on another cookie and let me think for a moment. At this point, I was as confident as she was that Brandi Sloan was in that cabin. Who else would it be? What else would explain Ingrid Sloan's secret houseguest?

I stood and went to the rear window of the small kitchen area, where I tilted the mini-blinds and peeked out. She was right. You couldn't see much, but you could see bits and pieces through the trees of the cabin behind her, including the porch and front door. This cabin was an ideal location for surveillance.

"So what were you doing in Ingrid's shop an hour ago?" I asked. "I mean, obviously, she recognized you."

"I told her that some of my medications had been interacting in an odd manner and creating some unclear thoughts, and I said I was sorry for having bothered her."

"How did she react?"

"We had a good laugh, but the relief on her face was unmistakable. She had probably been worrying that I was going to keep coming back."

"Or you were going to call the cops and say she was keeping your sister captive."

"Exactly. Think she'll move Brandi back to her place now?"

"Good chance, I'd say. Maybe tomorrow or the next day. She won't want to rush after you freaked her out."

Doris nodded.

Perhaps she hadn't done everything exactly as I would have done it, but everything appeared to have worked, and why argue with success?

I quietly let out a sigh.

Doris had been so forthcoming with everything she'd learned, I owed it to her to do the same. I turned back toward her and leaned backward against the countertop.

"There's something I need to tell you about Brent," I said.

Right about the same time, as I learned later, Mia was leaving the house to do some surveillance on the subject of her new case. This meant she drove her Chevy Tahoe rather than her 1968 Mustang fastback. That car alone turns heads, but when you put her behind the wheel, it's a wonder it doesn't make the six o'clock news. *A local beauty goes for a drive in a classic car. The story right after this break.*

The Tahoe, on the other hand, blended right in with the traffic, and the tinted windows provided concealment.

So why, just five minutes after getting on MoPac and going north, did she feel like she was being tailed? White Chevy truck, fifty yards back and three vehicles behind. Of course, I'd told her that Damon Tate drove a white Chevy, and I'd given her the license plate number, but she couldn't make it out at this distance.

She exited at 45th Street just to see what the truck would do. It followed. One vehicle—a purple hatchback—separated them.

Mia went east. So did the hatchback. And the white truck.

Could be a coincidence. There were literally thousands of white Chevy trucks on the road in Austin. Try to take a five-minute drive without seeing several and you'll fail.

She came to a four-way stop and turned north on Shoal Creek Boulevard. She was now in a residential area, so she had a good excuse to move slowly and see if the Chevy would keep following.

Glancing in her mirror, she saw the purple hatchback reach the stop sign, then proceed further eastward. Then the white truck appeared. Mia was tempted to pull to the curb and wait—force his hand—but she didn't want the driver of the truck to know she'd spotted him.

Then she realized a Jeep had just backed into the street in front of her, and she had to jam her brakes to keep from smashing into it. The driver gave an apologetic wave, then gunned it.

Mia caught her breath. Then looked back and did not see the truck. It had continued east, same as the hatchback. Now she did pull over to the curb, because she was more rattled than she'd realized. She had a .38 Special riding in a holster on her hip, and she found herself placing her right hand on it for reassurance.

Now she remembered that there was no reason to wonder if that had been Damon Tate's truck; she could know for certain. She opened the tracker app on her phone and checked his truck's location.

It was two blocks away on 45th Street.

That son of a bitch.

She remained parked there at the curb and watched the app until Tate's truck was a mile away. Then she proceeded back to MoPac and continued north.

I wish she'd called me right then and told me what had happened, but she chose not to, because I was 600 miles away and she didn't want to worry me.

I can tell you it isn't pleasant to snatch away a worried mother's last shred of hope that her missing son might still be alive. That's what I had to do, and I did it, telling Doris everything Mia and I had learned from our conversation with Lennox Armbruster, including the recorded conversation between Joe Jankowski and Brandi Sloan.

I was concerned that Doris might still refuse to believe that Brent was really dead, but as I spoke, I could see the acceptance settling over her face once and for all.

When I was done, she just began to nod slowly, staring toward the window behind me. Eventually she said, "Thank you for telling me."

"I wish I could have told you sooner," I said. "In this business, you can't always—"

"No," she said. "It's okay. I knew already. I might not have wanted to believe it, but I knew."

"I'm very sorry, Doris."

"Thank you."

There was enough light coming through the window behind me that I noticed her eyes welling up.

Then she asked the obvious question—"Why don't we tell the police?"—and I had to explain why that wouldn't work, because Armbruster would deny everything. When I told her about the threat toward Armbruster's nephew, Doris agreed that we couldn't risk it.

At the moment, she looked small and defeated.

"Can I get you anything?" I asked.

"How about a hug? And then I think the two of us should sit here, drink another bourbon and Coke, and figure out what we're going to do next."

What *we're* going to do next? I almost laughed.

Instead, I did what anyone would do in this situation. I gave her a hug and mixed her a fresh drink. Then we sat and talked some more. The conversation meandered for quite some time.

She told me about Brent when he was a little boy. The way he loved the Teenage Mutant Ninja Turtles and liked to dress as Leonardo at Halloween. He played Little League baseball for a few seasons but didn't really excel at it. He just wasn't a natural athlete. Wasn't much of a student, either, but he was good at making friends. Unfortunately, during middle school, he began to make the wrong kind of friends. He began to smoke and drink and cut class. Stayed out late. It was a textbook case of a troubled teenager. Doris knew that, too, and she tried so hard to get him back on track, but nothing worked.

Brent managed to graduate high school, and within weeks he moved out, only to be arrested within a month for possession of cocaine. Doris and her husband bailed him out. Looking back, she wasn't sure it was the right thing to do. He didn't seem to learn anything from the experience.

It went on from there. Highs and lows. Moments when Brent seemed like he might grow out of it...but didn't. More arrests. Long periods when Doris wouldn't hear from him.

I sat there quietly and let her unload all of it, and I felt honored to be the one who could do that for her.

She finished her drink. I finished mine.

"That woman," Doris said, pointing toward the rear window and Brandi's cabin beyond, "knows who killed him. Agreed?"

"Sure looks that way."

"The question is, how do we find out what she knows?" Doris asked.

"Not just that, but it has to be admissible in court later," I said.

Doris nodded and remained quiet for a moment, thinking. "Think her sister knows what happened?"

"Unless they have an unusually tight bond, I'd say no chance. I'd say Brandi made up a story explaining why she had to run. Same with her parents."

"I can't imagine a young woman carrying around such horrible information and not wanting to unburden herself," Doris said. "I'm assuming we shouldn't just walk over there right now and try to ask her. She wouldn't answer the door, and even if she did, she wouldn't talk. Right?"

"I seriously doubt it, and we'd be tipping our hand. She'd take off again and I bet we'd never find her a second time. I mean *you*. You wouldn't find her a second time."

"Got lucky," Doris said.

"Hell if you did," I said. "You did some great work. Beat me here, didn't you? And I'm a professional. You totally kicked my ass. Now I'm second-guessing my career choice. You've brought shame to my—"

"Okay," she said. "You've made your point. I accept your compliment. But as smart as we both are, I don't know what to do next."

"Well, then, stand back and give me room, because you're about to see how a paid professional does it," I said.

"I can hardly wait," she said.

32

"Sometimes I find it helpful to run back through everything I know," I said. "Sort of summarize the case to make sure I'm not forgetting anything, and to make sure everything fits with what we know."

"That might help me keep everything straight," she said.

I found a sheet of stationary with the Idle Hours logo on it and wrote the high points of the case.

—Brent tried a scam, but it failed.
—Jankowski pressed charges.
—Brent said he had a way out of the problem, but he went missing.
—Lennox Armbruster stole Jankowski's dash cam.
—He overheard Jankowski on phone talking about a body.
—Brandi Sloan was in the SUV. Having affair with Jankowski?
—Lennox began to blackmail Jankowski.
—Jankowski paid at first, until he could ID Lennox.
—He tried to intimidate Lennox at Randall's parking lot, then hit him with car.
—Simultaneously, Damon Tate broke into Lennox's apartment, got dash cam and laptop.
—Lennox has no other copy of the file from the dash cam.
—I got involved, so Jankowski sent Damon Tate after me.
—Lennox pressures Brandi at her house. She tells Jankowski.
—Tate brothers try to shoot Lennox on MoPac. He crashes.
—Brandi goes on the run, maybe fearing for her life.
—Jankowski threatens Lennox in hospital.
—Doris brilliantly finds Brandi in Ruidoso.

"And that brings us to the present moment," I said.

"It all makes sense," Doris said, "but there are still several holes."

"Agreed."

"Like who actually killed Brent? Was it one or both of the Tates, as you surmised earlier? Was it Brandi? Or somebody else we don't even know about?"

"All good questions. And I'm still wondering what Brent meant when he said he had a way out of the problem with Jankowski."

"Did you ask his friends if they knew anything?" Doris asked.

"Yes, several."

"They were cooperative?"

"Yeah, most of them. A couple didn't call me back, but some did. One guy named Raul was really chatty."

"Raul called you back? That surprises me."

"Why?"

"Brent told me they'd had a falling out and hadn't spoken for a long time. I only put him on the list because they had known each other for so long. What's that look on your face?"

"Raul didn't say anything about a falling out to me. In fact, he said he texted Brent the day after he went missing. And Brent had texted him two days earlier."

Doris was frowning now. "Why would Brent lie to me about that? Or did Raul lie to you?"

I thought about it for a moment.

"I'd guess Brent lied, because he was trying to protect Raul."

"From what?"

"Maybe Raul knows something, and Brent didn't want him to get caught up in the mess."

Now she was nodding slowly. "Brent had his problems, but that sounds like something he would do. He was very loyal to his friends. What does Raul know?"

"Maybe he knew about Brent's fraud scheme before he did it and Brent decided he didn't want Raul dragged into it as a witness."

"In that case, it would've been less about loyalty and more about covering his own ass," Doris said.

Which made me regret making the guess. "Might've been both," I said. "Anyway, we really won't know if Raul knows anything until we ask him. If he'll come clean."

"Let me just call him right now," Doris said.

"I'm not so sure that's the way to—"

"Oh, he'll tell me the truth if I put the heat on," she said. "I can promise you that much."

"Okay," I said. "Worth a shot."

She took out her phone and dialed his number, putting it on speakerphone so I could hear. But there was no answer, and it never went to voicemail. She finally hung up after a dozen rings.

"You have to specifically turn voicemail off," I said. "He doesn't even want to let people leave messages. Either that or he no longer uses that number."

She set her phone on the table. "Maybe he'll call back."

"Guess we'll see," I said, although I doubted he would.

"Okay, then back to Brandi," she said. "What are we going to do about her?"

Obviously, I'd been unable to pack an extensive amount of gear into the one small suitcase I'd brought along, so I went to a small outdoors-oriented store and managed to find a cheap trail camera with an infrared flash and a camouflage pattern on the exterior designed to help it blend in. Sixty bucks.

At the cash register, they were selling little tacky *Ski Ruidoso!* key chains, so I grabbed one for Mia, then I grabbed one for Doris. She was waiting back at Idle Hour, keeping an eye on Brandi's cabin through the rear window.

Next I stopped at a liquor store for more bourbon, because I'd noticed Doris's supply had gotten a little low.

I had one more stop. Doris had insisted I pick up some ground meat, tomato, spaghetti, and various spices, so that she could make us a home-cooked dinner. When I facetiously offered to stop at a McDonald's instead, she facetiously threatened to slap me.

When I came out of the grocery store and got back into my rental car, I texted Mia: *Okay if I spend the night with another woman?*

She called immediately and said, "What kind of shenanigans are you getting into over there?"

So I told her everything, shortening it to about five minutes.

She said, "Doris sounds like one sharp lady."

"She absolutely is."

"What happens if Brandi *is* in that cabin but she won't talk?"

"Still working on that," I said. "I have a plan brewing."

"You usually do," she said. "Gonna tell me about it?"

"Not yet. It's a work in progress. How's your case going?"

"Done," she said. "He went to Barton Springs Nursery and loaded about a dozen bags of potting soil into his truck this afternoon. Got it all on camera."

"You are awesome," I said.

"Don't you ever forget it."

She wasn't sounding as distant or preoccupied as she had a day or two earlier.

If Brandi Sloan were like most people, she wouldn't be able to stand being cooped up in a cabin 24 hours a day. She would feel the need to step outside every now and then, and she would almost certainly do that at night. She might sit out on the porch and enjoy a tasty adult beverage, or maybe just stare at the moon and wonder how in the hell she had gotten herself into such a pickle. I was counting on it.

After dinner, which was excellent, I slipped out the front door of Doris's cabin and went around back, through the trees, toward Brandi's cabin. Funny, I had begun to think of it as Brandi's cabin, even though we still had no conclusive evidence that she was in there. But we might have some soon.

It was just after dark and the waning moon had not risen yet.

As I got closer to Brandi's cabin, I stopped behind a pine tree and listened. Let my eyes adjust. The porch light was not turned on, but I could see that there wasn't anybody sitting in the chairs. There were no vehicles in front. All of the windows had blinds lowered, but light was seeping through them. Was Brandi in there?

I chose my steps carefully and moved forward until I reached a tree roughly forty feet from the porch, off to the left side. It was an ideal location, because anyone sitting on the porch would tend to face forward, toward the short drive leading to the cabin. Therefore they would be less likely to spot the camera.

I used the included strap to secure the camera to the tree trunk, choosing a spot where limbs hung low and would provide additional cover. Someone would have to be looking for it specifically to notice it.

A few hours later, Doris and I sat on the porch of her cabin with another bourbon and Coke. The woman liked her bourbon, but she held it well, with no visible effects, and she nursed each drink slowly. There was a slight chill to the air, but it was just right for a light jacket, which I'd brought along.

"I suppose you're right about Raul," she said at ten o'clock.

"About him not calling back?"

"Right."

"Maybe he'll call in the morning," I said.

"You don't believe that," she said.

Her tone indicated she didn't expect an answer.

I yawned. "I should go back to my cabin."

"I have an extra bedroom here," she said.

"Yeah, but my toothbrush and all that," I said. "And I've been known to snore. Just a little. Anyway, it's just across the road."

She nodded.

"You planning to stay here for a few more days?" I asked.

"Now I am," she said. "I want to see how this turns out with the camera."

"How would you like to be in charge?" I asked.

"You need to get back home?" she asked.

"Well, there's no need for both of us to be here," I said.

"You go," she said. "I can sneak over there and check the camera when you think it's time."

"Then I'll take off in the morning," I said.

"If I understand what you do for a living correctly, you aren't being paid for any of this," she said.

I didn't say anything.

She turned to look at me directly. "Am I right? You aren't being paid?"

"I'll get paid for the Lennox Armbruster case," I said.

"But your work is done on that," she said. "Isn't it?"

"Kind of."

"Yet you came out here to find Brandi Sloan, so you can figure out what happened to Brent."

"I'd like to know," I said. "It got personal when Jankowski sent the goons after me. I want to see them all locked up."

"I understand, but is there perhaps just a teeny bit of empathy for an old lady in there somewhere?"

"People in my line of work don't have empathy," I said.

"Yes, you do," she said. "A lot of it. But we'll keep that our little secret."

33

My flight landed in Austin the next day at two o'clock, and I drove straight toward Raul Ablanedo's address, which I'd dug up online. Along the way, I called him, but he didn't answer. No voicemail greeting, same as when Doris had called last night.

Then I texted Mia to check her status. She was waiting for me right where we'd agreed—the Whataburger parking lot just around the corner from Raul's place. He lived in a duplex off Oltorf Street, east of Interstate 35. Not the nicest neighborhood I'd ever seen, but I didn't see any dealers slinging dope from the curb.

I slid the van into a spot next to Mia's Chevy Tahoe. She hopped out, climbed into the van, and greeted me with a kiss that would've incapacitated many lesser men.

"Hey," she whispered.

"Hey," I said. "Nice outfit."

She was wearing a black leather skirt that landed at mid-thigh and an aqua V-neck T-shirt just snug enough to be a distraction. Her hair and makeup were at "date night" levels. She was wearing flats because heels would've rendered Raul speechless. We didn't want speechless.

"Think it'll get the job done?" she asked.

"It's working on me and I don't even know anything."

"Then let's go close this case and move on to better things, okay?"

I think she was speaking more broadly than just our work.

"Sounds good to me," I said.

I backed up and pulled onto Oltorf, heading east. We were three blocks from Raul's place, and now I was worrying he might not be home. That would suck. I'd had all I could stand of this case and everyone involved. Well, not Doris. She was the one bright spot.

I turned left onto Burton Drive, heading north, and that's when our plan got derailed. There would be no speaking to Raul anytime soon.

"There's a black GMC truck behind us," I said. "Damn it."

Mia glanced in the passenger-side mirror. "Nathaniel Tate is still in the hospital, right?"

"Yeah, but it could be Damon."

I skipped the turn that would've taken us to Raul's duplex.

"Now is probably a good time for me to tell you that Damon followed me yesterday in his white Chevy."

I looked at her, then back at the road. "What happened?"

"Nothing. He followed, but I took some turns and he stopped following."

"Because he knew you spotted him?"

"I can't be sure," she said. "But that would explain why he switched vehicles, if that's him back there."

"Jesus, Mia, why didn't you tell me yesterday?" I asked.

"Because you would've dropped everything and come home," she said. "Which means you wouldn't have seen Doris, so you wouldn't have found Brandi Sloan, and you wouldn't have learned that Raul was lying to one of you."

"But other than that," I said.

I turned left on Woodland Avenue, heading west. Most people going this way on Woodland would be headed for Interstate 35, about half a mile ahead. The truck turned, too.

"What's he doing?" Mia asked.

"Still back there," I said. "But he won't get close enough for me to read the plate."

I took a quick right on Royal Crest Drive. So did the truck. This would lead to Riverside Drive, maybe half a mile ahead. There was still a small chance the person in the truck wasn't following us, but was simply taking a shortcut.

"Oh, turn here," Mia said, pointing to our right before we reached Riverside. "This parking lot cuts through."

I did as she said, entering the south perimeter of an office complex, which would give us a straight shot back to Burton Drive. To our right was a tall concrete wall covered with some elaborate graffiti. To my left was a collection of unassuming one-story buildings painted beige. First office I saw was a cosmetology school. There were a lot of parking spaces on both sides, but very few vehicles.

I was moving slowly and watching my rearview mirror.

"If he turns here, it's him. It *has* to be him," I said.

Mia swiveled in her seat to look backward.

Now I was just coasting. Waiting. Hoping the truck would drive past the entrance. I wasn't in the mood for this right now. I passed a CrossFit studio that appeared to be closed, then a print shop.

"Here he comes," Mia said.

I glanced in the rearview again and sure enough, the black truck was still following.

"Any ideas?" I said. "Keep driving or finally deal with this head on?"

She knew as well as I did that the person in the truck—whether it was Damon Tate or someone else—had done nothing illegal at this point.

"Stop for a minute," Mia said. "Let's see what he does."

I noticed that she had grabbed her purse off the floorboard and was holding it in her lap now. I stopped the van exactly where we were.

I said, "If he starts to go around us…"

"Can't let him do that," she said. "We'd be sitting ducks."

"Doesn't matter, because he's stopping," I said.

He was eighty or ninety feet behind us. There wasn't another person to be seen coming or going from any of the offices.

"Got a good camera in here?" Mia asked.

A super-zoom camera or a decent pair of binoculars would give us a good look at the driver.

"Nope," I said. "Didn't want to leave anything good in here while the van was parked at the airport."

Unfortunately, that included the front and rear dash cams. The van has an expensive security system, but that can't stop a quick smash-and-grab burglary.

We waited a few seconds, both of us looking in the mirrors. Now he knew without question that we knew he was back there. Fine by me.

"He's just trying to intimidate us," Mia said.

"He needs to try harder," I said. "Should I back up?"

"I don't think so. He could claim later that it was an aggressive move."

We waited a few more seconds.

"Then I say we keep driving and see if we can confirm that it's Damon Tate."

"Works for me."

I began to ease forward slowly—not realizing I was about to make perhaps the biggest mistake I'd made in this profession. Stupid. Wasn't evaluating all possible risks.

The truck began moving again, too, just as slowly.

All of the doors on our left were unmarked—rear entry doors to offices that fronted on the other side of the building. No vehicles down at this end at all. We rounded the corner, went twenty yards, then turned right, which placed us at the exit onto Burton Drive.

The truck rounded the corner, too, and Mia said, "It's him. It's Damon Tate. I can see him now."

I looked to my left and saw an eighteen-wheeler coming this way, driving too fast for this particular street.

"Roy!" Mia said.

That's when I felt the impact of the truck's front bumper on the rear of the van.

I couldn't move forward. Couldn't move backward. I had only one choice—push the brake down as hard as I could.

Everything that followed took place in less than four seconds...

Tate obviously floored the gas in his truck, because I could hear his tires squealing as they spun and the van began to inch forward.

"Get out!" I said to Mia.

The front of the van was about to enter the street. The driver of the eighteen-wheeler laid on his horn.

Mia opened her door and hopped out.

Now I had one more option. Do the same. Open my door, bail out, and let the van get crushed.

Just as I reached for the door handle, I heard gunshots—four or five, or maybe more. Rapid fire. Loud.

The squealing of Tate's tires came to an abrupt halt. The speed of his roaring engine dropped.

I pulled the parking brake and killed the engine. Then I looked through the open passenger door at Mia. She was just lowering her .38 Special from the firing position. She appeared stunned, but not panicked. Not freaking out.

"Mia," I said. "I'm getting out. You hear me?"

She nodded.

I exited the van, breathing heavily, and began moving toward the black truck. The smell of burning rubber was overwhelming.

The bullet holes—five of them—were grouped in a tight cluster in the windshield. I saw no movement from Tate. His head was tipped backward. When I reached the driver's-side window, I saw that one of the rounds had caught him in the hollow spot below his Adam's apple. At least two more had entered his chest. It was remarkable shooting under pressure.

I started to reach in to turn his engine off, but I thought better of it. Don't touch anything.

I circled the rear of the truck and came toward Mia. The gun was dangling from her right hand. When I reached her, I gently took the revolver from her hand and placed it inside the van's glove compartment for now.

"Jesus, Roy," she said.

"It's okay."

Not a soul had exited any of the shops or come from anywhere else to see what had happened. The big rig had continued south on Burton. Either he hadn't heard the gunshots or he'd decided he didn't want to get involved. Maybe he was calling the police right now.

"Is he dead?" Mia asked.

"Yeah."

I wrapped my arms around her. She didn't move, except for a slight tremble. I was doing my best to remain calm, for her sake, but I could feel my heart hammering.

"Oh, my God," she said. "That was crazy."

"You did the right thing. He gave you no choice. I need to call 911 now. You understand?

She nodded.

"We tell them exactly what happened," I said. "Leave nothing out. He tried to kill both of us. We just tell the truth."

She nodded again. We were still alone. Cars passed and some of the people looked at us, but they didn't seem to understand what had just taken place.

"Roy, I killed him," Mia said. Her eyes were wide and unfocused.

"It's not your fault," I said. "And you saved my life. Here, sit down."

I helped her back into the van. Then I dialed 911.

Many violent crimes are solved quickly and easily simply because the perpetrator acts out of anger or impulse. That's what had happened here. Damon Tate had seen an opportunity and he hadn't been able to resist it. Same as when Jankowski had hit Lennox with his SUV. Stupid. It had cost Damon Tate his life. On the plus side for us, the physical evidence would be overwhelming, and it was well documented that Damon Tate had a reason for seeking revenge against me.

But, of course, we were both taken to APD headquarters and asked to provide a statement, which we did, separately. The woman interviewing me was an investigator named Delma Watson. I'd never met her, but she was friendly enough. Not pushy or officious.

It took me a while to explain all of the backstory leading up to the shooting, and she left the room a couple of times to check on things, but I was done within two hours—mostly because I told her at that point that I had nothing more to add and that I was not interested in repeating my story again. It's not that cops necessarily think you're lying, but they want you to tell your story several times so they can look for inconsistencies. My story was consistent, because it was the truth. Also, it was probably plain to Delma Watson that the Tate brothers were bad guys who brought trouble onto themselves.

When I stepped into the lobby and checked my phone, I saw that Doris Donovan had sent me a text: *I see a housekeeper at the cabin behind me. Should I check the camera?*

Honest to God, my first thought was, *What camera? What is she talking about?* That's how distracted I was by the current situation. Okay, the trail camera aimed at Brandi Sloan's cabin. If Brandi was staying in there, Ingrid would've requested a hold on maid service. If the housekeeper was in there, it was logical to conclude that Ingrid had picked Brandi up last night or this morning.

Yes, please, I replied. *But maybe wait until the housekeeper is gone. And let me know if you get anything good.*

She sent me a thumbs-up.

I'd left her with a card reader that could be plugged directly into her phone. Handy gizmo. Just take the SD card from the camera and insert it into the reader, and there you go—the photos can be viewed on your phone, then emailed or texted.

I was just about to text Mia when she appeared in the lobby and headed toward me. When she got close, I raised my eyebrows, saying, *Well?*

"It went fine. Let's go home, okay? I just want to go home."

We had to grab an Uber, because the van was in police custody for the time being.

At home, Mia wanted a drink, so I made her one, and a little later I grilled some chicken, but she only ate a few bites. Then she went to bed, and frankly, I had no idea if that was the best thing for her or not.

I sat down on the couch and pulled my phone out. I had turned it off earlier in order to give Mia my full attention.

First thing I saw was a text from Doris Donovan. No message, just two photos.

The first one showed Brandi Sloan standing on the porch of the little cabin she'd inhabited for a day. The photo had been taken this morning, not long after sunrise. It was a profile shot as she looked toward the little drive leading up to the cabin. The photo was crisp and clear. No mistaking who it was. She was waiting for someone. Easy to guess who.

Turned out a guess wasn't necessary, because there was Ingrid Sloan in the second photo, standing beside Brandi on the porch. Probably saying, "You sure you got everything?" before they loaded her suitcase into the car and took off.

I sent Doris a text: *That's what you call a slam dunk.*

A minute later, she said, *What now? Should I stay here?*

I told her I would think about next steps and call her in the morning, and she should come on home whenever she was ready.

Then I made another drink, this one for myself.

34

I know a lot of people—mostly men—who talk in cavalier terms about the circumstances in which they would kill someone. In some cases, they've even played the scene out in their heads. A burglar breaking in at night. A meth head robbing a convenience store. Mugger, carjacker, some scumbag running from the cops. *Oh, I'd totally blow that guy away. Wouldn't bother me in the least.*

But, yeah, it would, even if the person you killed was evil to the core. I've seen it firsthand in some cops I know, and now I was seeing it in Mia.

She slept late the next morning. Until ten o'clock. When she finally came out of the bedroom, she had bags under her eyes, but she gave me a weak smile. I offered to make her breakfast, but she wasn't interested.

I gave her a hug and she hugged back. Hard. Like she couldn't bear to let go.

"I'll be okay," she whispered into my ear.

I hadn't said anything, but she'd seen it in my face. We took a seat on the couch.

She said, "It's just that...I don't know what to *do*. What am I supposed to do?"

"Want my opinion?"

"Yes."

"I don't want this to sound callous, but you don't have to do anything. What I mean is, you don't have to feel a certain way about what happened. Whatever you feel is okay. You might think you're supposed to feel guilty or remorseful, but if you don't, there's nothing wrong with that. If you feel relief or anger or anything else, whose business is that but yours?"

"Do you feel guilty about shooting Nathaniel Tate?"

"Honestly, not really. Maybe I'd feel different if he'd died, but I don't know. The important thing is, you did nothing wrong, and he did everything wrong. I wouldn't be sitting here right now if you hadn't done what you did. I know how *I* feel about that, which is grateful. So thank you."

She grabbed my hand and held it.

"I don't want to do anything today," she said. "Just not think about anything or talk to anyone. Not go anywhere."

"I can understand that," I said.

"You do whatever you need to do," she said.

"Are you sure?"

"Yeah."

"I still need to track down Raul Ablanedo," I said.

"Just be careful, okay?" she said.

I nodded, but I wasn't worried now. Damon Tate was dead. Nathaniel Tate was still in the hospital. That left Joe Jankowski, and I doubted he had the guts to come after me himself.

"I've got some good news," I said.

"What is it?"

I showed her the photos Doris had sent earlier. Mia had never met Brandi Sloan, but she'd seen other photos, and she said, "No question about that, is there?"

"Nope."

"This Doris lady is going to steal my job," Mia said.

"Or mine. She'll own this outfit before long. You need to meet her when she gets back."

"Sounds good. What're you going to do with the photos?"

"Nothing right now," I said. "Not until I hear what Raul has to say."

I waited until Mia ate a small lunch, then I kissed her on the forehead and left to complete the mission we'd had to abort the day before.

I was driving my back-up vehicle, the Camry. Took Fifteenth Street over to Interstate 35, then down to Oltorf. Hung a left on Burton, same as yesterday.

Took two more turns, and then I was in front of Raul's duplex. There was one vehicle parked in front—a dirty Honda Civic. I'd checked my online resources and knew Raul owned a Civic. The plate matched.

I wasted no time. Walked to the front door and knocked. A man answered a brief moment later. Mid-thirties. Slender. Shaggy black hair and a goatee. A friendly, open face.

"Raul?" I said.

"Yeah?"

"I'm Roy Ballard," I said. "I talked to you the other—"

"Right. About Brent."

I was about to ask if I could come inside, but I was too impatient.

I said, "Last week, a man named Nathaniel Tate came to my house and tried to execute me. He is still in the hospital, because I shot him. You might recognize that name because his brother, Damon, works for Joe Jankowski. Excuse me, he *worked* for Jankowski. Damon Tate is now dead."

"Whoa," Raul said.

"He threatened my partner and me yesterday, so my partner killed him. She had no choice. Have to admit we're both relieved."

"I saw about a man getting killed on the news, but they didn't say who it was," he said.

"By the way, two days ago, I sat down with Doris Donovan and had a lengthy conversation. We came to the conclusion that you lied to one of us about Brent."

His expression clouded immediately.

He started to speak, but I said, "You told me you text back and forth regularly. You said he texted you the day before he went missing and you texted him the day after. But Brent told Doris the two of you had had a falling out and hadn't spoken in a long time. Why the different stories?"

He'd gone pale. "Doris is getting pretty old, so maybe she—"

"She's sharper than you and me put together," I said. "Don't try to play it that way. Here's what's going to happen. When I tell the cops about the discrepancy, they'll dig into your life in ways you wouldn't expect. They'll find the truth. The best thing you can do right now is decide to stop lying and limit the damage to your future. I know some cops pretty well, so I'll help you if I can."

He looked down at the porch and said, "Well, fuck."

"Do it for Doris," I said. "She deserves to know what really happened. She said you were a good person and would do what's right."

That was known as a fib. Whatever works in this kind of situation. And it did work. Nothing beats hearing a big, soul-cleansing confession that puts all the missing pieces of a case in place. Raul delivered in a big way.

"I helped Brent with the scam," he said. "In fact, it was kind of my idea."

"Tell me how that came about," I said.

"We'd sit around and drink beer and he'd bitch about his job. Most of his bosses were jerks, and they were pretty sloppy about all the safety requirements at the job sites."

"Such as what?"

"Like crummy eye and ear protection, or junky ladders and scaffolds. All kinds of shit. It was just dangerous working around there, you know? Brent said it was just a matter of time until someone got hurt bad, but the good news was, they'd probably score a sweet payday from it. And then an idea kind of grew from there."

"Grew how?" I asked. "You suggested it?"

"Kind of," he said. "I think I said, 'Why couldn't it be you?' I was kind of joking, but he asked what I meant, and I said he could probably figure out a way to get hurt—or probably fake it—and make them pay for treating their employees like disposable equipment."

People who committed fraud always had a way to rationalize it.

"And he went for it?" I asked.

"Eventually, yeah. Hey, it's not like I talked him into it. I just mentioned it and he ended up liking the idea. He went and did a bunch of research on the Internet and stuff."

"Okay, so he tried his little stunt with the concrete truck, but he ended up getting hurt worse than he intended. Then Jankowski pressed charges and all that. Doris told me Brent had a way out of all his troubles. What was the way?"

I had an idea what it was, but I wanted Raul to say it and admit his participation.

Raul shifted from one foot to the other, plainly agitated.

"Well, it was those same violations, man. All that safety shit. Brent told Jankowski that if he didn't drop the charges and pay up for his injury, Brent was gonna blow the whistle. He'd been taking pictures and videos for a couple of months on the job site, so all he had to do was send 'em to the state agencies that regulate all that stuff. Jankowski would've been looking at some serious fines."

"How did Brent tell him? In person?"

"On the phone."

"When was this?"

"Couple of days before he went missing."

"Did he say how Jankowski reacted?"

"Yeah, he said he was fucking screaming at him, but then he called back and said they could work something out."

Brent had gotten in over his head and didn't know it. Jankowski had never had any plans to "work it out."

"So what happened?"

"Nothing for a few days. Then we're sitting around on a Saturday and there's a knock on the door."

Here it comes, I thought. Damon Tate, most likely, possibly with his brother Nathaniel.

"Brent looks out the window and says, 'What the hell?' I ask what's up, and he says it's some chick from work named Brandi."

No matter how many cases I work, I still get thrown a curveball now and then.

"What did she want?" I asked.

"She said Jankowski wanted to work a deal out right now, and she'd take Brent over there to see him. She sounded real nice and apologetic, like it was her job to smooth this sort of thing over whenever Jankowski screwed things up. She said his temper made him say and do some stupid things, but she was on Brent's side, because she'd been to some of the job sites and he was right—some of them weren't safe. She was going to work on fixing that."

"And he believed her?" I asked, finding it hard to keep the incredulity out of my voice. It should've been obvious to Brent—and Raul—why she was there.

"Yeah, and to be honest, I did, too. She was pretty slick. She said Jankowski had cooled down and was ready to talk."

"Where were you during this conversation?"

"I was in the kitchen, but she couldn't see me. She never knew I was there."

"So how did Brent respond to the offer?"

"He told her he'd be right down. She went back to her car, and then he asked me what I thought about it, and every fucking day I wish I'd said he shouldn't go. But I didn't, and he left—and that was the last time I ever saw him."

Raul was tearing up, and his remorse was plainly genuine.

"I appreciate you telling me the truth," I said.

"Yeah," he said. "It feels good, to be honest. I've been carrying the guilt around. I don't know if I can ever make up for being so stupid. How would I do that? It's too late, isn't it?"

I had to hold my tongue. If Raul hadn't prodded Brent along in his stupid plan, followed by a second stupid plan, Brent might still be alive. But now was not the time for me to tear into Raul for failing to reveal this information when Brent went missing. I didn't want to rattle him, because there was another important step to take.

"No, it's not too late," I said. "You can still tell it to the cops."

35

I didn't mention that it might be smart for him to consult an attorney, but he did, and the result was that two days passed before Raul Ablanedo sat down with the investigators in the Brent Donovan case and told them what he knew—in a limited version. He left out his involvement in the scam and the subsequent blackmail. He only told them about being at Brent's apartment when Brandi Sloan came to get him.

I wasn't in the interview room, so I have no idea if the investigators were skeptical or not, but they immediately got a warrant for Raul's cell records and phone-location data, and when they received the data from his cell provider two days later, it confirmed that Raul was near Brent's apartment when he said he was.

I waited until then to call one of the investigators—a young guy I'd never met—and tell him I knew where Brandi Sloan was hiding out. I emailed him the photos while we were talking and he said, "These are dated five days ago."

"Better late than never," I said.

"You've been withholding information," he said.

"She had no warrants and wasn't suspected in a crime," I said.

"You should have told us anyway," he said. "She was a missing person."

"And I found her for you. You're welcome. Anything else?"

He waited a little too long to reply, so I hung up. Kids these days.

On a happier note, Mia seemed to be coping with her emotions better every day. She told me she wanted to talk to a therapist and I said I was all for it. I'd go with her, if she wanted.

We still hadn't had any further discussion about us. I was going to let her broach that topic again when she was ready.

That afternoon, while Mia was working out, I took an Uber to retrieve the van from a police impound lot. Then I stopped by to see Doris Donovan, who was back home in Westwood. After we'd settled in around the coffee table in her living room—with a plate of cookies, of course—she said, "Do you think we'll ever know the complete truth? I mean, I know Jankowski and the Tate brothers and Brandi Sloan were probably all involved, but will we ever know exactly what happened?"

"I wish I could say the answer is yes, but I just don't know. It might be that only one of them actually knows the specific details."

"About how Brent was killed?" she asked.

"Right."

"But Brandi Sloan lured Brent to his death," she said. "I assume we agree on that."

"She did," I said. "But she might not have known what Jankowski was planning to do. Maybe he told her he really was going to arrange a deal with Brent."

"I don't believe that," she said.

"I don't blame you. If she knew Jankowski's real intentions, there's almost zero chance she'll admit it, and it will be hard to prove otherwise. The problem is, when you have three or four people involved, each of them will tell the story in a way that minimizes their own involvement as much as possible. Brandi will blame Jankowski, and he'll blame the Tates, or just Damon, since he's dead. At that point, you just have to hope the cops can figure it out from the evidence."

She nodded and remained quiet for a long moment. "I need some tea," she said. "Would you like some?"

"No, thank you."

"Be right back," she said, rising to go into the kitchen.

I sat quietly and gazed out her picture windows at the amazing view of the Austin skyline. So much new construction in the past decade. I couldn't tell you what most of the new high-rises were. I found it all depressing. Sometimes change sweeps through our lives and there's not a damn thing we can do to stop it.

"You're off today," Doris said, back in the room.

"Pardon?"

She took her seat again and placed a tumbler filled with iced tea on the table. "You're not quite yourself. Something's bothering you."

It was weird—I started to dismiss it. Fake a smile, crack a joke, and move on. But I couldn't. In fact, I started to speak, but my throat caught. I was getting emotional. Doris waited as I gathered myself, and then I told her what had caused the recent distance between Mia and me. Funny thing is, I didn't feel awkward or embarrassed at all. Doris was the kind of woman who wanted to help you however she could. She simply listened.

Then she said, "I haven't known you long, Roy, but I suspect you and Mia will work it out, and later you'll wonder why you worried about this at all. You're a creative guy. Look at what you did with that trail camera. You're a problem solver. You'll come up with something."

"I hope so."

"And I would bet Mia is *not* thinking about leaving you. She just needs more time to accept what you told her. This is something you've been carrying around for quite a while, but she's only just learned about it, and now she's also dealing with the aftermath from killing Damon Tate. I can't even imagine what she's going through right now."

"She's thinking of seeing a therapist," I said.

"About the shooting?"

"Yes."

"I think that's a good idea. You know what else might make her feel better?"

"Cookies?" I said.

She laughed and pointed at me. "Exactly. Cookies. I'm going to bag some up for you to take home to her."

When I went out to the van, I checked my phone and saw that I had a voicemail from Randy Wolfe, the investigator who'd interviewed me after I'd shot Nathaniel Tate.

He was informing me that Nathaniel Tate had been released from the hospital and was free on bond for the charges against him for attempting to shoot me. Great. Wolfe also mentioned that the concerns about Nathaniel suffering paralysis had turned out to be unfounded. In fact, at this point, he was moving around fairly well. The subtext was obvious. *Watch your back, because you might have to deal with him again.*

Damn nice of him to give me that heads-up. I immediately texted Mia and let her know what was happening. This wasn't going to help her stress levels any, so I went straight home.

I found her relaxing in a hot bath, with a layer of bubbles hiding some of her best parts. Mostly. She had a single votive candle burning in a corner where the backsplash meets the wall. Classical music played softly from a Bluetooth speaker resting on the vanity.

"Hey," I said quietly.

"Hey."

"You're having some peace and quiet. Want me to come back later?"

"No, that's okay. How's Doris?"

"She's doing fine," I said. "She sent you some cookies."

"She did?"

"Yeah."

"Then where are they?"

"In the kitchen."

"They're not doing me much good in there," she said.

So I retrieved the plastic bag and brought it to her. Then I slid the Bluetooth speaker aside and took a seat on the vanity, between our twin sinks.

"Sweet Jesus, these are good," Mia said.

Watching a drop-dead gorgeous woman eat chocolate chip cookies in a bubble bath should be on everyone's bucket list.

"Want a glass of milk?" I asked.

"Absolutely yes."

So I got her a small glass of whole milk and rested it on the edge of the tub.

"Thank you."

"You bet. Anything else?"

"Yes. No snide comments if I eat half this bag."

"I would never."

"Want one?"

"I already ate about five."

I took my seat again.

Mia finished a cookie and said, "So…Nathaniel Tate is loose."

"Yeah. We knew this was a possibility."

"Think he'll do anything?"

"I really don't," I said. "But that doesn't make it any easier to relax, knowing he's out there."

"One of many," she said, referring to the scores of disgruntled individuals who held a grudge against us.

Yeah, I thought, *but we haven't shot any of those people, or killed one of their brothers.*

"I sent the photos of Brandi Sloan to APD," I said. "Some young whippersnapper on the case tried to lay some guilt on me for holding on to them until now. He sounded about twelve."

"So probably twenty-six, twenty-seven."

"Maybe," I said. "I should inform you that some of your bubbles are popping, and I can see some things I couldn't see earlier."

"Yeah? I guess you'll just have to look away."

"I'm not sure I can do that."

"Let's see how much self control you have," she said. "By the way, since we're talking about stuff, I found a therapist."

Mia hadn't mentioned this topic in several days, but I knew she still hadn't been sleeping well since the shooting, and I'd noticed she'd been avoiding violent shows on TV.

"That's great," I said. "Who is it?"

"My friend Dana sees her. Says she's great, and that's good enough for me. Her first appointment was in three weeks, so she's obviously in demand. Maybe I'll change my mind by then."

"I'll support your decision no matter what it is," I said.

"Thank you."

Half a minute passed. Some more bubbles popped.

"What time is it?" Mia asked.

"About two-thirty," I said. "Why?"

"The milk was fine," she said, holding the half-filled glass toward me, "but can I trade this in for a glass of white wine?"

"You bet."

"And when you come back, I'm thinking you should climb in here with me. I need someone to wash my back. Might as well be you."

For the first time in ten days, I was beginning to think everything was going to be okay.

36

The wheels of justice turn slowly, especially when a witness or person of interest in a case refuses to speak to the cops. That's what Brandi Sloan did.

The day after I shared those photos of Brandi with the whippersnapper, someone from APD made a call to the Ruidoso Police Department and asked for a favor. A few hours later, one of their investigators, a man named Peacock, drove out to Ingrid Sloan's house and knocked on the door. Ingrid answered and Peacock immediately showed her the photos. Why play around? Then he asked to speak to Brandi.

She came to the door but refused to answer any questions. Not much the cop could do. It was Brandi's right to keep her mouth shut. Damn Constitution.

That same afternoon, I drove over to JMJ Construction and found yet another young, attractive woman acting as the receptionist, this one a platinum blonde with severe black eyebrows. I gave her a big smile—which she did not return—and asked to speak to Joe Jankowksi.

"May I tell him who's here?"

"Roy Ballard."

"Do you have an appointment?"

"I'm afraid I don't, but I'm hoping he'll see me. I have something urgent to discuss."

"Please have a seat and I'll let him know you're here as soon as he gets off the phone."

She had an air about her that suggested she was doing extremely important work and I was lucky to have a few minutes of her attention.

"Always talking to someone, isn't he?" I said with a phony chuckle. "Quite the wheeler-dealer and go-getter."

"There's coffee over there if you'd like some," she said, pointing toward the waiting area behind me.

"Is it still over there if I don't want any?" I said.

"What?"

"I'll try some," I said. "Thanks."

Twelve minutes later, she led me back to Jankowski's office and closed the door as she left. He was standing behind his desk, backlit by the big window behind him.

"You got some *cojones* coming over here again," he said.

So we were abandoning any pretense about the situation. He knew that I'd shot one Tate brother and Mia had killed the other, and he certainly assumed that I knew he was behind those attacks and the murder of Brent Donovan.

I said, "Two, actually. I don't know if that counts as *some*. Do you have more than two? Because maybe you should see a doctor."

"What do you want?" he said. "Make it quick."

I didn't know if Jankowski was smart enough to be recording this conversation, but he'd had time to think of it, and his phone was lying on top of his desk. For that matter, he could be recording it with his computer. Easy enough to do.

"Nathaniel Tate got out of the hospital yesterday," I said.

"So what?"

"He tried to shoot me through my bedroom window a couple of weeks ago."

"I heard about that," he said, grinning.

"Apparently you think that's amusing," I said.

"A little bit," he said.

"I guess I need to tighten the choke on my twelve gauge," I said. "Anyway, now that his brother is dead, which is probably a bummer for ol' Nate, it makes me wonder if he might try something else."

"Why talk to me about it?"

"Do you remember what you said to Lennox Armbruster in his hospital room?"

"The fuck're you talking about? I never saw him in the hospital."

Which is what I expected him to say.

"You can deny it, but that thing you said to him—what you told him might happen to his nephew—that's what will happen to you if Nathaniel Tate doesn't stay out of our lives."

He tried to laugh. "Oh, really? So you're making a threat?"

"How can I be making a threat if you never said anything to Armbruster?"

"You're a punk," he said, "with a smart mouth."

"Yeah, probably. But you're the kind of scum that threatens kids."

"Get out of my office."

"You had Brent Donovan killed."

"Prove it."

"And everybody knows who you sent to pick him up at his apartment."

"I didn't send nobody to do nothing. Get the fuck out."

I could tell he was rattled. Now I wanted to push it further.

"Hang on a sec. Has she not even told you the police found her?"

"I don't know who you're talking about," he said.

"Think she'll spill the beans? I think she will, because there's something you don't know. There's a witness."

He snorted. "A witness to what?"

"To this particular young lady picking up Brent. So she'll talk, and the witness will back up her story, and that means you're totally screwed."

His face was getting bright red.

If my guess was right, he had a way to contact Brandi in Ruidoso, and he'd be doing that as soon as I was gone. She'd probably paid cash for a burner phone before she'd left Austin. He would call that number in a panic, wondering if what I'd said was true.

"You've got one minute before I call someone in here to throw you out," he said.

"One minute? Okay, cool. I'll take it. This chair is comfortable. An extra minute is like heaven."

He glared at me.

I said, "The alternative is for you to come around your desk and physically remove me yourself. Feel free to give that a try."

He didn't move. I stared at him, but he wouldn't hold eye contact.

I was feeling charitable, so I left after half a minute. My work there was done.

Before I got home, I pulled over and dialed the number I had for Brandi Sloan. Even if she hadn't taken her primary cell phone with her, she was probably using her burner phone to check the voicemail on that line now and then. Voicemail is what I got.

After the tone, I said, "Hey, Brandi, it's me, Roy Ballard, the videographer with the dreamy eyes. I have to admit I'm concerned about you. If Joe finds out where you are and thinks you might work a deal with the cops, well, that probably would not be good. In that situation, your best option would be to do just that—ask the DA for a deal, and then tell them everything you know, before they build a stronger case against you and the deal is off the table. I'm not saying Joe is going to find out, but these things have a way of getting out. So take care of yourself, you hear? Give my best to your sister."

Roy Ballard, puppet master.

It worked.

Three days later, I learned that Brandi Sloan had lawyered up and told her story in exchange for a deal. Nothing she said came as much of a surprise…

She had been sleeping with her boss, Joe Jankowski, for seven months, and in that time, he showered her with gifts and kind gestures. Paid many of her bills, including a new HVAC system and roof for her house. When he went to buy himself a new vehicle, instead of trading in his old Land Rover SUV, he "sold" it to her for $25,000, but no money actually changed hands. Yes, he was sort of rough around the edges, but she grew to love him. He was a different person when he was with her. Gentle. Sweet. He promised he was going to leave his wife, and then suddenly Brandi would be partners with a wealthy, high-profile businessman. It was hard to resist.

Then the problem with Brent Donovan came up—the fake job-site accident, followed by the threat to blow the whistle about safety violations. Jankowski paid Donovan some money to shut up and go away, but he didn't go away.

According to Brandi Sloan, that made Jankowski furious. Brandi said she had no idea if the job-site violations actually existed, but Jankowski downplayed them. Said they were minor—no big deal—and at most his company would get a warning. "Then why not just ignore the guy?" Brandi asked. Jankowski never had a good answer for that.

They didn't discuss it much after that, until one day Jankowski said he was going to try to strike a deal with Brent Donovan. Give him one more payment and say that would have to be the end of it. Cheaper than trying to fight off a bunch of worthless claims in court. And he asked Brandi to do him a favor. Would she mind going over to pick Brent up and bring him over to talk? The investigators asked her if she thought that was a strange request, and she said not at all. Joe told her she would be better at putting Brent at ease, so that he would be more open to a deal. She felt honored that Joe would trust her to do that.

So she did go get Brent, but after that meeting, he disappeared. At first, Joe denied knowing what had happened, but then he finally told Brandi his version of events.

Jankowski said he'd asked Damon Tate to come over to loom in the background—to intimidate Brent Donovan if he didn't go along. Unfortunately, that didn't work. Donovan got loud and mouthy. Started making all kinds of ridiculous demands. Then he got in Damon Tate's face, it escalated, and Donovan threw a punch. Tate punched back hard, and it proved fatal when Donovan fell backward and hit his head on the edge of the fireplace hearth. Joe said it was purely self-defense, but who would believe him and Damon Tate? There was only one way out. They agreed that Damon Tate would dispose of the body.

Tate happened to know the perfect place—a wooded area behind one of their job sites. Tate had explored the property a couple of times a year earlier when he'd seen a big ten-point buck on the other side of the fence. When he was looking around, he found a cave. Not a big one—the entrance wasn't much bigger than an armadillo hole—but when he went back with a flashlight, he could see that it was plenty deep. Maybe thirty feet. Couldn't tell how far it went horizontally, but he couldn't see the walls in any direction. Lots of cool air rushing out.

Caves weren't unusual in central Texas, but he was surprised nobody had ever boarded this one over for safety. He later found out that this property was a conservancy consisting of a thousand acres, and it was doubtful anyone even knew the cave was there.

Jankowski said fine. He didn't want to know where the body went, as long as it would never be found. Seal the hole up permanently. And that's exactly what happened, as far as Brandi knew.

There was only one problem with this account—a problem for Jankowski and Damon Tate, not for Brandi. According to location data for Damon Tate's cell phone, he went straight home after leaving Jankowski's house, thirty-seven minutes after Brandi had dropped Brent off. Damon Tate had never gone anywhere near a wooded former job site in the days that followed. So who had gotten rid of the body?

The cops decided to get location data for Nathaniel Tate's cell phone, too. That's when the picture filled in. Turned out Nathaniel had also driven to Jankowski's neighborhood before Brent Donovan arrived, and he'd left one minute before Damon did.

He drove south, to Manchaca, a small community about ten miles from downtown Austin. He parked behind a strip center that had been built by JMJ Construction. By then, it was nearly seven in the evening. All of the little shops and businesses in the strip center were closed. Nathaniel Tate's vehicle didn't move for one hour and twelve minutes. Then he went to his brother's place and stayed until three in the morning.

It was obvious what had happened, but it was still unclear who had done the killing. Legally, they were all culpable, and all of them could be charged with murder.

But first things first.

Three days after Brandi gave a statement, and one day after the cops had received the location data for the Tates' phones, they searched the property in question behind the strip center.

They quickly located a cave entrance that had been covered with a half-sheet of plywood, which had been piled with several large rocks and pieces of loose brush. Inside, forty feet down, they discovered human remains, and dental records later confirmed that Brent Donovan had finally been found.

Joe Jankowski and Nathaniel Tate were arrested the next morning. Both were out on bond by that evening. The process goes quickly and smoothly when you have money to spend on the best lawyers. I was assuming Jankowski covered the bond for Nathaniel Tate, if for no other reason than to keep him from talking to the cops.

I felt good about the progress in the case, but I had some worries, because I knew what the defense attorneys would say to a jury...

Brent Donovan's unfortunate death happened exactly the way Joe Jankowski described it—Donovan threw a punch at Damon Tate, who defended himself. Unfortunately, all three men made the bad decision to cover up the incident, and Nathaniel Tate volunteered to dispose of the body out of misplaced loyalty to his brother. That meant Joe Jankowski and Nathaniel Tate were guilty of crimes, indeed, but nothing nearly as serious as murder.

I could only hope the cops would keep digging until they had more. Or maybe they'd already found new evidence and were slowly building a rock-solid case.

I went to see Doris Donovan again that afternoon. I took some flowers and expressed my sympathy on the loss of her son. We had another long conversation with another glass of bourbon.

At one point, she said, "Honestly, I guess I shouldn't be surprised about this, but I'm feeling a certain amount of relief that I have an answer now. I know he isn't alive and he hasn't been for quite some time. All I can hope for now is that he died quickly and painlessly."

Maybe the autopsy would deliver that solace, or maybe it wouldn't. Or it might provide no answers at all. A body in a cave for that length of time would be in such a state that a lot of evidence could be lost.

I was glad to see that Doris wasn't dwelling on which of the three men actually committed the murder. My money was on one of the Tate brothers. That's why Jankowski had them around, right? To do his dirty work? And since Nathaniel disposed of the body, I figured there was a better than even chance that he did the killing. Or maybe he and Damon both did it together.

I gave Doris a hug as I left and she thanked me for bringing the truth to light. I reminded her that she had done most of that herself.

I was oddly calm as I drove through snarled traffic that stretched along Bee Caves Road and continued on MoPac.

When I got home, I noticed my neighbor Regina in front of her house, tending her flower garden. I was walking over to say hello when my phone chimed in my pocket. It was an alert from the app that monitors the GPS trackers we use. I stopped and simply stared at the screen, puzzled for a moment by what I was seeing. Damon Tate was dead. Why was I getting an alert that his truck was nearby?

I heard a vehicle passing and looked up to see a white Chevy truck rolling slowly past my house. Nathaniel Tate was behind the wheel, left elbow resting in the open window, and he gave me a grin that told me he wasn't going to go away on his own.

37

One reason serial killers often manage to evade detection for months or years is that they choose random victims. No connection. As long as the killer doesn't establish some sort of pattern or commit a really stupid mistake, it can be nearly impossible to track them down.

But most murders have a tangible motive. The victim is someone the killer hates. Someone who cut him off in traffic. Someone with a large insurance policy on his or her head. Someone who wouldn't cooperate as the killer committed a burglary or a rape or a carjacking against them.

Connections. It's how killers get caught.

If you decide to kill someone and you have a connection to the victim, well, first of all, don't do it unless you expect to wind up in prison or strapped to a gurney.

But if you *have* to move forward—if, say, a loved one is at risk—you have to make a plan. How are you going to do it? Where? With what? Leave the body where it is? Try to make it look like an accident? Suicide? Try to make it look like self-defense? Jankowski had gone that route and he'd still been charged—but it might work on the jury. Never know.

The odds are against you. You aren't as smart as you think you are. There are hundreds of ways to get tripped up. You have to be really dumb to go through with it.

Or desperate.

The day after Nathaniel Tate cruised our street in his dead brother's truck, I tracked the movements of the truck and followed it to an indoor gun range in Oak Hill. A gun range. Not a good omen. I was tempted to go inside and see what kind of weapon Nathaniel Tate was practicing with—handgun or rifle—but I knew this particular range had security cameras inside. But I did follow him to a pool hall that night and retrieve the tracker from underneath the truck.

The next day, I checked my phone and found a nearby garage sale. They had a table piled thick with clothes. What garage sale doesn't have clothes? I found a few things that would work, including a pair of New Balance walking shoes one size too large. Disposable clothing.

Then I let two more days pass.

I was riddled with doubt. But if I failed to act and something happened to Mia, I couldn't live with myself. And what could the cops do? Nathaniel Tate was already awaiting two trials, but those might be a year from now. In the meantime, no law prevented him from driving down our street. I could get a protective order, but why bother? That wouldn't stop him if he decided to act.

I had to act first.

Twenty-nine days after Jonathan had hired me to investigate Lennox Armbruster for insurance fraud, I told Mia I had a new case and that I had to conduct surveillance on a guy who worked the evening shift. I drove my Camry to a cheap hotel on Interstate 35. I'd checked it out the day before and spotted no cameras anywhere.

It was ten minutes past midnight.

I began to walk—four and a half miles to my destination. I kept to the shadows, cutting through alleys, avoiding any other humans I saw wandering the streets. It was fifty-four degrees, with no wind. I was wearing the blue jeans and dark long-sleeved shirt I'd bought at the garage sale. I had a lightweight ski mask jammed into my pocket, along with latex gloves.

Three miles to go.

I was carrying no phone. No wallet. No keys.

A compact Colt .380 was riding in a holster on my hip. Unavoidable. I'd considered other methods, but none were feasible. Too much could go wrong. This Colt was special. I'd bought it from a guy several years ago for cash via Craigslist. It was not connected to me by any paperwork or documented transaction. It would disappear permanently after I was done with it.

Two miles to go.

I was walking on a quiet street lined with warehouses and industrial complexes. Few streetlights. I could see a small fire burning in the center of a nearby field, with a dozen figures around it, some standing, some sitting.

A man approached me in the dark. Hard to see him well, but he was big. Dark clothes. Thick, unruly hair and a beard. I could smell him, and it was not good.

He said, "Hey, man, what's up?"

"Not interested," I said.

"Say what?"

"Keep moving."

"The fuck's wrong with you?"

I turned and faced him in a boxer's stance—left foot leading. Hands still down, but ready. My palms were tingling. I was sweaty all over. My heart was beating heavily.

"I thought you was Kenny," the man mumbled, and he retreated back into the darkness.

I considered calling it off at this point. The man was a witness. He could place me in the area, walking, late at night. But I hadn't gotten a good look at him, which meant he hadn't gotten a good look at me. And what were the odds the cops would ever find him? What were the odds he would remember our encounter, or be willing to talk about it?

I kept walking.

One mile to go.

The warehouse row turned into a strip of retail establishments, but they were all closed for the night.

At half a mile, I heard a gunshot in the distance. Then another. And a third. Probably not an anomaly in this area. Hard to tell which direction the shots had come from.

I turned right onto a residential street. I saw a car without tires. A window covered with a tarp. I heard people talking loudly inside a house with an open front door.

I was getting close. Maybe a thousand yards to go. There was still time to come up with a better idea or, to put it bluntly, to chicken out. Was I really going to do this? I thought about Mia back at home, likely sleeping right now. How could I not do it? She'd done her part, taking care of Damon Tate. Now it was my turn.

I was five hundred yards from Nathaniel Tate's house when I heard a siren. Again, probably not unusual around here. It grew louder. Then it died just as quickly and sharply as a snapped twig.

I stopped walking and waited. Was the siren related to the earlier gunshots?

Now I saw another dark form coming toward me in the darkness, roughly a hundred feet ahead. I ducked behind a truck parked along the curb. It was just one person, walking quickly.

I drew my .380, just in case. I don't know why. Nerves, I guess. I kept my thumb on the safety.

The house behind me had a porch light burning, but a large tree in the yard kept me bathed in shadows. I was well concealed.

The person was fifty feet away. Then thirty.

Maybe I was overreacting, as I had with the man earlier who'd been looking for Kenny.

I held my breath as the person got within ten feet, still in darkness, and then, for one brief moment, light flashed across a familiar face.

Raul Ablanedo.

Wait. Wasn't it?

It sure looked liked him, but now he was gone. Had I seen him well enough to know for sure?

I let out a long breath. My hands were trembling.

Half a minute later, red and blue lights began to bounce off the houses and trees, and then a patrol car—possibly the same one that had been sounding a siren earlier—zipped past me and continued down the street.

I slipped into bed at 2:49 and Mia didn't budge. I knew she'd been taking something to help her sleep lately.

I wasn't destined to sleep at all. Too much adrenaline flowing. Too many decisions to make. Too worried that an investigator would be knocking on our door at any moment, asking me to account for my whereabouts in the past several hours. What could I say? And they'd want to speak with Mia, too, to see if my alibi added up.

The minutes and hours moved painfully slowly.

Mia finally stirred at 6:14. She stretched her legs, then rolled onto her left side, now facing me.

"Hey, there," she said. "I'm surprised you're awake. How was your case?"

"There was no case, Mia," I said. "I made that up."

"What are you talking about?"

I said, "I need to tell you where I went last night, and what I saw. And then I need you to help me decide what I should do next."

38

The knock on the door came at 1:47 in the afternoon. Two detectives—Billy Chang and Randy Wolfe. Made sense. Chang had investigated when Damon Tate had accosted me on my porch, and Wolfe had investigated and cleared me on the shooting of Nathaniel Tate outside my bedroom window.

"Mr. Ballard," Chang said.

"Hi, guys," I said, standing in the doorway in shorts and a T-shirt. "I was wondering when you were going to show up."

"Why's that?" Wolfe said.

"I heard Nathaniel Tate was killed last night. I figure you're working your way through a long list of possible suspects."

"Who'd you hear it from?" Wolfe asked. "The name wasn't on the news."

"Yeah, but they mentioned the address—Tate's address," I said. "And now you're showing up here. That means it was Nathaniel Tate."

"We need you to come down to the office and chat with us for a while," Chang said.

I tried to appear appropriately ambivalent—like I really wanted to go, but there were too many other considerations. I said, "Look, the truth is, I'm a total dead end. I didn't do it. So I'm going to save us all time by skipping the interview. You'll thank me for that later."

"Mind telling us where you were last night?" Wolfe asked.

"I have no comment on that," I said.

"So you went somewhere, but you won't tell us where it was?" Chang said.

"I didn't say that."

"You stayed home?"

"No comment."

"Who were you with?"

"No comment."

"You and your fiancée spend the night together?"

"Mia? We usually do, because we live together."

"No, I mean were you with her all night?"

"No comment."

Wolfe was shaking his head, plainly irritated. Chang was glaring at me.

"We need to talk to her," he said.

"She's not here," I said. "And she has no interest in answering any questions."

"You speak for her?" Wolfe asked.

I laughed. Totally genuine.

"What's so funny?" Wolfe asked.

"If you knew Mia, you'd know I don't speak for her. But she knew as well as I did that you'd show up, and she told me that she wouldn't answer any questions."

"It's not a big deal if you went somewhere last night or early this morning," Wolfe said. "But we need to know where, so we can rule you out."

"I'm ruling myself out. You can trust me. Really. Save yourself some man-hours."

"We can get a warrant for your cell phone," Chang said.

"Waste of time."

"You didn't take it with you?" Chang asked.

"No comment. Hey, I'm not trying to make your lives difficult. I just don't want to answer any questions because I didn't do anything to Nathaniel Tate last night or early this morning. Wasn't me."

"We checked his cell phone data and saw that he drove through this neighborhood four days ago," Wolfe said.

They both looked at me.

"Yes?" I said.

"Did you see him?"

"No comment," I said.

"Was he harassing you?"

"No comment."

"You are only harming yourself by refusing to talk," Chang said.

"I tend toward self-destructive behavior on occasion," I said. "It's the result of some deep misgivings about my own self-worth."

"If you had some words with him, now's the time to tell us," Wolfe said. "Did he threaten you?"

"No comment," I said. "I did not kill Nathaniel Tate. I can't make that any more clear."

"Do you know who did?"

And, finally, we'd arrived at the most pertinent question of all. What was the answer? I mean, *did* I know? Had I really seen Raul Ablanedo, or was it someone who simply looked like him? It was dark out. Perceptions can be altered by nerves and adrenaline and fatigue. Let's say it really wasn't him, but I told Chang and Wolfe what I thought I'd seen. I might be putting an innocent man—a man with a motive—in serious legal jeopardy. That wasn't just a rationalization, it was the truth, and I had to take that into account.

What's more, if Raul *had* killed Nathaniel Tate, some people might argue he deserved our thanks, not our judgment. Should I protect him? Risk my own neck to save his? Mia and I had talked about it at great length. And we'd agreed on what I would tell the cops.

"No," I said. "I don't know who did it."

I would look back in the months that followed with some measure of satisfaction that the murder of Nathaniel Tate went unsolved. Maybe the killer would get caught eventually, but I found myself hoping the detectives working the case would simply move on.

I kept remembering one thing Raul had said to me when he'd confessed his part in Brent's scam…

I don't know if I can ever make up for being so stupid. How would I do that? It's too late, isn't it?

I didn't realize it at the time, but looking back, was Raul signaling an intent to take action? Did it matter now?

Finally I had to let it go, because I had more important things that needed my focus.

Four days after Nathaniel Tate was killed in his home, Mia came home from her appointment with the therapist.

I met her at the door, unsure of what to ask or whether I should even bring it up. But, no, I shouldn't avoid the topic, right?

"How'd it go?" I asked after she'd set her purse down and gone to the refrigerator for a Dr Pepper.

"I don't think I've ever talked so much in my life," Mia said, leaning against the counter with the can in her hand. "I liked her. I'm glad I went."

"So you, uh, talked about the shooting?"

"We did, yeah. I told her exactly what happened. In detail. And it—"

Her voice caught and she stopped talking.

I gave it a moment and then said, "Did it help?"

She nodded as her eyes began to fill.

"Do you want to tell me more?"

"Not right now. Maybe later. Or maybe not."

"Are you going back?"

"I think so, yes. Maybe for a few weeks. I don't know. I need to think about it."

"Do you want me to go with you?"

"Possibly. I'll let you know."

"I'll go," I said. "Whatever it takes."

"I appreciate that."

I grabbed a box of Kleenex off the kitchen table and offered it to her. She took one and wiped her nose.

I leaned sideways against the counter, right beside her.

"I want to ask one more question," I said.

"Okay," she said.

"No matter what the answer is, I can take it," I said. "You understand that?"

She nodded, and now she was crying freely. She knew where I was headed.

"Did you talk about us?" I said. "About me and you?"

She nodded again.

I waited for her to say more, but she didn't.

I couldn't leave it at that. Couldn't wait to hear more later. I had to know now.

"Are we going to be okay, Mia?" I said.

Now she quickly turned and wrapped her arms around me and buried her face beside my neck. I could feel her warm tears on my collar bone. I could feel her heart beating against my chest.

"Of course we are," she said. "Of course we are."

Want to know when Ben Rehder's
next novel will be released?

Subscribe to his email list at www.benrehder.com

Turn the page for an excerpt from

THE DRIVING LESSON

By Ben Rehder

THE DRIVING LESSON

1

If, during the last week of my freshman year, you'd asked me what I was planning to do that summer, I can guarantee you that becoming a fugitive would not have made the list. Not even a really long list. Especially if you'd told me that I wouldn't be alone, that it would be me and my grandfather—seriously, my Opa—together, on the run, the subject of a nationwide manhunt. *Yeah, right*, I would've said. *Are you friggin' nuts?*

But, as we know now, that's exactly what happened. Events sort of conspired, as Mr. Gardner, my English teacher, would say. And before the entire fiasco was over, we'd become an international phenomenon. The chaos would grow to include...

Cops across Texas asking the public for help in tracking us down.

Newspapers from Los Angeles to New York plastering our photos all over the front page, me with my baby face and blondish-white hair.

John Walsh talking about us on *America's Most Wanted*, stressing that we were most likely unarmed. Most likely?

People tweeting about us, talking about us on Facebook, posting videos on YouTube that supposedly showed us eating breakfast at an Iowa truck stop or camping out at Big Bend National Park.

My parents, Glen and Sarah Dunbar, appearing on CNN, Mom pleading for God to deliver "her baby Charlie" home safely, while Dad sits there looking uncomfortable and the smoking hot newsbabe nods with sympathy.

So, yeah, you can kind of understand why I didn't see any of this coming. Silly me, I thought the highlight of my summer would be getting my learner's permit.

~

The last Saturday in May plays an important role in this story, because that's when Matt, my best friend, talked me into doing something really dumb. Actually, two dumb things in a row, the second one worse than the first.

It was about thirty minutes before dark and we were walking to the bowling alley. Yeah, it sounds lame. Who bowls, right? But it's something Matt has done since he was about five, and I've known Matt since third grade, so I usually tag along, and sometimes I bowl, too. My high score is 114. Matt's is 223. So you can tell which one of us applies himself.

Anyway, we were walking past a home under construction on the edge of the neighborhood where we both live. There aren't many empty lots left in our subdivision, but every so often, one of the remaining lots sells and a new home gets slapped up in a matter of a few months. We're not talking high-dollar mansions, just tract homes that look like all the rest in the area. This particular home was nearly complete, and there was already a for-sale sign stuck in the freshly sodded yard. *I'm gorgeous inside!* the sign proclaimed. (My dad joked that that sounded like the title for a book designed to build self-esteem in teenage girls.)

That's when Matt stopped walking and said, "Charlie, check it out." He was looking at the house.

"What?"

"The front door is open."

And it was. Wide open. Like somebody forgot to lock it and the wind had given it a shove. The construction workers were gone for the day. The place was quiet and still.

I stopped, too. So what if the door was open? Nothing good could come from going inside a home under construction, especially since we'd gotten into trouble less than a month ago for skipping an assembly at school. Under those circumstances, only an idiot would go inside this house.

Matt said, "Let's go inside."

"Forget it."

"Just for a minute."

"Why?"

"Why not?"

"It's stupid."

"I just want to look around."

"Be my guest."

"Come with me."

"Nope."

"It'll be fun."

"It'll be trespassing."

"Don't be a pussy."

And there it was. Matt's trump card. Whenever he wanted to push my buttons, he'd call me a pussy. I *hated* it and he knew it. But, of course, my only option was to act like I didn't care, or he'd still be calling me that name when we were living in a retirement home. So I said, "Whatever, dude."

"Pussy."

"Real mature."

"Pussy."

"Jeez, Matt, grow the hell up."

"Pussy."

"You might want to broaden your vocabulary."

"Pussy."

I knew from experience that it wouldn't do any good to keep arguing with him. He can be a persistent little jerk. So, even though I wish I could go back and do that night over—use some common sense—instead, well, you can probably see where this is going.

~

We closed the front door behind us and stood there for a few seconds in the tiled entry hallway, which would be called a foyer in a larger home. I have to admit, my heart was pumping pretty good. We weren't supposed to be in here, but we were, and it was exciting. Exhilarating, even.

"Come on," Matt said, and he stepped slowly into the living room, onto the carpet, which was clean and perfect. The entire house was spotless. I could smell fresh paint.

But something was strange. Sort of familiar. Then I figured it out. I whispered, "You know what? This place has the exact same floor plan as my house."

And it did. Dining room over there. Three bedrooms down that hallway. Fireplace with a window on either side. Weird. It made me wonder how many other homes in the neighborhood were just like mine—except maybe with a different coat of paint on the outside, or bricks instead of plywood siding.

Matt didn't say anything. He was just looking around with this odd little grin on his face. Enjoying the rush. The light was fading as the sun was beginning to set, but I noticed that his sneakers were leaving smudges on the carpet.

"Let's go, Matt," I said.

"Not yet."

"There's nothing to see in here. The place is empty."

No response.

"Matt!"

He moved toward a swinging door on the other side of the living room. I knew that was the way to the kitchen, just like in my house. Matt went through the door, but I stayed behind, near one of the windows, so I could keep an eye on the street.

I was starting to get nervous. What if someone had seen us come in? It wasn't like we were real sly about it, walking right up to the front door. Anyone watching would've known we didn't belong in here. Which could mean the police might be on their way right this very minute.

"Matt!"

If we got caught...I didn't even want to think how my mom would respond.

Suddenly Matt, still in the kitchen, said, "Sweet!" And here he came through the door again, holding something. "Dude, look what I found."

It was a cordless drill. My dad had one like it, but a different brand. Yellow instead of blue. I was with him at Home Depot when he bought it. Nearly two hundred bucks, which is a lot of money.

"Put it back," I said.

"Somebody must've forgot it."

"Quit screwing around."

He pulled the trigger on the drill and it made a powerful whirring sound. It seemed awfully loud in the quiet house.

"Man, I could *use* this!" Matt said.

"For what?"

"Stuff."

"Don't even think about it."

But he had that grin on his face again. Sometimes I hate that grin.

At this point, I should mention that I outweigh Matt by about thirty pounds. I'm nearly six feet tall, one of the biggest kids in the freshman class, and sometimes my size has its advantages. Like making nose guard on the football team. Or like right now. If I had to, I could wrestle the drill away from Matt and put it back in the kitchen. Then we'd leave. Sure, Matt would be pissed, but he'd get over it. Later, he'd realize how dumb it would've been to steal the drill. He'd realize that I'd actually done him a favor. So that was the plan, to try to talk him out of it, and if that didn't work, to use my superior physical attributes to impose my will.

And that's when we heard the car door out front.

~

Here's what would happen if I got caught.

I'd get grounded, for sure—probably for at least a month, and maybe for the entire summer. No cell phone, no computer, no video games, no TV, no iPod. No hanging out at the mall, no riding my bike, no going to the movies, no having friends over to share in my misery. Guess what I'd be expected to do instead?

Read the Bible.

Seriously. My mom would insist on it. Didn't matter that I'd already read it several times, cover to cover, in my nearly fifteen years. When I was younger, parts of it sort of freaked me out, especially in the Old Testament. I mean, come on—people think *Mortal Kombat* is gruesome? The Bible has this big long list of reasons to stone people to death. It's got plagues, brought on by God, that wipe out entire cities, plus human and animal sacrifices, fathers having sex with their daughters, and a bunch of other bizarre events. Kind of disturbing when you're a kid. Now that I'm older, frankly, it just bores me. But Sarah Dunbar—that's my mother—is a firm believer that reading the Bible can cure all ills. The King James version, of course.

Any time I got in trouble, even for something relatively minor, like being tardy to class, she'd say something like, "I didn't raise you to be a juvenile delinquent," and then she'd pronounce my punishment. Could be a few verses, a couple of chapters, or even a full book. If she was really angry, I'd have to write a report about what I'd learned, assuming I'd had any luck deciphering what I'd read.

So maybe you can understand just how badly I didn't want to get caught in that house.

~

Matt's eyes got really big. I'm sure mine did, too.

I peeked out the window and saw a green Ford Explorer parked at the curb. A woman was coming around the front of the SUV, walking slowly, because she was in the middle of a conversation on her cell phone. She was about my parents' age, dressed nicely in a skirt and high heels. Everything about her said real estate agent. She was in charge of selling this house. She probably had some clients coming to look at the place right now.

"Oh, crap," I said, because I'm such a master of the English language. Now my heart was really pounding.

"Who is it?" Matt hissed. He hadn't moved.

"Some lady. Maybe a realtor."

"Is she coming in?"

"She...she..."

"She what?"

"She's stopping at the for-sale sign. It has one of those little boxes for flyers. She's checking to see if there are any flyers left."

Matt came up behind me and peeked over my shoulder. I was beginning to feel sick. "This is your fault," I said.

"Maybe that's all she came for, to check the flyers. Maybe she'll drive away."

The real-estate lady, still talking on her phone, let the metal lid slap shut on the rectangular box. Then she started up the driveway toward the house.

I turned quickly. "Follow me," I said.

He did, too. Amazing how, all of a sudden, Matt was willing to listen to a pussy like me. He was too frozen with fear to realize that all we had to do was go out the back door, which we did, closing that door just as we heard the front door opening.

It wasn't until we'd ducked through a gate in the privacy fence and started jogging down the street that I noticed Matt was still carrying the cordless drill.

~

I got home around nine-thirty, and I halfway expected my parents to be waiting for me, looking stern, ready to tear me a new one, because I just knew the cops had already solved the crime and had come to the house looking for me.

I'm a wimp that way, a total bundle of nerves when it comes to the possibility of getting in trouble—so much so that my mom can usually tell just from looking at my face that I've been up to something.

But that didn't turn out to be a problem tonight, because my parents were nowhere to be seen when I came through the front door. Normally, one or both of them would be hanging out in the living room, watching TV or reading. Or mom would be busy in the kitchen while dad was in the study working or just goofing around on the computer.

Then I heard them, just a low murmuring from their bedroom. The lights were on in the hallway. I decided I'd just duck into their doorway, say a quick goodnight, and go to bed before my own behavior gave me away. Then I began to wonder if going to bed so quickly would be a giveaway in itself. Maybe it would be better to talk to them for longer than a few seconds. Sheesh.

I started down the hallway. *Just act normal. Be yourself. Don't be an idiot.*

I was literally two steps from their bedroom door—and they still didn't know I'd come home—when I heard my mother say, "Here? Honey, you know that won't work. He'll have to end up in hospice."

Now she saw me in the doorway, and I saw them sitting on the edge of the bed, holding hands.

"Charlie," she said. That, and nothing else. It was strange, the way she said my name, and the odd expression on her face. Like she was surprised to see me. No, that's not exactly right. She looked like I'd caught her doing something she shouldn't be doing, or maybe saying something she didn't want me to hear.

"I'm home," I announced. Well, duh.

My dad looked up and caught my eye, but only for a second. He was acting weird, too. Angry about something? Sad? Were his eyes red?

"How was bowling?" Mom asked.

"Okay." Not really. I'd scored an 82, with three gutter balls. My mind had been on other things, like the fact that I'd taken part in a burglary.

Dad got up and went into the bathroom. Mom looked at me and gave a weak smile. "How is Matt?"

"Fine." *Despite being a felon in training.*

"Are you hungry? There's some pizza left in the fridge."

She's always trying to feed me—I'm a big guy and I burn a lot of calories—but I got the distinct impression she was making small talk to sort of gloss over the odd vibe in the air.

Had my parents been arguing about something? Or about somebody? And what in the heck was a hospice? I knew it had something to do with nurses or hospitals. Which meant there could only be one person they were talking about.

2

My phone chimed at 8:37 the next morning. A text message from Matt.

Any prblms?

I'd been awake for nearly an hour, but I was still in bed, just thinking about things. About last night. Not so much about the stolen drill, but about "hospice care." I'd looked it up on the Internet and was not happy with what I'd learned.

Yeah, there are problems, I thought.

That was made even more obvious by the fact that church started at nine and it appeared we weren't going. Mom hadn't even knocked on my door to get me up for breakfast. I didn't smell bacon frying or coffee brewing. In fact, I didn't hear any movement or talking at all in the house.

I lay there for several minutes, just feeling crummy. To be honest, I was kind of enjoying leaving Matt hanging. He was always doing stupid stuff and somehow getting me involved. Like this thing with the drill. So I texted him back.

Cops came this morning

His reply came within fifteen seconds:

Srius?

I could picture the panic he was feeling. Pretty funny.

I denied evrythng

Not funny

Not a joke

I put my phone on silent mode because I knew what he'd do next, and sure enough, it rang. I let it go to voicemail. Thirty seconds passed. Then he sent a text:

Where r u

Cant talk now

Im freaking out whats happening

Cops r chcking the nborhood door 2 door

U r lying

Wish i was

OMG 4 a stupid drill?
Doesnt mttr its stil theft
The door was open
Rmembr whn ur bike was stolen?

Now there was a long pause and I realized I had a huge smile on my face. I was getting him good. Last year, somebody had taken Matt's mountain bike when he'd left it in front of a convenience store. His dad had been really pissed that he'd left it unlocked and wouldn't buy him a new one. That's why we walked everywhere now—Matt had no bike.

Finally he said: *Shld we put it back?*

That caught me by surprise. Put the drill back? I thought about it, then said: *Door wont be unlocked now*

Cld leave it on back porch
Might get caught
We'd b careful
Not we, u
U wont go?
No
Plz go w me
U stole it u return it
I need a lookout
Good luck
Y r u being such a jerk

Was I? Maybe I was. Regardless, I was tired of stringing him along. And he deserved to know what was really going on, since he was my best friend. So I said:

Think my g'father is dying

~

Later, I found Mom in the living room, folding sheets and watching Pat Robertson, and she acted as if everything was fine. When I asked why we hadn't gone to church, she said Dad hadn't been feeling well when he woke up, so she let him sleep late. Then she asked if I was hungry, and before I could even answer, she said, "Of course you are," and went into the kitchen to make me some breakfast.

She seemed awfully cheerful. Maybe I was wrong about Opa. That's what we called him, because of his mother's German ancestry.

Maybe I'd misheard what Mom had said last night, or maybe they'd been talking about someone else.

I was even more convinced of that when, a couple hours later, Dad finally emerged from his bedroom—fully dressed, apparently feeling much better—and said, "Grab the keys, Charlie!"

"Huh?"

"Time for another driving lesson!"

~

"Parallel parking," Dad said very seriously, "is the most important part of the test."

He was bending down to look at me through the passenger window. It was a long way down for him, because he's six foot four. I get my size from his side of the family.

Dad continued, saying, "When I was your age, it counted for a full thirty points. So if you screwed it up, the best you could get was a seventy, which meant you were just one point—one measly point— from a failing grade." His voice was rising with mock outrage. He was kidding around because he has a weird sense of humor. I think he got it from Opa, who is even more of a goofball. Dad went on. "It didn't matter if you drove with the precision of Richard Petty and the skill of Dale Earnhardt, if you couldn't parallel park like you'd been doing it all your life, you didn't get your license. Personally, I don't think that's very reasonable, but that's the way it was. What're you gonna do? Bunch of bureaucrats."

I couldn't help grinning at him. "That's what happened to you, huh, Dad?"

"Is it that obvious? Yeah, well, my instructor was a hard-ass."

He used words like that sometimes when Mom wasn't around. It was understood that this was a guy thing, only between us.

"Okay, you ready to give it a try?" he asked.

We were in the huge parking lot of the exposition center on the east side of town. This is where they held the rodeo, dog shows, tractor pulls, and various concerts, but no events were taking place today, so it was a ghost town.

The parking lot was basically a wide-open expanse of pavement, with the occasional curbed island of concrete here and there to divide the big lot into smaller sections. We'd come here for previous lessons, and Dad had taught me the basics—shifting gears smoothly, braking hard without locking up the tires, backing up for a long distance—all the things that would be on the driving test.

Today, Dad had placed a pair of orange traffic cones exactly twenty-five feet apart, with each cone about six feet out from a long, straight section of curb. It was my job to parallel park our Toyota between those two cones.

I didn't know why he was making such a big deal out of it. It looked simple enough. He had already demonstrated for me a couple of times. As you back up, he said, you whip the wheel this way, then, at just the right moment, you whip it the other way, and presto, you slide right into the slot. Take it slow. Keep an eye on the cones.

Piece of cake, I thought. *No problem. It's not trigonometry.*

On my first try, I totally crushed the cone in front.

Dad was ready with some sound effects. He screamed like I'd just run over a pedestrian. "Aaah! Oh, my god, help me! My leg! You crushed my leg!"

Yeah, okay, I'll admit I laughed. Then I pulled out, he stood the cone up again, and I gave it another shot. I whipped it too late and rolled over the rear cone. Another pedestrian. It was like I was playing *Grand Theft Auto.*

Dad said, "For the love of God, somebody stop this maniac! An ambulance! I need an ambulance!"

Right about then, I was grateful there wasn't another soul within a mile of us. It was embarrassing.

The third time, with some verbal coaching from Dad, I did a little better. Didn't hit a cone, but wound up parked about three feet from the curb. You're supposed to be eighteen inches or closer.

But I got better with each try. After about a dozen attempts, I finally nailed it.

"There you go! Now you've got it!"

Three more times in a row, I managed to park without sending any imaginary pedestrians to the hospital or the morgue. It felt good.

Dad climbed into the passenger seat and closed the door. "You know what? I'm thinking you should drive us home today."

"Really?" That would be cool. I hadn't driven on any real streets yet, just this parking lot.

"Yeah, we'll take the back streets. No highways. Think you can handle that?"

"I think so, yeah."

"I do, too. You're getting the hang of it. I'm proud of you. But first, why don't you cut the engine for minute. We need to talk about something."

I knew immediately what was coming.

~

The word "grandpa" might bring to mind a certain image for some people: a little white-haired guy with arthritis and poor hearing. My grandfather wasn't like that at all. Not even close.

Yeah, he was sixty-three years old—getting up there—but he was very active, always running around doing something. Like he was a big-time swimmer. Went to a public pool in his neighborhood four or five mornings a week. He played the guitar and wrote his own songs. He attended political rallies and book signings and all kinds of fundraisers.

He dated a lot, too. He and my grandmother had gotten a divorce before I was even born, and Opa had never remarried. Instead, he had what my mother called "lady friends."

He traveled with some of these friends to other states and even other countries. Just last summer, he went to Ireland with a redheaded woman named Linda. A couple years before that, he went to Africa with a woman whose name I can't remember. For a while after that trip, he wore a shirt called a *dashiki*. It had all these wild colors, and I thought it looked pretty cool, but my mom always said he looked like some old nut. Other times, when she was being nicer, she used the word "eccentric."

My point is, he wasn't some decrepit geezer ready for a nursing home. Heck, he had more energy than me and most of my friends. Or he used to.

~

"You know that Opa hasn't been feeling good."

I nodded.

Dad said, "He...well, for a while, nobody could say what was wrong with him. The doctors didn't know. He just didn't feel right, so they ran various tests, and everything looked okay. They said he was probably fine, just getting old, and he shouldn't worry too much about it. We told you about that. Remember right after Christmas?"

My face was starting to feel very warm. I nodded again. I did remember. First they told me Opa might be sick, then they said maybe he wasn't, then, just before spring break, they said it was a "wait and see" type of thing. We hadn't really talked much about it since then.

"In early April," Dad said, "he went to a special hospital in Houston. It's one of the best in the country. They ran even more tests, different tests, and this time they were able to figure out what the problem is." He paused for a second. "Unfortunately, it wasn't good news. He has a type of bone cancer that is very aggressive. It's already in the advanced stages."

Does it make me a pussy to admit my eyes were starting to fill with tears? A real tough guy, right? Big football player. Macho and all that. But cancer is scary. Everybody knows that.

I was looking down at my lap. My dad had his arm on the driver's headrest behind me. Now he placed his hand on my neck, rubbing it, trying to make me feel better, but I was this close to bawling like a baby. Some snot dripped from my nose and landed on my jeans.

Dad said, "It gets a little more complicated, because Opa has some wild ideas about what he should do next. He isn't thinking straight. Maybe it's his age, or maybe he's just scared, but he's decided that he doesn't want to undergo the treatment plan the doctors are recommending."

Now I looked up. "Why not?"

"Well, it can be pretty rough on the patient. And the chances that it would be successful are pretty slim. It comes down to what they call 'quality of life.'"

I knew the answer, but I asked the question anyway. "Is he going to die?"

I don't know whether my dad had decided hours ago to be completely honest with me, or if he made the decision right then and there. But when I think back on this moment, as painful as it was, I'm glad he didn't sugarcoat it or give me any false hope.

He simply said, "Yeah, he is."

Now the tears really began to flow.

He said, "I'm sorry, Charlie. I'm really sorry. Even with the treatment, he...that would only delay it, or maybe it wouldn't even do that."

Now he was getting emotional, too, and I couldn't bring myself to look at him. I looked down at my lap again, and we just sat there for another minute or two, neither of us saying anything.

Then, when I thought I could talk without blubbering, I said, "How soon?"

~ ~ ~

ABOUT THE AUTHOR

Ben Rehder lives with his wife near Austin, Texas, where he was born and raised. His novels have made best-of-the-year lists in *Publishers Weekly, Library Journal, Kirkus Reviews*, and *Field & Stream. Buck Fever* was a finalist for the Edgar Award, and *Get Busy Dying* was a finalist for the Shamus Award. For more information, visit www.benrehder.com.

OTHER NOVELS BY BEN REHDER

Buck Fever
Bone Dry
Flat Crazy
Guilt Trip
Gun Shy
Holy Moly
The Chicken Hanger
The Driving Lesson
Gone The Next
Hog Heaven
Get Busy Dying
Stag Party
Bum Steer
If I Had A Nickel
Point Taken
Now You See Him
Last Laugh

Made in the USA
Coppell, TX
11 November 2024

40066001R00148